adverbs

ALSO BY DANIEL HANDLER

The Basic Eight

Watch Your Mouth

adverbs

Daniel Handler

The author would like to thank the following people:
Lisa Brown, Charlotte Sheedy, Ron Bernstein, Dan Halpern, Susan Rich,
Josh Greenhut, Darla Spiers, Kezia Pearlman, Paula Sharp, Ayelet Waldman,
Helena Echlin, Dan Clowes, and Amanda Davis, much missed.

Portions of this book appeared in *ZYZZYVA,* Zoetrope: All Story, West, the Sunday
magazine of the Los Angeles Times, and in a privately printed chapbook, in different
form. The author is grateful to editors Howard Junker, Michael Ray, Amy Tan, and
Rick Wartzman for these indulgences.

HarperCollins books may be purchased for educational, business,
or sales promotional use. For information please write: Special Markets Department,
HarperCollins Publishers, 10 East 53rd Street, New York, NY 10022.

FIRST EDITION

Designed by Claire Vaccaro

Library of Congress Cataloging in Publication Data is available upon request.
ISBN-10: 0-06-072441-2
ISBN-13: 978-0-06-072441-2

06 07 08 09 10   BVG/RRD   10 9 8 7 6 5 4 3 2 1

for Rook—

for whom else the book on love?

What do you mean where does the music come from? Where does the

music *ever* come from? The guy says to the girl Something is on my mind

and the girl says Really? What is it? and somebody in the orchestra hits a

note and they sing. That's where the music comes from.

——MORRIE RYSKIND ON THE SET OF A MARX BROTHERS MOVIE

Adverbs:

adverbs

immediately

Love was in the air, so both of us walked through love on our way to the corner. We breathed it in, particularly me: the air was also full of smells and birds, but it was the love, I was sure, that was tumbling down to my lungs, the heart's neighbors and confidants. Andrea was tall and angry. I was a little bit shorter. She smoked cigarettes. I worked in a store that sold things. We always walked to this same corner, Thirty-seventh and what's-it, Third Avenue, in New York, because it was easier to get a cab there, the entire time we were in love.

"You must be nervous," she said when we'd walked about two puffs.

"Yes," I said. "I *am* nervous. I've never been to a reading of a will. I didn't even know they still did things like this, read wills. I thought it was, I don't know, a movie thing. In a movie. Do you think everybody will be dressed up?"

"Who cares?" Andrea said. She threw down her cigarette and ground it out with the heel of her shoe like a new kind of halfhearted dance. "Look," she said, and shaded her eyes with her hand for a minute like she was actually looking at something. I turned my head to see. "I just mean, *look*," she said, cupping my head with her hand. "The expression I mean. *Look*, I'm trying to be nice, but I'm *scatterbrained* right now, if you know what I mean. I'm *frightened* by your behavior. I woke up this morning and you said good morning and I said good morning, what do you feel like doing today and you said well I sort of have to do this thing and I said what thing and you said go to the reading of my father's will and I said what are you talking about and then you told me your dad died. *This morning.* I mean, he died two weeks ago but that's when you told me. That's when you *told* me. I'm trying to think that you just must be *in shock* that your dad died but it's very, very, very, very, very, very difficult."

"He's not really," I said, "my dad."

Three cars went by.

"What do you mean?" she asked. "What are you talking about? What could you possibly mean? He is your biological father and raised you, along with your mother, in the same house, for eighteen years. He carves the turkey at Thanksgiving and when I met him three years ago I said it's so nice to meet your father and he didn't even blink. How can you say that? What can you mean?"

"I don't know," I said, and we reached the corner. The street was a yellow streak, however many yards wide, cabs and cabs and cabs and the occasional car that wasn't a cab so the whole thing looked like a scarcely-been-touched ear of corn. I put my hand up and one stopped. I opened the back door and Andrea just looked at me. I put one knee into the cab, half-sitting in it, almost kneeling as if the cabdriver, whom you'll meet in a minute, had just brought me up curbside to ask this tall angry woman to marry me. She wasn't going to say yes, I realized. She was never going to say yes.

"Why are you acting this way?" she said. "You've never acted this way. Usually you're, I don't know. Usually we're eating at diners and taking money out of our ATM machines, a normal person. What is—"

"You don't have a chance," I said, "to act like this in a diner."

"Please stop," she said. She smeared one finger underneath her eye, although she wasn't crying, just finishing a finger painting of herself. She was done. "This is worse than the last time," she said.

"I think I should go to this thing by myself," I said, and sat more. "I think you should go home to the middle of the block and I'll go someplace in this cab. I'll be back later or something."

"What do you—" She stood on the corner and wiped her eye again but now she was crying. Somehow she was crying by the time we reached the same corner and were almost all the way into a cab. "I'm going," I said, and shut the door. She stared at me through the window like I was maybe nothing. The cabdriver asked me where I wanted to go and I told him Seventy-ninth Street and then I apologized for making him wait like that at the corner and told him I would give him an extra couple of bucks or something. "Don't worry about it," he said, and looked at me in the rearview mirror, a polite smile. His eyes veered off my reflection and onto the reflection of the traffic behind us, so we could merge, and we merged, and that's when, immediately, I fell in love with my cabdriver.

"I changed my mind," I told him. Then I decided I shouldn't

tell him, not yet. His cab number was 6J108. His first name was Peter, I saw, and his last name looked like somebody had just dropped their forearm onto the typewriter keyboard, someplace in Europe I guess. "Penn Station. I have to go somewhere." I felt the weight of the lie I had told Andrea, enormous and unde-served, and vowed I'd never do something like that again. But not telling Peter everything that was in my heart wasn't a lie, right? That was just good timing. That was just being sensitive. "I don't have to go somewhere," I said, "not really. But I think I *should* go somewhere."

"Okay," he said. It didn't make a difference to him, and I loved him all the more for it. We turned left.

"You have pretty eyes," I said.

"Yeah," Peter said. "It's pretty nice. Since they cleaned it up."

"So you've had surgery?" I said. "That's okay. Some people think it's vanity, but I don't think it's any more vain than buying a sweater. It's funny we're talking about sweaters, because I lost one in a taxi once. It was blue, a nice shade of blue. Andrea and I—that's the girl, Andrea, who kept you waiting because I was breaking up with her—we were first going out. This was maybe three years ago. We caught a cab at the very same corner, actu-ally, where I met you, Peter. And we were chatting about this and that, on our way to a party. I think a party, and we started kissing, and you know how that goes."

"Shit!" Peter said. Somebody in front of us had done some-thing.

"I'm sorry," I said. "I don't mean to distract you. To make a long story short we lost the sweater."

"If it's okay," Peter said and pulled up to the curb. To my dismay we were there already. I rolled down the window to get a better look. Penn Station swerved to the left, and for a moment I thought there had been another catastrophe, but it was just me, swerving to the right. Peter was parking the cab in a rare empty spot across the street, one kernel of corn sticking in the gap between somebody's teeth. "I gotta have a cup of coffee," Peter explained. "So I'm going to stop here, if it's okay?"

The clock in his car hadn't adjusted to daylight saving time yet and said it was four-fifteen when it was really five-fifteen. Peter probably didn't have time to fiddle with it, or it was tricky, as car clocks are. I didn't mind. You can't mind these things, you just can't, for to dislike what makes a person human is to dislike all humans, or at least other people who can't work clocks. You have to love the whole person, if you are truly in love. If you are going to take a lifelong journey with somebody, you can't mind if the other person believes they are leaving for that journey an hour earlier than you, as long as truly, in the real world, you are both leaving at exactly the same time.

He turned to face me and I saw what I owed him. "Here you go," I said, opening my wallet and handing him something. It was risky not to look at the bill, but I wanted him to know that I considered the commercial aspect of our relationship over and done with. "Here you go," I said again, because a garbage truck was going by and I couldn't be sure he had heard me the first time, "and *yes*. It's *more* than okay. I would *love* to have a cup of coffee with you."

Peter was already outside, looking up and down the street

and waiting for me to leave the cab and join him. I stepped out and everything looked ugly, spots of gum on the street and smoke in all the oxygen. They say that when you're really in love, the world becomes gossamer and gorgeous, but in my experience—with Peter, and, I suppose, in a more naïve time in my life, with Andrea and Bob Dylan—the world gets grimy, and the love object is in stark relief from the surroundings. This is love, a pretty thing on an ugly street, and why wouldn't you pick it up if it appeared in a cab? Finders keepers is what they say, and I wanted to be kept. I could see, in this stark relief, every inch of Peter's clothing as he nodded politely to me and began to walk toward a grimy little diner place, Sal's. Black jeans. A sort of olive-green jacket, with a rip on one of the elbows covered in masking tape. Pretty, pretty, pretty.

I won't bore you with the details of Sal's. Peter walked ahead of me to a booth and, after wondering if I dared sit next to him rather than across, I slid into the across seat. Best to give him space. I didn't let the fact that I apparently no longer lived at Thirty-seventh and what's-it pressure us into moving in together. I knew I could probably find a studio, month-to-month. Ridiculous maybe, but if you live in New York, real estate decisions can often supersede any other issues in a relationship, and it can be ugly, ugly. "Two coffees," I told somebody who worked at Sal's, and they brought them at the *exact same time*.

"Um," Peter said. He looked confused.

"I understand," I said. "It's overwhelming, isn't it? I'm sorry, I'll shut up. You talk. Milk?"

"I don't have a lot of time," Peter said, taking it black. I made a note for the coffees we'd drink in the future. "I'm sort of on a schedule."

"I understand," I said. "We can just take it easy. I should probably catch a train at some point, see my dad, tell him what happened."

"Okay," Peter said, but I could tell it wasn't okay. He was looking over my shoulder, making a little jiggling motion with a clasped hand, like he was running a pen through the air.

"I guess I could say it in a letter," I agreed, "if that would help things any." The check came and I threw another bill on it without looking. "But it's really quite simple. Amazing, isn't it, that something like this happens so frequently yet it boils down to three simple words."

"Yeah, um, okay," Peter said, and swallowed the rest of his coffee. He was bracing himself, I realized. He thought maybe I would reject him. I reached across the table, over the bill, which I now noticed was a five, and tried to take one of his sweetly veined hands. He pulled away, stood up, snakebit.

"What are you," he said, "some kind of faggot?"

"Not if it upsets you so much," I said. I remained sitting, looking up at him like a visit to a volcano, my Vesuvius, my Mauna Loa, spouting love lava all over this ugly, ugly town. "*Labels*, Peter. That's all. *Labels*. You know?"

"How the hell you know my name?" he asked and backed up five steps. He bumped up against somebody, turned around quickly with a half-wave of apology. It was somebody he didn't know. He had bumped up against a stranger. "How the hell you know my name?"

"Peter!" I cried out, and he left me in Sal's. I hurried the length of this stupid restaurant. Why had I come here? Why not show him a little respect, a salad, sushi? I had the money. I could spend it all on him, my Fuji, my Etna, what did it matter? My father wasn't dead, but when he died I would surely get something, and by then, I was positive, I'd be assistant manager. We could manage. This real estate jungle couldn't tear us apart. "Peter!"

But Peter was already at his cab, looking at the ground and shaking his head in a tired, self-hating gesture. Denial, probably, the great exhauster, or maybe just a weary glance at all that sidewalk gum. The world was caving in on him, too, but my love wanted to run for it. Afraid of commitment, like all single men, he wanted to slipstream forever, picking up whatever stranger spotted him first. "Peter!" Without answering, he took his black jeans and jumped into his cab and merged, looking, I knew, into his rearview mirror at the reflection of traffic swarming around us.

"I love you!" I called. Peter went by, and then a bus, with black smoke behind it like the appearance of an evil queen. For a moment Penn Station shook in turmoil, a bubbling and gaseous Penn Station, but then the smoke cleared and the building was fully upright, proud as the truth printed out in big bright stencils: 6J108. I would find him, my Mount St. Helens, I could find him anywhere. He was a landmark. I waved both arms in the air, joyous giddiness for all the cars to see: *Peter, Peter, Peter*. I stood at the curb and waved, semaphored, signaled. I hailed him, my active mountain, my hole in the sidewalk that led to the center of the world. I knew if I waved long enough he would pull over and take me where I wanted to go.

obviously

The movie was kickass, which was appropriate, because tonight it was called *Kickass: The Movie*. It was a sort of action-adventure thing starring two women and one man, and another man who was the villain, and they all said funny lines sometimes, so I guess you could call it an action-adventure comedy except it was not a comedy in the traditional, classical sense, not in the way Ms. Wylie called it. Lila and I were in the same English class and we both worked Saturdays and Thursday nights at the Sovereign Cinemaplex, and I guess if I were a little braver I would have asked her something like, "Do you think Ms. Wylie, who we both have fourth period, would call *Kickass: The Movie* a comedy in the traditional, classical sense?" and we could have that conversation, and it would lead to other conversations, during the flat and lonely times in the Sovereign, when all the people had paid their money and bought their girlfriends popcorn and handed their tickets either to Lila, if they used the right-hand escalator, or to me at the left-hand one, to be torn in half, the emptied-out times when all the happy people were happy in the dark, and Lila and I just stood around at the bottom of the whirring escalators, taking nobody up and up and up for the big show. But the thing is, that line about Ms. Wylie is sort of lame, and I think Lila would just roll her eyes, which are green and thick with black eyeliner and beautiful.

Ask me why people go to the movies. You won't ask, right? Because it's obvious. There is nothing complicated about why people would stop driving around Mercer Island, staring out their car windows at those black, petrified parking lots with the birds sulking in the garbage, and come inside where it's warm and where *Kickass: The Movie* is playing on two screens at 11:00, 11:45, 1:00, 1:45, blah blah blah, you can see it very clearly from the left-hand escalator and I've looked at it a million times. It's not complicated. First you meet these two guys, one famous and one black, and guess which one dies in the first five minutes? Obvious. And they're partners, I forgot to say, and the big white guy who always plays the Chief is playing the Chief, and he says the famous guy has to train these two women rookies, one of whom used to be a stripper and the other one I forget. I mean, it's based on practically the most famous TV show ever, so even if it was complicated you could just stay inside your crampy house and flip channels for five minutes and find an episode which would explain it all for you in about ten kickass seconds, and it's not complicated. It's not. Even on Thursdays it's packed. The villain wants to blow up a stadium full of innocent baseball fans, and guess if he succeeds or if the two women who have to wear tight leather pants as part of an undercover operation manage to stop him, and guess if the famous guy gets to use that top-secret mini-submarine we got to see in the opening credits. Right? Right? Right? Right? Right? Obvious.

The only reason I'm blah-blah talking about it is so that you get what kind of night it was. Late, is what kind, but also obvious, and the obvious part was sort of messing with the kickass part, if you know what I mean. Like, just for instance, standing ten feet away from Lila was sort of kickass, with her nails drumming on the box with the slot in it where we put everything that we rip in half, and with her blue-eyed beauty and with the gum she was chewing and with how lovely she was, in that way that makes you want to find something else lovely just so you can give it to her and see how really kickass it is to have two lovely things next to each other in the Sovereign Cinemaplex. But the kickassness of Lila was a sort of muted kickassness, a kickassness tainted with melancholy, because there was also the obvious part, which was named Keith.

Keith. Unchivalrous Keith. Keith who picked her up from work every night, and who, if this was *Kickass: The Movie*, would have a little fuzz of mustache so that we would know what an asshole he was, except this being the real-life Seattle Metropolitan Area there was no way anybody could tell and so he just drove up to the Sovereign and beeped his horn and Lila just pushed open the swinging glass doors with the stupid stickerheads of all the famous people stuck to them and ran out into the night of Keith without anybody running after her and saying, "Don't go out there to Keith! The boy who has stood by you, at the left-hand escalator, for nine Thursdays and eight Saturdays, loves you very much, plus his chivalry!" Which is the kickass part on my end, the part I think about every Lila moment, from the first bell for Ms. Wylie to the tearing of every little ticket that is handed to me: the total King Arthur chivalry that sits deep in my puny, frantic heart. Example of chivalry, why am I working at the Sovereign? What is the money for? To buy flowers for Lila and to give them to her. Keith? Honk honk honk, please come running out of the Cinemaplex doors and jump into the seat next to me where there are no flowers and I won't even tell you how nice you look, I bet. But my secret special kickass chivalry is tainted, obviously, by obviousness. And it's the obvious thing that it's not going to happen. Because there might be a suburb of Seattle where a girl says, "Oh my god! Flowers? You are chivalrous, Joe," and then I win and she doesn't care that Keith has one of those all-terrain things that will come in so handy when the world ends and we need a nine-thousand-cylinder engine to drive over the hordes of bloodthirsty mutants crawling all over the video-game landscape, or maybe there's a suburb of Seattle where Lila wouldn't care whether or not her chivalrous suitor was wearing a fucking WELCOME TO THE BIG SHOW! button on a red why-the-hell-is-it-fireproof Sovereign Cinemaplex vest which is sort of blocking the signals of that hungry heart of mine, and Lila and I drive around this other suburb of Seattle in a car I take care of myself on weekends and tell each other a big bag of secrets we've been hiding underneath the beds our parents bought us, tossing and turning over its poky burlap creases and staring out of the window screens at a spooky blue moon that is beaming down secret New York bus tickets of a grown-up love future, and then someplace where the sun is setting or rising she takes her top off, but I don't live in that suburb of Seattle. I live on Mercer Island, and here we just tear tickets and wait to watch her go home.

Here I was maybe forty minutes ago, sort of claustrophobed in the gap between the kickass movie world where Lila dumps the guy with the smarmy mustache and the obvious one where it just keeps getting later. It was the last show and were I to guess it was just the moment where the stripper woman is forcing the hired-sunglasses dude to tell her who sent him to mess up all the chrome in her apartment where she sits in a towel and stares at a picture of her brother who was killed in a motorcycle accident, when Lila and I see this guy with his hands behind his back walking very slowly across the Sovereign carpet staring straight down like the chivalrous code of the wisdom of the ancients was encoded in stray kernels of popcorn that it was my turn to suck up before closing.

"At this point," says the woman who I'm beginning to remember was in the air force but was thrown out for insubordination, "we are departing for regions unknown."

This guy was not from Mercer Island. He was older than me. He was the age where chivalry has rewarded you, I hope I hope I hope, and he was carrying a jacket. When he reached the two escalators, he stopped looking at the carpet and looked at both of us, and then he did what I would have done, which is go over to Lila.

"Hey," he said, "has anybody turned in a pair of keys? Two keys, on a ring?"

"Turned in?" Lila said, chewing her beautiful gum. "I don't think so."

The guy frowned and then looked at me and I made a face to the guy like I don't have your keys either. "Is there—could I check the lost and found or something?"

"We don't really have like a lost and found," Lila said. "We have a box with some sweaters in it, behind popcorn. But nobody turned in anything tonight. Did you lose them tonight?"

"Yeah," the guy said. "I don't know when, but tonight. Two keys on a ring. I can't find them. I've been looking all over the parking lot and I went back to the restaurant where we ate so, um, I thought I'd try here."

"Sorry," Lila said. She looked at this guy and shrugged just a little little bit. It was sort of a gorgeous sneak preview of the "Sorry" shrug supercombo that I would get some day if I actually bought the flowers and laid them at her gorgeous hardcore rap-star sneakers, and maybe that's why I spoke up. Or maybe, probably, it was the jacket. Maybe it was the pretty dream of a time when my fireproof vest would be nowhere and if someone asked me, like at a party where everything is poured into real glasses, did you ever work at the Sovereign Cinemaplex, I would call across my chrome Manhattan place to my wife and say, "Lila? Remember like a hundred years ago when we used to rip tickets in half? This guy in the jacket wants to know about it," and we'd all shout the healthy, excited laugh of people with ice in their drinks who can stay out as late as they want, a time in my life when sorry wouldn't be good enough when I've lost my keys and I'm looking for them on the filthy floor and hoping against hope against hope for a chivalrous squire to say "What movie were you in?"

"What movie were you in?" I asked. Yeah.

The guy sighed. "That one with all of those skinny women kicking things," he said. "You know, *Kickass*."

"*The Movie*," I said, and I said it perfect. I know because the guy gave me a little smile like he and I knew the same perfect code of: this world is suckier than we are, and the best thing to do is keep moving and find your keys. The kickass rookie women smile at the famous guy the same way after the three of them break up a fight at the biker bar where they go to get to know each other over a product-placement beer by pounding this bandanna asshole against a heavy metal jukebox playing a song that was popular a million years ago when my parents roamed the earth free and loose. "Let's get to work," the famous guy says, and the women nod, like yeah I know, I know so well that you didn't need to say it but you're not at all geeky and overtalkative for saying it anyway. I walked over to Lila's escalator and reached down to the flashlight they make us wear, clipped to my belt, bouncing along my thigh like a bonus helping of embarrassing. I held it up for the guy. "Let's get to work, check it out. We can go in there and see if it's on the floor. See if you dropped it."

"Yeah," he said, smiled again, my chivalrous compadre. "Thanks."

Lila was looking at me with some gorgeous indecisive loveliness, like she couldn't decide if I was cool because I could talk to this guy, like we were two cool guys standing near her, or if I'd just dragged him down and we were two lame guys who weren't Keith and that was all we had to offer. "There's people in there," she said. "The movie is playing."

"We won't bother them," I said. "We won't bother the movie patrons." I said a bullshit word like *patrons* so the guy would know that I didn't think those people would stop us for a second. "This guy lost his keys," I said. "It's more important than a movie. We'll be quiet."

"Thanks," the guy said, nodding at me.

"Okay?" I said to Lila, and I watched her consult. She consulted the same imagination that bought that lipstick, and made her face a sexy promise for anyone who happened to have at least one working eye in their yearning little head. *What principles from the life of Sir Gawain do you see practiced in your own life?* asks Ms. Wylie's essay question which is due on Monday, and I watched Lila consult her imagination. I might be the guy practicing chivalry, I hope I hope she was thinking. "Okay?" I said. "Okay?"

"Whatever," she said. "Be careful out there."

By this time the threesome had cornered the main suspect, but it was so early in the movie you knew he couldn't be the right guy, even if you didn't actually see that the real mastermind had created a false digital trail by utilizing the satellite time he exchanged for rubies in the shadowy scene they filmed in a hurry. "Your training is over," the famous guy tells the slightly hotter of the two women after she kicks in the door before he can, and we opened the swinging doors at the back of the theater and cast a fine yellow slice of light, all laid out as a triangle on the carpet like a big piece of pie. Some heads swiveled and swiveled back to the sputtering wrong suspect, who they made a sissy for comic relief.

"Where were you?" I said. "Where was your seat?"

"She wanted to be toward the back," he said and his jacket

shrugged in the closing light of the door. "She said it was going to be loud."

He led the way. "But there are like fifteen speakers all over the walls," I said. "You can't escape a movie loud like this."

"Don't I know it," he said grimly.

"Shut up," said someone who got himself an aisle seat so as to show the world, *Hey, I got boots.* The guy glared and for a minute I thought that *Kickass* might start playing on one more screen, if you know what I mean. Wicked boot man didn't want any real-life audio to interfere with the famous guy saying, "Of course! It's a false digital trail," but my guy was all set with the chivalry secret weapon.

"I'm very sorry, sir," and in the light of the next morning in front of police headquarters I was so fucking proud of him. Chivalrous chivalrous with the "I'm very sorry" and the "sir," and without a sword being drawn my man Gawain made the guy embarrassed *and* wearing boots. "I heard about your shenanigans last night," the Chief said all grumpy on the screen, but I knew my guy was shenanigan-free.

He stopped in the aisle. "Here I think," he said, and it was pretty empty. He moved my flashlight slightly and we saw some couple making out and a few bored alone men. "Or a row up or down, or two rows, I don't know."

"We'll find it," I said. "We'll look."

"I hope so," the guy said. "I got a girl outside and she's not that happy at me about it."

"Outside?" I said. It was cold outside, what else is new in this part of the world.

"Smoking," he said. "She's a smoker. A smoker, and she's a dream, and I think she might vanish if I don't find those god-damn keys on a ring if you know what I mean."

I knew what he meant and felt for him, to get a girl and then not be able to bring her indoors. My pal Garth blew it almost the same way after a girl he met at camp invited him down to San Francisco for a weekend. He has the kind of parents who always said no, so he saved the money himself and took the bus down, listening to a mix I made him over and over, while I stood by the phone to vouch that he was in the shower if they called. My man Garth slapped on aftershave in the station rest room so the smell of his sweat would be invisible. Picture it like a movie. Play it like a movie in your head, the montage of his Saturday, of a brunch with her parents and a walk alone across that beautiful bridge, kissing with tongue in the exact middle of it, like a love song playing for the lovely parts of the movie, some obvious love song previously unreleased by the original artist and now a theme for Garth's motion-picture weekend with Kate, with the lyrics all hooked up to them so if it was "Everything I Do, I Do It for You," it would be "Everything Garth Does, He Does It for Kate."

But then he lost the fifty bucks. He took her to the movies for some French thing she wanted and had already called down on his parents' phone to the French restaurant to reserve a dinner afterwards and was prepared to catch hell for it when the phone bill came. But the hell of losing one of his hard-saved fifty-dollar bills and to scour the floor as the audience poured out, willing himself not to cry as he brushed the spilled kernels of someone else's date to look for it in the nothing and gum spread out before him, while Kate stood embarrassed with her purse and finally stammer to admit the dinner couldn't happen? Who can fucking dare to tell me that love is intangible when it's so obvious that it's not? The people who say *intangible* have places of their own. It's not intangible. Garth felt it. He felt it with the lost fifty dollars on the floor. I felt it. Garth and Kate did not have sex that weekend and never wrote again in their embarrassment. "Get down!" the hero says as the windows explode, and everyone ducks so the shatter won't rip them up. I got down on the ground all fierce with fucking chivalrous determination to find this guy Gawain's keys, because the good guys have to be teammates or the masterminds like Dr. Drecko will make life permanently harsh, Esmeralda!

I've seen this movie so many times.

Gawain ducked down one row ahead of me near the makeouts, and I scanned the ugly floor with my flashlight with an imaginary rap song fired up in my head about motherfuckers finding motherfucking keys boy, as the water rose in the basement chamber with the girls all chained together and their costumes getting wet and sexy, and I found them right as the handcuffs broke.

"Hey," I said, and swallowed my Gawain and offered a gratitude prayer someplace that I hadn't said it out loud. "Hey, I found your keys."

The makeout couple stopped with the tongue to shush me and it was a miracle like the ignition keys being in the helicopter when they finally reach the roof without a second to lose. It was

Keith and some other chick. She had a scarf draped around her and he was all guilty with the lipstick and he stared, knowing me, seesawing between humble and angry. He made the wrong choice.

"Shut up, *Joe*," he said. "And stop shining that light or I'll kick your ass. Go sell popcorn or whatever. You're the *usher*."

"And you're Lila's boyfriend," I said.

"You don't know what you're talking about," said the girl, and then it popped into her head to play with Keith's hair.

"Lila and I have an arrangement," Keith said.

"Then you won't mind me mentioning that," I said, "when I return to the escalator, *sir*." I made good with my posture. "Lila is a lady," I said, "kind and true. The most beautiful here is Lila, flashing her gray eye. No one has ever seen anyone lovelier in his day. The first I gazed upon her face I knew. It was in sixth grade and that girl Allison was crying about something in the stairwell, and Lila was hugging her so tight and nicely. She was hugging her out of *kindness*. She even said *ssh*, a person who has the kindness to say *ssh* when someone is brokenhearted. I watched her kind small head tucked on top of Allison's shoulder and noticed for the first time the lovely story of her, and how gorgeous it would be to stay on this island with her throughout high school, quietly loving her all this time. It's obvious she's a person to love and obviously I love her. Love is this clear thing of revering her, lending your chivalry to her pretty pants and the way she tosses her hair up behind her on rare sunny days and those gray eyes, the luscious gray of them like when the clouds are beautiful even if you're not buzzed, and so how fucking dare you, Keith. How dare you with the insults to her character by saying there's an arrangement. Lila has *honor*, Keith, so how dare you, and with this girl I think I recognize from the winter musical!"

By now people were shushing us and plus I didn't really say all that, especially the parts I stole from *Sir Gawain and the Green Knight*. "You don't have to say it," the stripper spy says at the end of the movie and ruffles the famous guy's hair all shiny in the spinning red light of the sirens. It wasn't the end yet but I knew what was coming. Keith stood up and sort of punched me like pizza dough at my old job, right on WELCOME TO THE BIG SHOW!

"If you fucking tell Lila *anything*—" he said.

"What's up?" my guy said, standing up with a handful of something. "*Hey*," he said, because Keith was still grabbing my vest. The guy reached out quietly and Keith put his hand down.

"This is *personal*," Keith said, suddenly all whiny.

"He was bothering us," said the temptress.

"This guy's here because of me." My man Gawain stepped into the aisle right beside me as if almost for color guard. "He's helping me. Just chill. The villain gets his ass defeated, if you're worried."

"I'm not *worried*," Keith said, and sat down.

"Then sit down," Gawain said.

"I found your keys so let's go," I said to him. We paused anyway and looked down at the couple writhing in the light of the big boom as the truck went off the bridge. It looked dangerous but the hero whooped like a rodeo. "Enjoy the show," I said calmly, "*sir*."

We strode the aisle like we were medals of honor, or at least deserved them. We stopped underneath the EXIT sign to share the spoils, the light emerald on our faces like the whole night was green. It was a pretty green night.

"Do you really have my keys?" Gawain said.

I held them out to see and then tossed them into the air for him to catch with confidence and he did. "Thanks," he said, "and I found something for you."

He held a hand in front of my eyes like he'd caught a frog down by the old-time creek, and then unfurled his fingers for me. Inside was a thing of beauty. It was a chain, of some dark metal, tiny thick links all wrung together so it looked like an elegant kind of tough that's hard to find outside of certain album covers. The chain was all curled around itself like something sleeping in a lair, but at rest in the center was the beautiful pendant. Shiny with special curlicues and all ornate like a palace, it was caught mid-prance for the world to see: a unicorn, man, mighty and lovely, with some kind of tiny semiprecious stones, one on the eye, one on the tip of the horn, and a three-stone glitter of a neck harness. Fucking wow.

"I thought you could give it to the girl," he said. "You know, by the other escalator. Looks like something that might win her heart."

"You could tell I like her?" I asked him.

He closed his hand and then held it over mine and dribbled the necklace into my sweaty palm. "It's obvious," he said, and then nodded back to Screen Four. "And now maybe you have a chance, huh? With that guy Keith blowing it."

"You heard?" I said. "You heard me?"

"I thought you did well," he said, reshouldering his jacket. "I only stepped in when it seemed like you needed backup."

The unicorn was cool and safe in my hand, but still it felt like it might be wrong. Some wow object like that would take me nine more evening shifts, minimum, the saving up slowed by the gas that the Sovereign commute required of me, and still I'd have to bribe my sister to help me choose and then again to shut up about it. "I can have this, really?" I said. "Are you for real?"

He swung the door open and we blinked like new babies in the lobby light. "It's yours," he said, "and she's yours too, and I gotta run or else mine will kill me."

He ran and left me with wonder in my pounding heart as he vanished, because how could this have happened? It's not an obvious thing. Obviously what should happen is the unrequited. Obviously Lila will never notice and our chrome apartment will never appear. You dream forever of the girls who stood next to you and didn't notice, as far as I can tell so far in this rainy life, or if you're gay maybe a boy in a locker-room glimpse or a wine-soaked memory of something furtive in a sleeping bag, although nothing like that has ever happened to me and I don't care what fucking Tomas says. No matter how solid and glittery the unicorn appears, it does not come true. There are no fanciful creatures from the world of epic poems prancing around Mercer Island, no matter how I dream them up. I'm not allowed them. I have a paper due on Monday. Tonight I saw Lila walk through the doors, singing along with the headphones, one of those gloomy tracks she loves with the British singer not making any sense. "You've got green eyes, you've got blue eyes, you've got gray eyes," he says to her, some guy dreaming with his band, but Lila isn't going to turn her eyes to me because if you saw it in a movie you would say, "How did Keith bring another girl to the movies without passing either Lila on the right-hand escalator or Joe on the left?"

So I must be dreaming, however sure the necklace feels in my hands. As the story comes to this Sovereign moment I must descend back down to where they tear the tickets. *I was all led astray by women I had known, and if that has happened to me perhaps I may be forgiven.* Even Gawain didn't get her all to himself for longer than a second, so let me believe in mine for a second, as I stand in my vest, before I turn the corner and go down down down. Obviously life and its bad times are around that corner, more of the real yearning for Lila and the loud and clear of it not happening and all my chivalry rewarded only by Ms. Wylie in an essay no one else will read. Don't break my heart just yet, or ask me to lose my reverie on the sticky floor. Grant me one more kickass moment on my island, and hear the boom-boom music muted behind the theater door, and let me believe I'm the guy they all paid to watch all big and mighty, in the dark where I guess I belong.

arguably

Money money money money money money money money. Let no one say it has no place in a love story. It has a particular place. It is something on the right shelf. When Helena bought the chianti, there was no question which shelf she'd take it from. "We have the cheap stuff on the right, and then it gets more and more expensive as you go along," said the liquor guy.

"You don't say," Helena said. She took a cigarette out of her ripped purse and lit it because she smoked. She was a smoker.

"I like to put the expensive stuff here where I can keep an eye on it," the guy said.

Helena blew a smoke ring, which was illegal in this country. "Well," she said, "I'll be over here, as far as possible from you."

"You have a sexy accent," the guy said. "Are you from some-place?"

"Yes," Helena said. "I'm from Britain, originally."

"I told you," the guy said. "Because you can't smoke in a liquor store in San Francisco. In *California*, and everyone knows it. So I figured you're new."

"I guess I am new," Helena said and walked toward him with

a bottle. "I imagine you have a lot to teach me," and this is a good example. Why would she say this? Helena was a young woman, originally from Britain, whatever that means. She was a smoker. She had a sexy accent and a bottle of wine in her hands. The wine was chianti, also from Europe, and very cheap in this case, but that was no excuse for the "I imagine you have a lot to teach me," or that milder, less scrutable joke about being cheap herself. Why behave this way? Helena was beginning to think there was no particular reason. Arguably, of course, there was a particular reason that Helena could not find. Perhaps she had left it in Britain. She paid for her wine, in American currency. Money money money money money.

Helena had moved to New York first. She planned to stay there and work on a new book until her money ran out. Her money ran out in nine days. Prices will have changed as people read this book, so I'll try to explain it this way: let's say Helena arrived in New York with money from the American publication of her first novel in the amount of seven hundred billion dollars. She found a hovel of an apartment, crawling with grimy American insects, that cost five hundred billion a month to rent, and half a million usually went to the taxi driver who took her there. Milk—*milk!*—cost a hundred thousand dollars. A pair of smashing, striking new boots cost over a billion. Nine days was actually something of a miracle, although not the miracle Helena was hoping for. Unfortunately this is also the way she explained it to her husband.

David sighed when he heard it. "You really shouldn't say smashing or striking," he said, possibly to change the subject. "Those are terms from Britain, really. In America smashing or striking means something different, sort of violent. You know, *I'm smashing and striking you.* It's all the same to me, but if we're going to live here—"

"We can't afford to live here," Helena said in her boots. "To live in New York for nine days costs more than the gross national product of my country of origin."

"Have you written anything?" David asked.

"Yes, I've written something," Helena said. She had two drafts of the first sentence of a novel, on the index cards taped to the end of the tub, where she could look at them in the bath, if that's the expression. One was, "I imagine you have a lot to teach me," and the other was, "I imagine you are going to teach me a lot." She hadn't decided between the two, but she also had something a little longer written in a four-hundred-thousand-dollar notebook.

"Take it to your editor," David said. "Show your editor what you have written and he'll give you some money."

Helena knew that's not how it goes but she went to lunch. "Something new?" the editor said with a frown. He was Caucasian, or white, and it was almost Christmas. Helena forged ahead with her plan of reading it out loud.

Dear Mother,
I am about to run out of money. Please send me some money.
I need a lot of money. Please send me all, or nearly all, of
your money. Money money money money money. Please,
Mommy. I love you.
Love,
Helena

"And," Helena said, "in parentheses, *your daughter*."

The editor took a bite of paid-for cheese but he didn't look content. "That's from your new novel?"

"No," Helena said. "That's a letter to my mother. My new novel is a love story, but the love story, your editorship, requires money."

"The thing is," the editor said, and Helena waited for the thing. "We're still waiting for your first novel to really catch fire."

Helena liked this guy, and the idea of her novel catching fire, like a virgin thrown into a volcano, if one were available, the heat from the center of the earth catching first the pages and then the cardboard cover and the dust jacket until her entire career was in ashes. It was a lovely idea but it didn't sound like a money-maker. "What's the problem?" she said. "Why hasn't it caught on fire?"

"Just *caught fire*," the editor said, "is the American term. The title might be a problem. You called your novel *Glee Club*."

"I didn't just *call* it *Glee Club*," Helena said. Speakers embedded in the ceiling of the restaurant began to announce that they were dreaming of a white Christmas. "It's *called Glee Club*. That's the *title*."

"It's a British term," the editor said, "and I think Americans might not know what it means."

"The term *glee*," Helena said out loud, "is derived from the Anglo-Saxon *gliw* or *gléo* (entertainment, fun) especially as connected with minstrelsy—playing, singing, dancing, and perhaps even acrobatic feats. Until fairly recent times it was in this spirit that *American* college glee clubs, with rare exceptions, interpreted the term." This was from the *Harvard Dictionary of Music*, second edition, revised and enlarged, by Willi Apel, the Belknap Press of Harvard University Press, Cambridge, Massachusetts, fourteenth printing, which she threw at David for no particular reason she could think of, even that night in the bath. "See, they know it. They've had two hundred years to know it. Britain and America are exactly the same. I'm tired of people saying they don't understand, and that it's a British expression. I *know* what expression it is."

David had made some phone calls that afternoon, which again was a miracle. It was a miracle that the American government, in its two hundred plus years of ruthless history, did not have the common sense to shut down Helena's phone line when there was no way in heaven or on earth that she would be able to come up with the millions of American dollars required to pay the bill. "Do you remember my old girlfriend Andrea?" he asked.

"Whom you loved," Helena said, "and, who you told me once in a fit of pique, gave you the best blowjobs of your life?"

"That's the one," David said. "She works for an arts something in San Francisco and thinks she can get you a gig at a school."

David had this kindness thing he did which occasionally drove Helena up a wall with jealousy, if that's the term. She loved him, but arguably this wasn't enough. She had failed him, because her novel, *Glee Club*, first edition, St. Martin's Press, New York, New York, first printing, had failed to catch fire, and there were all these inexplicable things that came out of her mouth. Outside the restaurant she said to her editor, "What would happen if I slept with you?" The editor, to her relief, gave the question the same false consideration he had given the two index cards she had slid his way over dessert. "I'd probably ejaculate," he said, and got into the waiting taxi. "I'll speak to you soon, Helena." And look at her now, saying, "What's the difference between moving to San Francisco and staying here in New York in utter misery without any money money?"

"It's all the same to me," David said, "but San Francisco is warmer and apparently the people are more something. A credit card could fly us there. Andrea was telling me about a great bar she went to, and an apartment she used to live in, and there's a rumor that the entire city is resting on an active volcano they just discovered. Everyone's skittish so the rent is low, and plus, of course they're afraid of terrorists."

"I am," Helena said, "also afraid of terrorists. And I'm afraid I don't know what a gig is."

"It's a job," David said. "A teaching job in San Francisco. We'll kill two birds with one stone."

"Dead birds everywhere," Helena said out loud. "Littering that famous bridge they have over in San Francisco. The Gate Bridge."

"Golden." David was picking off the traces of tape Helena had left at the end of the tub, as if they were already hoping for the security deposit back. "I think we might do better there, scrape scrape scrape," he and his fingernails said, "and your mother scrape scrape thinks the same thing."

Helena's mother. Helena's mother. Mother mother mother. Helena thinks of her mother visiting, and that she could throw her into the active volcano. But what if these arguments were wrong? She leaned toward her husband and gave him a big kiss where the book had hit him. This is love, moving to where the money is, and all the while a volcano or an ex-girlfriend might blow the whole thing to hell, as the Americans say. As everybody says. Arguably there was more to this story, and there is. "But what if there's no volcano?" Helena said. "What am I going to do then?"

"I imagine," David said, "you are going to teach."

particularly

The sign in the teachers' lounge said YOUR MOTHER DOES NOT
WORK HERE, presumably referring to cleanliness. At the
word *lounge* Helena had imagined a dark, lovely place, with elegant cocktails and drapery, perhaps an old black-and-white
movie on a screen without sound. Instead this was a room with
some chairs in it and things taped on the walls. Love is like this,
plenty of places to sit but an overall feeling that the room needs
a good uptight scrubbing until everything that mentions your
mother has been washed away. "I imagine you don't have a
teachers' lounge in Britain," said Andrea, Helena's supervisor.

"We do not," Helena said, moving one of the chairs.

Andrea moved it back. "I imagine you'll enjoy this job," she
said. "I imagine you have a lot to teach them. We're giving you
afternoons and mornings. In between you can be here, or outside
if you're a smoker."

"I'm a smoker," Helena said. It was true. She was from Britain originally and had published a novel entitled *Glee Club*. This
had led to a position in a creative expression program in a private
school, although *led* was not the right word for how she ended up
here, and *gig* was sometimes what she called it. The answer was
money, which had a particular place in Helena's love story. She

and her husband needed to buy things pretty much on a regular basis. This teaching job did not pay a lot of money, because, let's face it, nobody gives a flying fuck about education, but it was a temporary position. Helena had been told it would last until the money ran out. From Helena's experience, she would say that the money was going to run out in about nine days.

"It's a temporary position, like I told you," said Andrea, who had said no such thing. "Pretty much what happens is, you facilitate the creative expression part. You're a creative expression facilitator. Get it?"

Andrea was an ex-girlfriend of Helena's husband, so she said "Get it?" like one might say, "The same man has seen both of us naked, and prefers you, bitch."

"Of course I get it," Helena said, but she sighed. Things like this had not happened to her in England. She could not explain the difference, perhaps because there wasn't one. Certainly England had castles, but Helena had not lived in them, although memories of her British life had become more and more glamorous the longer she hung out at hideous places like this.

"The first thing is, a field trip where the children will see what's-its on migration. Magpies. It's sponsored by the Men's Organization for Magpie Migration for Youth, who are donating their services for free. That'll take place tomorrow, unless the volcano erupts." This was a San Francisco joke due to some rumors of a volcano lurking underneath the city. They had just discovered it, a volcano that had gone unnoticed but was now given official membership in the geological phenomenon known as the Ring of Fire. It was one of those news stories that made everyone giggle but might also be true. It was like love in that way: Look at this! What's going to happen here? "Unless the volcano erupts" became a joke, like "See you Friday, unless the volcano erupts," or "I'll love you forever, unless the volcano erupts."

"So tomorrow I take them to see birds?" Helena said, thinking of what to wear.

"But today," Andrea said, "you do a lesson on birds. Magpies in particular. Do you know anything about magpies?"

When my mother was young she went to Thanksgiving at a friend's house and asked her friend's mother what she could do to help. "You can make a butter bird," the mother said to my mother, and handed her two small paddles and a mound of butter. A butter bird is, butter shaped into the shape of a decorative bird, but the point is, why is there cruelty? Why do people ask other people to do impossible things? Why behave this way? Why is there mean, when there are better things than mean, love particularly? "Oh, I know everything about all kinds of birds," Helena said, like it might be true. "At university I studied ornithology before switching to poetry."

"In America," said cruel Andrea, "we don't say *at university*. We say *in college*. Do you have information about magpies specifically?"

"I know a thing or two about magpies," Helena said helplessly. "A thing or two."

"Then I'll keep all the brochures the Men's Organization sent me," Andrea said, standing up smug and skinny and smug. "We're combining both grades, so it'll be fifty kids, in one hour from now. You can't smoke in here."

"I just like to keep a cigarette in my hand," Helena said, putting it back in the pack. "It helps me think. Tell me, what happened to the last woman who had this job?"

"She did a unit on idiomatic expressions that went way over the kids' heads," Andrea said, "so I fired her."

The door shut and Helena was alone in the lounge, wishing it were legal to smoke so she could light a cigarette and put it in her eye. Instead she ran to the school library where there was a miracle: *The Magpies: The Ecology and Behaviour of Black-billed and Yellow-billed Magpies*, by Tim Birkhead with illustrations by David Quinn, T & AD Poyser Publishers, London, England, first printing. By the time the hour passed away Helena had a list of interesting facts which she said out loud, and when Andrea came to check on her the fifty children were silent and interested, working hard on a creative expression exercise. "Attractive, artful, and aggressive are all terms which have been used to describe magpies, and they are all accurate," is the first sentence in *The Magpies: The Ecology and Behaviour of Black-billed and Yellow-billed Magpies*, and Helena told them they could write a story which was either attractive, artful, or aggressive, their choice.

"That worked," Andrea admitted, giving Helena a shiny smile as the students filed out of the room. "Of course, it was probably your accent. The kids love foreign accents like that."

"That would explain America's rabid interest in audio recordings of Winston Churchill's speeches," Helena said, but Andrea was telling her to watch her purse.

"Watch my purse," Andrea said, "while I get your paperwork. I'm afraid you won't get your money for twelve weeks."

"Okay," Helena said, but when Andrea left the room she

opened the purse and found the wallet. There was a ridiculous amount of cash money and she took all of it. It was gone and in Helena's pocket long before Andrea returned with a plastic cup.

"We have to test you for drugs, is how we do it in America," Andrea said. "You have to pee in this."

On the way home Helena bought a magnum of very expensive champagne from a liquor-store guy who flirted outrageously with her. She flirted back and drank most of it on the way, the bottle as heavy as a pair of twins. "How did you drink all that without peeing?" her husband said, when she walked in the door.

"Oh, I peed," Helena said. "Don't worry about that."

"Everyone I've ever gone out with," David said, "has drunk too much. Your mother told me you'd probably be tipsy when you got home from your first day of new work. You're British but even all the Americans I dated, they all drank too much."

"What are you saying?" Helena said. "That there's no difference? With magpies even, there's different what's-it, between the British and here in California. *Plumage.*"

"What I'm saying," David said kindly, "is that first thing tomorrow morning you have to take fifty children out to the hinterlands to look at black birds. Andrea says to meet at the place at eight sharp."

"They have *yellow breasts*," Helena said sourly, "and don't tell me you don't notice, David. Andrea's got enormous ones."

"It's all the same to me," David said, and then sighed very kindly, too. "I don't think this conversation is going well," he said. "You're being a little aggressive."

"You're being a little *artful*," Helena said, "and Andrea's being a little *attractive*. I can't believe you talked to *my* mother and *your* ex-girlfriend while all the while I was buying you a bottle of expensive champagne."

"Which you've drunk most of," David said, "and I don't like."

"Look," Helena said. "*Look*, I love you and I don't know what to do. I'm worrying about money. That can't be love." She slunk down on a chair she had bought on a whim. It cost let's say three million dollars. Her mother told her that you can't live on love, but Helena could not find anything else to live on. This is love and its trouble. You can earn it but it may not come for twelve more weeks, so you take it from other people and buy gifts for your lover he does not like and you drink most of. You take it to live on and you worry there's never enough. Helena could not stand this line of reasoning, but the trouble was, not standing this line of reasoning didn't pay anything either.

"I love you, too," David said, and took the bottle.

"I want you to love me in particular," Helena said. "I'm not the same as an American. I'm my own species and I want you to be picky about it, if that's the expression. How can it be all the same to you? What is it, did we move here so you could be with Andrea again?"

"*I'm* not with her," David said. "She gave you a job."

"Her and her jobs," Helena said. "Just tell me you love me."

"I love you," David said, "but I'm not sure that's enough for the likes of you."

"Then tell me you love me and give me a hundred billion dollars," she said, and David shook his head. In the morning there was no field trip, but not because the volcano erupted. There was no field trip due to weather, if that's the expression. Rain fell all over the windows and Helena had the class write letters to her mother and read them out loud for creative expression. Helena wrote a list of things that had to be in the letter, but they could be creative.

Dear Helena's Mother,
It is expensive to call from San Francisco to London so you should call. After all you're the mom. Is my husband David sleeping with Helena's boss?
Sincerely yours,
Laurie

Dear Helena's Mother,
You sound mean. Helena is doing the best she can. Maybe you should yell at David for once.
Love,
Mike

Dear Mommy,
Stop making Helena call the other way. You can't live on love. You are a mean mommy and David and Andrea might be kissing. Oh, what shall I do?
Your Friend,
Todd

Dear Mommy,
I want a horse for Christmas.

It was possible Margaret didn't understand the assignment, but it didn't matter because Andrea came in halfway and put an end to the entire program. "The money is gone," she said, with a significant look in Helena's dismayed direction. "You can throw those letters away, kids."

Helena would never have called them kids, but maybe this was an American thing. "Don't throw them away!" she cried. "I'm going to send those letters to my mother!"

The kids for some reason were cruel, and Helena was bombarded with balled-up letters and paper airplanes, like a terrorist action from a country not known for terror. "Look," Andrea said, when they all had left. Helena looked where Andrea was looking, at some rubbage of letters on the floor. "I just mean, *look*," Andrea said, picking up after her. "The expression *look*. The gig's over. The money is gone. Get it?"

"My mother doesn't work here," Helena said, "and neither do I."

Andrea sighed. "You're fired," she said, "I'm fired, we're all fired without the money."

"We're part of the ring of fired," Helena tried, and put an airplane in her purse. "Like the song. I fell into a something ring of fire. Johnny Money."

"*Burning*," Andrea said. "*Cash*."

"*Aggressive*," Helena said. "*Artful*." This was the creative expression part, the part they were going to pay her for. What was the third word? She felt fat. "Money," she said, and looked out the window. The rain was spread hard all over like an ocean of cheap wine, wet and seasonal, and this was like love too. We love someone in particular, but without money it's all the same to us; we're in despair. Without money we can stand next to someone else's girlfriend instead, for all the love it brings. This wasn't enough for the likes of Helena, and every word of the love she was losing was sadder as she said it. Every word got sadder, every letter nothing in her purse. "Money," she said again. "Money money money money money money money money."

briefly

Golfing today I beheaded a magpie. Yes yes yes, oh baby yes. Some kind of bird, anyway—grant me this—midair in the curve of the ball I hit. It fell. I walked across the lawn wondering what it was I had seen, some small glop of something fallen. It was a good swing and my eyesight is strong, but there are moments it doesn't matter if you look or not. The magpie's mouth was open like it couldn't believe it either. I picked up the ball and looked at the stain of blood in a perfect square. I sort of nudged the body with my foot, rolled it over into a thicker part of the grass. It was all alone, the bird. And here I bury you, O thing who winged your way into my path. Only I know of your poor little murdered head.

I grew up in the sort of house with a pool out back, and a small shack to shower and change into clothes to swim in the pool, and my older sister. She had boyfriends. Usually I went someplace else when they came splashing in, because my older sister grabbed boyfriends in ways that meant no girls came around the house. I was fourteen. The girls were at the pool at the club, so I went to the pool at the club, and there they sat, the girls older than me, rows of legs, rows of sunglasses, rows of laughing together. They let me sit knowing I was staring at them: a meager insult to my older sister, the only boy they could keep. Yes yes yes, oh baby yes. I handed them the lotions. Yes yes yes, oh baby yes. This was my summer, my two summers, my long weekends, all the sudden sunshine veering into town without reason, and all of it has abandoned me. I have loved none of those girls. I could not picture for you what any bathing suit revealed, although that's where I must have been looking, fourteen years old, all that skin that crossed my path. Yes yes yes, oh baby yes.

What I remember is named Keith. By all means he was not the favorite because my older sister had no favorites. Anybody could hand her snitched rum in the good glasses while she lay out and waited. By agreement, on these rare afternoons without the club I was changing in the shack and then would swim alone at the deeper end, while the boyfriend would stray at the shallow where my older sister dangled herself, and cup handfuls of the pool and let them run down her legs until dusk, while I treaded the surface of nine feet of water and pulled myself out on the shaky ladder when my skin couldn't wrinkle any longer. Four steps on the ladder, three steps on the ladder, five steps, I could not tell you now. That ladder has abandoned me, some maybe moment when I could have pulled myself out. That was the last time, when I emerged myself out of the pool and went to the shack to change forever, the moment before I fell, if fallen is what I am feeling, if fallen is what I am.

Show me the man who would not love the man who stepped out of the shower and put on his briefs, because I would love

that man too. Yes yes yes, oh baby yes. Soaking wet the shoulders, the hair spiked with water, pushed back with his hand
which had a hippie ring on it of thick pewter, silver, some girlfriend gift, some souvenir of a place he went before he walked
into my path forever once. Hair the color of the hills surround-
ing the club when the droughts hit, but nothing would get me
to the club again. His breathing chest rising carelessly from the
rest of him, but the desire here like nothing I can type: grant me
this. Yes yes yes, oh baby yes. Five years older, arms from the
shoulders with the careless towel hiding nothing, the chest
swelled and flat with impressing my sister, hair I had yet to
grow trailing toward me like warm smoke from someone's
mouth. Down to the legs, down to the penis, thick with sitting
all day near something he wanted but showered calm, never
something I had seen before. Oh, certainly: in locker rooms,
textbook something, but to no avail. Yes yes yes, oh baby yes.
There was no one I loved before Keith and his arms, his face
scarcely glancing at me, the thin line of not smiling as he shook
off water without fear. Where do they come from who can do
that, step out wet and share a small nude space with someone's
brother, cup his own penis for nothing, sit on the redwood
bench and dry his feet where I would never walk, wreck my life
like a pop song can wreck your brain? At fourteen I couldn't tell
you "swoon" and now I cannot remember any love but the
swoon of him until he picked through the scrabble of his
clothes and stepped into his underwear, and there was that little
stumble into my path. He nudged me on the spot on the side of
myself below my armpit oh my God. He nudged me and I oc-

of him for years? Yes yes yes, oh baby yes. Is it possible to lose someone who only stepped in front of you once in a towel? Yes yes yes, oh baby yes. Grant me this, this brief murdered moment, and then I will bury it sadly and go on with my game.

soundly

L et me explain what is happening to the Jewish people," the guy said. He had just come out of the lounge, and had spilled maybe coffee all over his vest, so recently that it still glittered and beaded on the ugly puffy fabric of it. He was speaking very loudly over music coming from his headphones, and this did not make him the best spokesperson as to what was happening to the Jewish people. We listened anyway. Lila and I had been Jewish all our lives and we were curious about what would happen to us.

"They want the money, right?" the guy said. "Let me explain it. They want all the world's money, right?"

"Right," we said. I was almost out of money myself and soon would be chained to a student loan. All the world's money *was* something I wanted, come to think of it.

"And the world's money is down in San Francisco," the guy said, "or San Fran, as everybody says. I'm going down there myself as sort of a freelance guard. Something terrible is going to happen down there that the Jews will use as an excuse. Maybe a building, like with terrorists, will . . ." The guy plucked his earphones from his ears and dropped them around his neck like one of those stupid pillows people wear on airplanes, and then spread his arms out like he was tossing handfuls of flour. He made a noise like a ten-year-old boy pretending to blow things up which is always the trouble. It was very pretty to look at, but then again I was drunk. I don't know why Lila was listening but she has always been kind.

"It'll either be guys with bombs or a volcano is my theory," the guy said. From his earphones we could hear an old song sung enthusiastically by the original artist. "You know how I know it?"

"I'm guessing a pamphlet you read," I said.

"I'm going to go with the Internet," Lila said. We turned to see if there'd be a guess from the only other person in the lounge, but the bartender was still cranky at the both of us and he stacked napkins to show us it was so.

"Both of you big-breasted girls are wrong," the guy said. "I did it by reading birds. They behave badly when disaster is going to strike. You know, like with earthquakes."

"Wouldn't an earthquake be more likely," Lila said, "in San Francisco?"

"Not in my theory," the guy said proudly.

"Well, that's a great theory," Lila said. She made a gesture like she might put her hand on the guy's stainy vest, if she weren't all the way across the lounge.

"Yeah," I said. "Go tell someone that theory and they'll interrupt the Super Bowl."

"You think I'm hilarious and crazy," the guy said, in that sudden spooky clarity only exhibited by crazy people. He walked backward toward a pair of swinging doors. "I'm just wrecked up. I've been beaten down by the knowledge of all the terrible things happening, and my theory is to tell my fellow man. In San Francisco my fellow man will see how wrecked I am and he'll treasure all the time he has before the Jews take over. So you're welcome, even if you don't love me and never will."

He put his tunes back on his head and left us there. We shifted in the booth of the lounge and I raised my finger to the bartender, who brought me another bourbon. "San Francisco," he said, shaking his head. "And I was just going down there to work in my brother's bar with better tips."

"We're going to tip you," I said, "at the end of our day."

The bartender snorted and caressed a blank TV which hung silent near the ceiling. He touched it like he could bring it back to life. "Not like you said," he murmured sadly, and Lila changed the subject.

"Everybody has a theory today," she said. "That woman leaving as we came in? She had a blackjack theory, how to win. It also had to do with birds, come to think of it, but they were her own birds, in cages."

I took a delicious sip. The bourbon was perfect but then it almost always is. "My theory is," I said, "pay no attention to theories in bars."

Lila patted my hand and took a fake sip of water. "You should get a guy like *that*."

"You just like him because he said you have tits," I said.

"No no no." Lila shook her head very carefully. "Clean him up and turn off his music and he's the guy for you. I always thought you'd do well with a guy who was apocalyptic. It would remind you nothing is the end of the world."

"Except when it is," I said, too quietly with my mouth full of drink. I ordered another. She was comforting me, which made me sick. Lila was the sick one, the one who ought to be comforted. This was an old song, too: she was sick and dying, for sure, in a lot of pain. We couldn't drive north enough to escape this: young people in a deserted bar, drinking as death approaches, and still the men come at us and still we notice them. The only thing you haven't heard about it is how rare she was, such a rare gastrointestinal thing that the doctors could never hide their excitement when they were called into the room. There had only been eight previous cases, one of them Lila's mother, who had died helpless, aching and coughing all over and finally screaming, Lila told me, when Lila was the only visitor left to her.

It had been Lila and her mother; today it was Lila and me. Lila had undergone one operation that had been invented since, when they rerouted a part of her intestines or some such shit, and for a while there'd been a capful of hope, sort of. They thought in a couple of years she might be able to eat, and when she farted the doctors opened a bottle of champagne to celebrate. They poured it into urine sample cups in the hospital room, except she couldn't have any and the doctors were on duty, so I finished the bottle myself and watched her doze in the upright bed. But it's always dawnest before dark. Now she had a beeper clipped to her waist, for when some poor soul with the same blood type stepped in front of a bus and offered up a digestive system, but even this was not the sort of hope one hopes for. This was hope that the operation would work for a few weeks, so that the doctors could learn something and maybe fix the next person. Lila herself would be granted more pain and a few months unless she died first. Hope was now hitched to the doctors, who were handsome to a fault and wore leather jackets when I saw them walking in the parking lot. Hope was hitched to them, and not to Lila, who rarely got to leave the room.

She wasn't supposed to be here, of course, but it depended on how you phrased it. Lila and I had phrased it as "Can we take a walk around the block and maybe even sit out on the spiky hospital grass?" The nurses were glued to the TV and gave us an absent okay, but instead we got into my car and left Seattle in the belly of a ferry across Puget Sound. It wasn't far, but it was far away, the ferry line the only thread which would lead us back. We drove north past Bainbridge and Kingston in search of the name that always cracked us up: Point No Point. There was a new casino, who knew? Inside it wasn't easy to find a place that didn't have the Super Bowl blaring on the screen. We weren't interested in the year's big football contest. We didn't think those guys needed any more encouragement. It took me waiting for the bartender to slip out for something, and taking one of the heavy chairs, lifting it over my head and banging it against the bottom of the TV over and over until it spat sparks, while Lila stood underneath the green EXIT sign and watched for his return. If she saw him coming she was going to give me the password. The password was, "Shit! The bartender's coming!"

Let us have our fun. By Super Bowl Sunday there was no one

to stop us. Lila's father had died when someone had killed him, and her husband had shot himself long before she even got sick, after a nervous breakdown that left him weeping and playing golf by himself in the rain. It was something else we had in common. She and I were cut from the same cloth, an angry odd quilt, and then she went and got sick just like her mother and I had to start drinking for both of us. *"Sick?"* I would hear myself yelling to the late-night science television. It was the only thing worth watching after visiting hours were done. "Why haven't we fixed *sick* yet? You scientists there—put down those starfish and *help us*. I hereby demand that all people who are good at math make the world free of illness. The rest of us will write you epic poems and staple them together into a booklet." Then I'd weep, finally, and fall asleep in Adam's sweatshirt and wake up and quit my job.

"Tell me a story," she said. "You're thinking about Adam, I can tell."

"Then I'll tell you a story about him," I said. "Once upon a time it was morning, and the two of us were hungover in Steven's old apartment on South King. It was when Andrea visited with that boyfriend of hers who turned out to be loopy."

"I've heard he's since straightened himself out," she said.

"You heard it from me, who's telling this story," I said. "The point is, five pitchers of margaritas is plenty. Andrea and what's-his-name were asleep on the couch and you in your room and by some miracle I was getting it together to make us a pot of coffee and banana waffles."

Lila smiled at the waffles, curling her beautiful lips in fond remembrance of having something to eat. "And?" she said.

"And bacon," I said, although this wasn't true. Bacon was my gift to her. "And there was a knock knock knocking on Steven's door. And behind the door was Adam, without a shirt on and holding his very old shoes."

"And so how could you not," Lila said, "take him and kiss him and live with him for six years? I mean, no shirt alone would be enough for most girls, Allison, but no shirt *and* holding old shoes? That's better than a Jewish doctor."

"Better than your doctors," I said. I could say this, and not just because it was true. I wasn't the only one who knew where the hope was hitched.

Lila dribbled her water into a potted plant above her on a counter, and then held the glass against her cheek like she'd downed a drink. "You know when I stopped with the doctors?" she said. "You know when I gave up on my life and just thought, *Well, if it makes the docs happy to learn something . . . ?* It was when that handsome one, except for the pimple under his eye, looked right at me and said *binomial nomenclature*."

She'd told me this story a thousand times. "Two-word name," I said.

"Two-*name* name," she said. "To look at me dying and waste breath with the Latin, and it's not even Latin. 'Okay, okay,' I told him, but he didn't get it, which was another bad sign."

"Like a bird behaving badly," I said.

She smiled right at me. "Or a chain saw," she said, "outside the window." Lila and I shared a room in college and spent one night drinking round after round of a 1930s drink recipe called the Suffering Bastard. We were almost out of bitters and brandy when we heard an evil buzzing outside. Boy oh boy was it very,

very late. We peered out the window and two boys were standing in the parking lot, holding chain saws and staring at us. We screamed and called the campus security, who arrived enthusiastically only to find the boys were holding remotes with antennae poking out of them, while miniature sportscars buzzed around the concrete, and that they were staring at us because we had thrown back the curtain and stood there in our underwear screaming at them. Also we knew these boys, Joe and Joe's friend what's-his-name. Our position was not one of strength, but Lila argued with campus security anyway.

"You were fierce," I told her, another bourbon gone.

"I was," Lila agreed faintly. "The point, as I saw it, and I still see it this way, is that they were dumb guys and ought to be rounded up, chain saws or no. I mean look, it's more than ten years later and the Super Bowl still exists. Do they honestly think I don't know why there were scarcely any doctors on my floor today?"

I looked at her: she was tops. She made me want to have a hero. "Who's your hero, Lila?" I said, hearing my bourbon on the lilt of her name.

She gave me the look I would have given me if I were me. That was the last fun night we really had, with the chain saws; her mom died two months later, and after that, no matter where we drank or what, we were the Suffering Bastards. "You're my hero," she said, "for driving me here and for lack of a better guess. Finally getting to Point No Point is the last thing that makes sense. You know how the nurses started asking me to rate my pain one to ten? I just started giving them random numbers.

You can't get to ten, I told the one with those earrings I want to yank out. You can't get to ten because someone might slap you and that would hurt more."

"I won't slap you," I said.

"Someone put 'Jewish' on the chart," she said, "so they sent in a rabbi who I swear looked pre–bar mitzvah."

"They sent you a *rabbi*?" I said.

"You must have been putting money in the meter," Lila said. "He had that rabbi curly hair, and it was his first gig after wherever you go to be a rabbi."

I signaled the bartender, who hung up a phone and sulked over without a bottle. "What did he say?"

Lila blinked very slowly, which she also did when she was drunk, like the move with her empty water glass. "He said I was a very pretty girl," she said. "He said I was beautiful."

"Let's go, girls," the bartender said. "Bar's closing."

"It's noon," I said, "or something."

"Tony says I can close it up," he said. "Super Bowl Sunday, even the Indians aren't drinking. I'm full of hard times today. TV goes on the fritz, and I'm the only man on earth who's in a bar and can't watch the game. I have to call Tony every five minutes to know what's going on."

"There's no justice in the world," I said.

"Yes, I know, I know," the man said, "but it really bugs me when the game's on."

"We don't want to watch the game," Lila said. "We want to talk to each other before I die."

"Listen to you with your drama," he said, and walked away

from us to reach behind the bar for a bottle of lotion. "Don't pretend like you like me, okay? When you came in here you *strongly implied* that we were going to have a threesome if I gave you a round of drinks. As soon as I did, even though one of you wanted water, you laughed your asses off at me, so shut up with the *There's no justice.* Justice is you leaving the Point No Point Casino Lounge Number Six right now."

Lila stood up and tottered, which was a new thing lately and couldn't be good. The bartender frowned and spread his gob of lotion between his hands. "You don't get it," she said. "Let me explain what is happening to the Jewish people. Girls are never never never never never never never never going to walk into this place or another place and sleep with you in pairs"—she looked at his name tag—"*Gus.* It's over. Stop with the porn imagination and the men tackling each other outdoors. You need to call Tony every five minutes for the score? Go score with Tony. If men went out and had sex with each other every time they were angry there'd be so much less pain in the world."

"What the hell?" the man said. "You're crazier than our friend Headphones and you're not even drinking. What's eating you, anyway?"

Lila gave him the same smile she gave her husband when he bought the gun. *For hunting*, he had said. *To kill birds*, and she unbuttoned her blouse. It was a green silk thing, bad for rain and it always rained in this part of the world. There was a row of gorgeous outfits hanging in her hospital room closet, ready for the nightlife like a sick joke. Whenever I opened the doors the hangers would ping and rattle in the breeze, like Lila was dead already and her ghost was deciding what to wear. "Check it out," she said, unbuttoning further. She wasn't wearing a bra and had never needed to, although of course she'd worn one for two years in junior high until I told her, in the soccer field out back as the drizzle spat into our rum, that she should just give it up. Beneath the silk was the scar from the last time, snaked between her breasts, and a spiral, wide and bearing nasty teeth, down to her pale belly, in a way that made her navel no more. For some reason they had to spiral it. For some reason this was necessary. I'd seen it a thousand times, from that day in the waiting lounge when they wouldn't let me in, and I heard her surface from the anesthetic and cry and cry and cry until I pushed through anyway. The waiting lounge felt like a blind date on the sixth floor, with everyone staring and wondering what was wrong with one another, but Adam was gone by then, and Lila's unmentionable husband, and so I was the only one out there for Lila and she was the only one in there for me. Every time I saw the scar I thought of what they showed on the TV in the room. Some nurse had turned it on so Lila could have company, while I magazined in the lounge because I wasn't a relative. The TV told a science story of some people who had found a wounded bear in a faraway forest and had used science to trick it back into healthy. Now it traveled with a show and balanced objects on its head. Why don't they leave them alone? Why don't they ever leave them alone? I couldn't believe my eyes, that they would show such a thing on a screen, and neither could Gus believe his eyes as he saw it. Without a rude word he left us and Lila sat down and pulled her shirt shut. "I have to go to the bathroom," she said, and reached into the rip in her purse.

"Do you want me to come with?" I said. Terrible things happened with her in the bathroom, as you might imagine, and I had seen them all.

"Just to brush my teeth," she said, taking her toothbrush out. "Bad taste in my mouth."

She walked off behind the plants and I put my head down on the table and cried. When Adam moved in we bought a globe at a garage sale and would spin it together in bed. I'd stop the world with my finger and Adam, the drugs racing through his teeth, would tell me things he knew about where my finger landed. Some of them he made up but most of them he remembered from a grade school teacher of unspeakable power. Still nothing in this world prepared me. In all the world I couldn't guess this moment or what it looked like, so I thought I'd cry about it for a minute until I heard the bottle set on the table and Lila sit down beside me.

"I'll make you a drink, dear," said Lila, but it wasn't Lila. She was older, much older, and vaguely cool, wearing a shawl I might buy if my loans ever let up. Her fingers looked like trees in the park, and she clutched everything at once: vermouth and Campari and a cocktail shaker and three dainty glasses by their stems.

"You're the woman on the way in," I said. "We saw you."

"I talked to your friend," she agreed, unscrewing the cap of the vermouth. "I told her my blackjack theory."

Drink was making this difficult. "Do you *work* here?" I asked.

She made a noise so much like a barnyard hen that I missed Lila's mom all over again, the way she always got pesto on her shirt but never stopped ordering it. "I wouldn't call it working," the woman said. "I'm wasting all my money away. It doesn't pay much. As you well know, it's quiet today, so I stumbled in here and saw you crying like you couldn't go on. So I'm here to serve as an example, and I'm going to make you a drink called an Old Pal, Campari and vermouth and bourbon like you like, but served up so you look better drinking it, as you well know."

I looked at this woman and saw also the bored nurse, and Adam and those boys who liked to run tiny cars at four in the morning. It was the usual revelation: *everyone's crazy*. "There was another guy in here serving as an example," I said. "He had a theory."

"Everybody has a theory," the woman said. She started shaking the shaker and I could hear that ice was already inside. "This other guy, what did *he* make you?"

"Nervous," I said. Lila was taking a while—I felt the prickle of deciding whether or not to worry—but then she appeared like a miracle and tottered past the plants to our table.

"It's a party!" the woman said, adding the Campari.

"I'm back and so are you," Lila said, putting the toothbrush where it belonged. "This is the blackjack woman, Allison. We talked on the way in about her theory."

"As you well know," the woman said, "I have these birds in cages given to me by a dear young man who draws things. He's the sort of boy you girls would like."

"I'm done with boys," Lila said, "except Sidney Poitier."

"I met him once in my Hollywood days," the woman said. "He's not for you." She turned to me and her eyes looked icicle shiny, sharp and pretty and not likely to last. "You want my bird friend," she said. "Sometimes he behaves badly, like his birds, but you would like the likes of him."

"I was telling Allison she needed someone apocalyptic," Lila said.

"Maybe she needs both," the woman said. "An apocalyptic boy who draws."

"Even with the right boy I'd wreck it," I said. "I'd join the navy on impulse and sail off right when he needed me, or we'd have a baby and I'd accidentally put it in my purse. The right boys I always toss and the wrong ones I keep on top of me like paperweights. I know they're the wrong boys and I just go to them." I balanced my finger on the square of a napkin and moved it down the table like a barge. "I just go," I said.

"It's true," Lila said. The talk was cheering her, I could tell. When she first got sick there was a very popular book about heaven. While she languished in the hospital I stayed up all night on espresso, taping the word *heaven* over with the word *Las Vegas*, everywhere it appeared in the book. *Sometimes when I'm alone I get a warm feeling inside me and I know my mother's in Las Vegas thinking of me.* She was smiling like that now. "What's your name again?" she asked the woman.

"How about Gladys?" Gladys said.

"Well, Gladys," Lila said, and draped an arm around me. "Allison here once met a boy named Adam. He was all pepped up on drugs when he knocked on the door desperate for money. 'I need money,' he said, and do you know what Allison did?"

"Fed him waffles," I said. "He kept saying 'I need money'

and I told him if he picked up all the leaves in my yard I'd give him a dollar."

"It wasn't even her yard," Lila said. "She just wanted to see him bend over." Gladys laughed and slid the Old Pals over. They looked rosy in the indoor light. "I can't drink," Lila said.

"I thought you looked too sick to drink," Gladys said gently. "Never you mind, dear. As you well know, a woman looks good with a drink in front of her whether she's drinking or not. You keep it." She raised her glass to start a toast. "Good times around the corner," she said.

"I don't know," I said. "It's a long corner, Gladys. How about 'Confusion to the Gentiles'? That was the toast we learned in sixth grade."

"Allison was a gloomy Gus then," Lila said. "She would wander the halls like a ghost. She had a theory that she should be wearing men's neckties, but it wasn't going over well at Gene Ahern Preparatory School. People would laugh at her and she would cry at them back. She was a sore thumb."

"And what changed the tide?" Gladys asked.

I looked at Lila and saw her mother's chin, the crease of her mother's brow when we stayed out past curfew and snuck in the back. It was all that was left of her. For a while in college I was an experimental filmmaker, if that's the word for it. We'd get drunk and rip up pages in the *Norton Anthology of Poetry* and read them into her dad's video camera in funny voices. There was no point to it, but we loved those movies to tears. They were for a select audience, but then again we were the Chosen People. What would happen to us? What would happen? "It was when I met you," I said to her. "It all changed then."

"Birds of a feather," Lila said, and took my hand.

Gladys sipped her drink. "And what happened to your boy who wanted money?" she asked me. "Did he change you, too?"

"He was a mistake," Lila said quickly.

"He was," I said, but this didn't help, or the drink I finished. It's one thing to forgive yourself a mistake. But if you knew it was a mistake at the time, how do you forgive yourself then? That boy Adam had left a spiral scar as he tripped through my life, but you'd expect a clumsy passage from someone who showed up carrying his shoes. I looked at Lila, who couldn't drink what was in front of her. I thought we wouldn't have times like this, me drunk and her sober, until she was pregnant and a boy was gone from my life. But instead she was sick and he was gone from my life. "He's dead," I said.

"He's nothing," Lila corrected me. "He's less than nothing."

"You can't be less than nothing," I said. "Thank God. He killed himself without caring about me. He shed me like skin." I heard the talk. You can be talking, just talk, and you wish you were conveying something at the same time, but you're not. How could you be? "He said he felt happy whenever he looked into my eyes," I said, "but he scarcely ever did. I said I'd hold him all night and make sure nothing happened to him, and sure enough nothing did. I thought I'd keep him because everybody should have a true love you can't be with, but he lay in the bathtub and got gone, all guilty over something I didn't even know about. Six years. I thought I'd be doing this with Lila when she was pregnant, not sick. Point No Point, we always said. Point No Point or bust someday." I stood up and rested my hand on the wrecked TV just for peace and quiet. The ceilings were mirrored, with cameras behind them probably to keep all the money safe, and still I didn't have any. "How dare he admit there's no point?" I said, and sat down again to drink Lila's Old Pal. "There's no point to drinking, either, but look—I'm doing it."

Gladys didn't look surprised. She finished her drink too, and gave me an otherworldly sigh. "And you'll die too?" she said to Lila. "When is that, dear?"

Lila gave her the smile again, the gorgeous one. "You're not supposed to ask me that," she said. "A month maybe, unless this beeper goes off, and then there'll be another operation and one more month. And then Allison will go to grad school without me and study poetry. She has her loans, she's all set to go, we just have to wait me out."

"Poetry?" Gladys said. "You're wasting money quicker than blackjack."

"In high school it was Wallace Stevens instead of Sidney Poitier," Lila said. "You know that poem about the different ways to look at a bird? She knew them all by heart. How many was it, Allison?"

"Thirteen," I said. "*O thin men of Haddam, why do you imagine golden birds? Do you not see how the blackbird walks around the feet of the women about you?*"

Lila took my hand and squeezed the thumbnail until it showed a white blob. *A ghost,* she taught me the day we met on stairwell B. *A ghost in your fingernail.*

"Are you ladies hungry?" Gladys said.

"I can't eat," Lila said.

"Don't drink, don't smoke, what do you do?" Gladys said, a song from prep school days. "If you could eat, dear, what would you, for a wish?"

"Cake," we both said. It was her favorite forever.

"You don't say," she said, chuckling. She reached under her shawl and brought cake to the Point No Point Casino Lounge Number Six. It was a small piece on a paper plate, covered in clear plastic like a birthday leftover. This woman was a prophetess. "A bite won't kill you," she said to Lila, "no quicker, anyway."

Lila tore the plastic off and licked a bit of icing from her finger. "What other wishes can you grant, Gladys?" she asked.

Gladys reached down to Lila's waist and pointed to the beeper. "You won't believe me," she said, "but I can make this go off and extend your life if the operation works."

"Bullshit," I said.

"I made the cake," Gladys said. "I made you a drink, as you well know. That's no less a miracle. You want to live longer, Lila? It won't be fun, but it seems like you girls could use the time."

"You're crazy and I wish you would stop," I said.

"I don't think so," Gladys said. "I don't think you're ready for it to stop."

Lila looked at Gladys and me and then the cake. It felt like waiting for Adam to say it back, those quiet times when all of a sudden nothing's a joke. We'd had these moments before, usually in bars. This was like all of them. "Yes," Lila said finally, "but can you really?"

"There's only one way to find out," Gladys said, and stood up. "No, what am I talking about? There are lots of ways. It's a gamble."

"It was a gamble to come here," Lila said. "What are the odds?"

Gladys didn't answer, or maybe we didn't hear it, not over the beeper. It was working. It was beeping. "Oh my god," Lila said quietly. "I have to call the hospital if this is real. I have to call in and see."

"Phone around the corner," Gladys pointed.

"I'll go with you," I said. She tottered up and leaned against me, staring at the old woman at our table, and I felt a warm rush those cocktails couldn't touch. It was love, not that I didn't know. We left the lounge and never saw Gladys again. It could be a malfunction, I knew, but that's always the case. Lila tossed coins into the phone which sat near the slot machines because the world doesn't care how exactly they get your money. I watched Lila talk to someone like she'd shown her scar to Gus, and loved her way up north. This is love, to sit with someone you've known forever in a place you've been meaning to go, and watching as their life happens to them until you stand up and it's time to go. You don't care about yours. Why should it change, the love you feel, no matter how death goes? She smiled at me and stuck her thumb up and hung up on the guy at the other end of the line.

"They're real mad at you," she said with a grin. "It's real, though. We can catch the last ferry and I can be in tremendous pain by tomorrow afternoon."

"Then what are we waiting for?" I said.

"Do you think Gladys," Lila said, "is some sort of—"

"She said she was here to serve as an example," I said. "I promise I'll do a thorough investigation while you're under anesthetic, Lila, only please let's go let's go let's go."

"Listen to you," she said, and led the way. "You're too drunk to drive." She clapped her hands like she used to do every birthday when the candles arrived in a halo of light, and her dwindling friends sang the same old song. "I haven't been behind the wheel in forever. Hooray!"

Hooray. We were outside in the weird afternoon, damp and hard to breathe in. Some seagulls from someplace were eating fried chicken that the casino had thrown away, and up near the spiraling clouds I saw some other kind of bird flap against the wind only to go the opposite direction. Lila took the keys.

"Come on!" she cried. "Come with me!"

The same album was on, of course, from the giddy ride up, and I drummed my fingers against the window as Lila threw us into gear. "You don't know what it's like," said the singer, who had probably done worse things than wrap Adam's seeping wrists with towels left over from Lila's mother. "You don't know what it's like to love somebody the way I love you." The original artists were a bunch of grinning white men, but the version Lila and I listened to was by a woman who made the whole thing fierce and wise. I turned it up and let it speak. I'd spent my life driving around my city with Lila while the pop music told us what was happening and what it was like, and never wished I was doing anything else. We merged to the bigger road and flew south, the winter weather getting crankier around us as we sang

the song together. "You don't know what it's like to love somebody the way I love you," and we retraced our woodsy steps
down the only road back. We filled up the car without paying in
Bainbridge, which is getting harder and harder to do, the gullible
men hunted to extinction, or maybe hiding in difficult parts of
the globe. Lila spun the wheel around each corner as the album
ended again, but even this turned out to be a wrong dream. The
girls don't win on Super Bowl Sunday, no matter how the game
goes.

The Jewish people are not islanders, except Manhattan and its
many bridges of escape, its secret underground railroads and its
taxis that must take you anywhere you want by law. We prefer
the mainland, as we have never been able to leave someplace easily. We linger in the entryway at the end of my parents' dinner
parties, and we clutter up the aisles of the synagogue, and the
bribes at the border don't work, and we end up surrendering our
shoes and boarding the train. No one has fixed this, this plague
thrown down upon us, and when we turned the last corner Lila
threw on the brakes for the mass of traffic stopped on the road to
the ferry. All the red lights of automobiles stretched out like a
holiday I didn't celebrate. "What's going on?" I called over to
the guy in the rusty sedan.

He rolled his window down too. "There's no way across," he
said. "The last ferry's canceled, is what I heard anyway. I'm trying to hear on the radio. It's an emergency, I guess, but nobody
knows what to do."

"There must be someone who knows," I said. I got out of the
car with bourbon bravado and gave Lila a thumbs-up.

"Come back," she said.

"The ticket booth guy," I said, pointing down the red light district. "He'll know something. I'm going to walk there and see."

"I mean," Lila said, and wiped at her eyes without knowing it. "I mean, come back after that. Don't fall in love with the ticket guy and leave me here in the car." There was a noise above us like an airplane zoom, but it was getting too dark to see. People started laying on the horn, braying like bad geese in a panic. "I am here," Lila said with a trembly smile. Our driver's ed teacher had told us that's what the horn should mean. Not *Move along, buddy* or *I am displeased* but *I am here. I am here, I am here, I am here!*

"I will come back," I said to her, shut the door, and ran down the asphalt to the booth where they took your money. A woman in sweaty overalls was already arguing with the guy. His name tag said Thomas but he'd crossed out the H in ink. Behind him I could see what he brought to work: a cup of coffee and a tattered black sketchbook, and he smoked, and on a grimy counter was a TV with its back to me. I heard the dim sound of a crowd. He was watching the game.

"I'm telling you I can't tell you, like I said," he told Overalls.

"How can I get back to the city if there's no ferry tonight?" she said. "I'm a florist. I have flowers in the back."

There was a loud, loud horn blast, and we all turned around to see who was there. First in the line at the booth, its bumper growling at the roadblock, was a station wagon, but through the windows all I could see were stacks and stacks of newspapers, yellowing now and yellowing more with every passing moment.

Couldn't anybody do anything right? "There must be a way," I said.

"That's what I keep saying," said the other woman. "If the ferry's broken there are other boats, like a charter."

"Only if you have a lot of money," the guy said, "and maybe not then. Look, I don't know anything." There was another roar above us and we looked up and waited. "They told me to let no one through and that there'd be more information on the radio. Will you *please* go back and sit in your car."

"I have a friend," I said, "who will have an operation tonight."

Even the other woman looked at me funny. "I've heard every emergency," the guy said. "Every single person in this traffic is urgent."

The TV squawked and the guy looked. "These guys are really taking a beating!" an announcer said. He sounded more panicked than usual, maybe. "I've never seen this kind of thing from the Magpies!"

"Shit!" the guy said, and waved us back. "Please, ladies, it's an emergency catastrophe. Go back and sit down and soon we'll all know."

"You could at least tell us something helpful," said the overalls woman, and looked at me to see if I was on her team. I shook my head and walked back, the liquor fading with every step. Again there was the roar above me, but why notice the thunder when it only turns out to be rain? There wasn't anything helpful to tell us. It was raining and it was going to rain. Everybody was honking so loudly I had to get back in the passenger seat to tell

Lila I didn't know, but she'd ejected the album and was fiddling with my radio which was almost always not working much.

"Tell me something," she said, and winced toward her belly. She undid the seat belt, took a deep breath, and faced me. "There's no football team called the Magpies, is there?"

"I don't know," I said. "There's the Eagles and some Orioles, I think. And the Anti-Semites. I don't know."

Lila winced again and then looked out the wet window. "Because the radio said something."

"Holy motherfucking shit!" the radio said suddenly, and then disappeared into a depth of static.

"I think something is happening," Lila said. She gave me a grim smile I hadn't seen in months, a smile of trying to be brave. "I don't think I'm going to make it. What did the guy say?"

"He didn't know," I said, "but he couldn't spell his own name, either."

"No one can spell my name," Lila said, "and it's a four-letter word. Don't leave again. With all this traffic you'll never find out. It'll never stop and I don't want to sit here without you."

She opened her door briefly to the loud of the rain and the cars and she spat onto the ground, a white glob of her bite of cake. "It's the end!" the radio shouted again, and I turned it off and reached across her to shut the door, so at least we could be quieter, a little. Emergency or football I wasn't sure, and Lila didn't seem up for either.

"They said this was my only chance," Lila said quietly. In the lounge maybe it was worth it, to sit free at Point No Point rather than linger someplace to teach something to doctors, but now in the traffic we couldn't bear for anything to end here, not a single thing.

"You won't die in this car," I said. "It's not like that anyway. We need to get you back, that's all. There's a way. We'll find it. I'll find it while you sit tight."

"No," she said. "The window's only open a few hours, is what they said. If I don't get there they can't do the operation and that guy will be dead for nothing."

"Listen to me," I said, and I felt the fury in my throat. The weight of the world isn't worth it, not even with the love which will die and go away, but each moment with Lila was worth everything, to talk to someone I'd known forever like an old song. Listen to it. Love was all we had left, all of us, as we sat beaten down with the knowledge that there wasn't a boat for the rescue. "They don't know anything," I said, "those guys. They think a leather jacket looks good zippered up all the way. A few-hour window? If you hadn't come to stairwell B I'd be crying there still, and if we hadn't left our keys on top of the jukebox the ambulance would have pulled Adam out of the bathtub alive, but then I would have married him like an idiot, and lost touch because you hated him. I would have lost touch with you in a few-hour window, what were the odds? We can do this. That guy's dead for nothing anyway, all the deaths are dead for nothing, but you're not dead at all."

"You're drunk," she said, crying very hard. "I wish I could get drunk with you again. But there's no way across."

"We can dream up a better time for you to die than stuck in traffic," I said.

"No," she said. "Not if I can't get to sleep."

"Then we'll stay up all night," I said. "You'll stay up all night with me. We've done it before, lots of times. I love you so soundly and I will do anything to drag you forward. You're mine, Lila. You're my star quarterback."

"I fucking hate football," Lila sobbed. "Blow up the game for me when I'm gone."

"I won't do a thing," I said. "Without you I'm not moving." Through the front window was another cliché, rain raging while the women inside wept like girls. The traffic screamed its emergency around us, but we could do this thing on our own. She was all the world's money, and I would spend it with her, my sharpest friend who changed the tide, my only comfort from the brutal gamble of the world and the wicked ways of men. I grabbed her hands and clasped them together over her scar into a position of strength, like a prayer we wouldn't be caught dead saying. *Gather around us, heroic women of Haddam. Gather around us and put us under your silken wings. We are here, we are here, we are here, won't someone take us across the sound together.*

frigidly

What a bad day it was, the clouds low and cloudy, the rain no fun, the dark as it hit late afternoon thick like someone who stops by your place and just won't leave. The day was canceled, almost, on account of the rain spilling itself all over everything. Everybody was eating at the diner where the food is lousy but you go there anyway. Everything was lousy about it. The chairs and tables stayed sticky, if you know what I mean. If you know what I mean there were five people inside the diner, plus a couple way off in the corner bickering together about something and the cook. Behind the counter was the guy who owned the place, with an apron on. He was let's say polishing glasses with a white rag. Sitting on one of the stools was a woman who had been drinking. Near her lurked a young boy who didn't belong to her. The boy was named Mike. Someone was supposed to meet him and hadn't shown up and Mike, bored, just stayed around anyway, pressing the buttons of the jukebox without putting money in and slurping the leftover ice from a glass of soda the owner had given him out of pity. Mike didn't mind it. Mike was ten years old, and already lots and lots of interesting things had happened to him in his life, so he could take a break this afternoon and punch nothing into the jukebox for a few hours. Nobody was worried about him. Mike was worrying nobody sick.

Down the counter a ways were the two detectives, who automatically make a story get interesting, even though the only interesting thing they were doing was eating waffles, both of them, at five-thirty in the afternoon. They had taken off their hats and lined them up together on the counter like two very short additional customers. This was how it was, the five people, Andy and Mike and the woman who had been drinking, Andrea, and the two detectives, while the couple bickered in the back and the cook stared into space at the grill, thinking, Well, if I took my goddamn spatula and scraped at that piece of burnt cheese, if I scrape it right there it would look like the state of Nevada.

This was that day, if you know what I mean. Outside it was dark, and what with the rain you might not even know Andy's was open. This was when there was a power shortage in California. It turned out to be corporate greed but at the time it seemed like there might be something to it, so everybody tried to be careful. All the neon signs were quiet and it was hard to see what was open and what wasn't. The Andy's sign was off. It definitely wasn't Christmas and yet the snowman and the wreath were still painted on the windows. Outside garbage blew, running stop signs and red lights. We've all had days like this. If you know what I mean it felt reckless, the rain and whatnot, but only if your idea of reckless is sitting at a diner and having whatever you felt like. There were limits to the menu, of course, and on days like this that hurt. You wanted to go do something and nobody would help you. It was a bad day for love. Andrea in particular was taking it hard.

"I want an Angel's Nipple," she said to Andy. "It's rum and heavy cream and an egg white with a floater of maraschino liqueur. I want a Louisiana Flip or a Neptune Fizz."

"We don't have those party drinks," Andy said. "You know that, honey. I'll bring you another half carafe of the house red if you want."

"If I want," Andrea sneered. She moved her hand down the counter like a spilled something, honey or milk. Mike watched her because it was a free country. "I want a Do Be Careful. I want a Pimm's Cup. I want a Delmonico with a twist, served up."

"I'll serve you up a half carafe of white or red," Andy said patiently. "Come on now, Andrea. They don't have those things at a diner. It's not the end of the world."

"When they say it's not the end of the world," Andrea said, "it usually is."

"The world can only end once," said one of the detectives, and then he raised a paper napkin to his mouth and wiped himself a false, hearty smile. "I know!" he said. "Here's something we can do! What is your name, Andrea? You want to do something? You want to look at a picture?" He turned to the other detective, who was already taking a photograph out of his jacket. It was not in an envelope. "Let's show her the picture," he said, and put the photograph down on the counter where it would probably stick. Andy frowned even before he saw it.

You love once and then maybe not again. Not on a day like this. The rain, the rain, the rain. You can't even hear it outside the window but still it's a sad thing. Rain, the grade school teachers say, makes the trees and flowers grow, but we're not trees and flowers, and so many grade school teachers are single. Even

Mike's teacher got lonesome brokenhearted like this. Her husband left and took all the red wine and even the salt, on the grounds that it was his. No, if you loved once and then kaput, then it looks like rain in your life. At least an Angel's Nipple would make it taste better, if you know what I mean. If you know what I mean the picture showed an old woman looking steadily at the camera in black-and-white, almost a formal portrait. Andy put a half carafe of red in front of Andrea.

"Who are you guys?" Andrea said. "I think I'll have a half carafe of red, Andy."

"We're detectives," the detective said. Mike looked up from the jukebox because it was interesting now. He looked at the picture. *Murderer?*

"I thought you weren't supposed to say 'We're detectives.'" She said "We're detectives" in the tone of voice someone might use to say "Making you happy isn't making me happy."

"You're thinking of spies," the detective said.

"I'm thinking of leaving, is what I'm thinking of," Andrea said.

"Don't leave, lady," the detective said. "We're just showing you a picture. We flew all the way out to San Fran and came to this diner."

"I hate when people call it San Fran," Andrea said.

"San Fran is what everyone calls it," said the detective. "Like the song says, I guess when it rains it pours."

Andrea poured more from the carafe into the glass and then, less successfully, back again. "Why don't you leave her alone?"

"It's Gladys," Andy said, turning his head so he wouldn't have to look at the picture upside down anymore.

"Gladys, the man says." The detective turned to the other detective, as if they were partners. "She's calling herself Gladys now." The partner took out a pen and then looked around. Their two hats were sitting in front of a paper place mat the diner used. He slid it on over and wrote Gladys, G-L-A-D-Y-S, in big pen letters.

"You asshole," Andrea said to the owner of the place. "You asshole jerk Andy."

Andy raised his hands very mildly and Mike blushed back by the jukebox. "She comes in here all the time," he said to the detectives, and poured them more coffee.

"Much obliged," the detective said about the coffee, and then turned to his partner. "Man says she comes here all the time." The other detective nodded and wrote "comes here all the time" below "Gladys" on the place mat.

"Why'd you tell them that?" Andrea said. "God, I want a drink." She slugged her wine down which didn't take long. "I want a Hong Kong Cobbler. I want a Gypsy Rose. I want a Mother's Ruin or a Singapore Sling, either one. They're both gin-based although I forget which one has ginger beer."

"We don't have those party drinks here," Andy said patiently. "This is a diner. I thought about opening a bar but that was a long time ago."

"Seems like even a bar wouldn't have drinks like that, more's the pity," the detective said. "Times have unfortunately changed."

Andrea stumbled up off her stool and went and sat closer to the detectives. She tried to pick up the picture but it stuck to the counter like I told you. "I've never seen this woman before in my life," she said. "I come in here all the time."

"Usually drunk and sad," Andy said.

"When Andy said she comes in here all the time he meant me," she said, tapping the place mat with a nail she broke on a man's door. "I come here all the time and I've never seen Gladys in all my life."

"Don't get like that," the detective said. "This other guy and me, we're detectives. Our client wants us to find the woman in the picture. There's only one of them. We flew out here, we ask around, and she's calling herself Gladys now and she comes here. We wait, she comes in, we got her and it's kaput, kaput, kaput. Cake."

"Cake," the partner said, also.

"She *always* calls herself Gladys," Andrea said, slouching back to her place.

"Cake?" Andy said. A very bad covered cake was nearby, and some lonely doughnuts.

"It's an expression detectives use," the detective said, "like easy as cake."

"Pie," Mike said. At school he'd just had a test on expressions like "easy as pie" but he said it so quietly, only the jukebox heard.

"Another one is 'southside,'" the detective said. "It's a detective expression if someone is, what's-it-called, fleeing. If they're fleeing, a detective will say 'southside,' because where do birds go?"

"Southside," Andy tried, and Mike murmured it to himself. "I wish all my troubles'd go *southside*."

"Southside," the detective said. "All the birds end up in South America, not a lot of people know. Every bird in the world.

They say in Peru you can scarcely walk in winter without step-
ping on a bird of some kind. Of course some birds are evergreen
but the rest are in South America."

"Is that so?" Andy said. He'd heard a lot of bullshit as part of
owning and operating a diner but speaking of cake this took it.

"No," Mike whispered, and then turned around and said it.
"No. Birds migrate according to a variety of patterns. I learned
about it, and we saw some magpies on a field trip two and a half
days ago, or we were supposed to but didn't because of the rain.
The yellow-billed magpie can be found exclusively in the coastal
valleys south of San Francisco Bay, and there are three common
words beginning with the letter A that describe it. The first is
'attractive.'"

"Don't you have someplace to go?" the detective said.

"No," Mike said, and Andrea finished her wine and raised her
fist in a salute. "It's a free country."

"If you're gonna tell my customers to leave," Andy said, "I'll
have to ask you gentlemen to go southside." But then Andy ruined it and winked at the boy, telling Mike there wasn't anybody
on his side after all.

"We're *detectives*," the partner said.

"What do *detectives*," Andrea said, using the word *detectives*
like she had used the word *your wife Helena* not so long ago,
"want with Gladys anyway? She's a nice old lady and she doesn't
have any money probably. She used to be an actress."

"She works I think at a store someplace," Andy volunteered.
"I heard her say 'the store' once, or 'back at the store.' She's not
bothering anyone, or you."

"What business do you have?" Andrea asked.

The detectives looked at one another like this was their least favorite part of the job. "Our client," said the one who keeps talking, "says this woman Gladys is the Snow Queen."

"The Snow Queen?" Andy said. "Who the fuck is the Snow Queen? Excuse my language, kid."

"It's okay," Mike said. "I've heard people say fuck a bunch of times."

"Don't say fuck," Andrea said. "Once you say fuck it's all over and your life has changed. Andy, how come you don't say excuse me to me? I'm a lady, with your language."

"How 'bout you give me another soda," said bold bold Mike, to Andy, "for swearing." Andy set him up, of the opinion that sugar didn't hurt kids one bit. That was a rare commodity and Mike was learning to appreciate such people.

"The Snow Queen, if anybody cares," said the detective, "is an agent of the netherworld of Kata. In human form, she takes the human form of a woman. As her name implies, she can control all types of weather especially snow."

"Gladys is making it rain," Andy said, thinking, And I didn't even open a bar to hear this kind of crazy talk.

"That's what the man says," said the detective.

"And what man is that?" Andy said.

"My client," the detective said. "Our client, my partner and me."

"And what does your client," Andy said, "want with the Snow Queen?" and cleared the waffles.

"He's in love with her," the detective said. "We get paid by the hour."

Love is hourly, too. There are stories about people who have loved someone forever after laying eyes on them for a few minutes and then nevermore, but these stories have not happened to anyone we know. No, when you love someone you spend hours and hours with them, and even the mightiest forces in the netherworld could not say whether the hours you spend increase your love or if you simply spend more hours with someone as your love increases. And when the love is over, when the diner of love seems closed from the outside, you want all those hours back, along with anything you left at the lover's house and maybe a couple of things which aren't technically yours on the grounds that you wasted a portion of your life and those hours have all gone southside. Nobody can make this better, it seems, nothing on the menu. It's like what the stewardess offers, even in first class. They come with towels, with drinks, mints, but they never say, "Here's the five hours we took from you when you flew across the country to New York to live with your boyfriend and then one day he got in a taxicab and he never came back, and also you flew back, another five hours, to San Francisco, just in time for a catastrophe." And so you sit like a spilled drink, those missing hours in you like an ache, and you hear stories that aren't true and won't bring anyone back. Things happen and you never get over them, and through the door came Gladys, the woman in the picture, and this is something none of the five people would ever get over. She was older than you might think but she looked good, and she did not look around, but went straight to the counter and sat down and put an arm around Andrea.

"It's good to see you, Andrea," she said. "I thought I might not see you. This place doesn't even look open, what with the sign dark."

"Hello, *Nancy*," Andrea said, and Andy poured half a cup of coffee.

"You're drinking more than usual if I'm Nancy," Gladys said. "Well, never you mind, dear. I know you're sad. What you need is a Gene Ahern Gloom Chaser. It's two kinds of rum, and cognac, Cointreau, lemon juice, and a bit of sugar, all stirred up and served in a highball glass with cola."

"That sounds terrible," Andrea said, "but I guess it might be good."

"It's delicious," Gladys said. "If I were you I'd order one."

"We don't have those party drinks," Andy said, breaking someone's heart every day. "This is a diner."

"I know what it is," Gladys said and drank her half coffee in one gulp. "As you well know, Andrea, the Gene Ahern Gloom Chaser was invented by Gene Ahern, the author of the comic strip——"

"I don't know it," Andrea said, with a shrug and an empty carafe. "Why do you say that, as you well know?"

"As you well know," Gladys said. "It's an affectation of mine."

"What is the comic strip?" Mike asked. Even Mike had recognized Gladys but maybe could not believe it, that something so interesting would happen after all this jukebox, after waiting for that guy to show up who never did, and the detectives. He had given up the day for lousy, and now, the woman they were looking for? *Now?*

"The comic strip," Gladys said, moving her coffee cup to Andy like a chess piece, "was called *Room and Board*, and as you well know it was not funny at all. There was one I remember, a man in a clown suit, big red nose, big long beard, big tall hat with a tassel like they do. He is looking in the mirror and the speech bubble says, 'I can't go to the masked ball like this! I need a shave'—something like that. Not funny, as you well know, but for a while there was talk of a movie, and I was going to be the ingenue."

"What's the ingenue, *Nancy*?" Mike asked. He got the code, the Nancy strategy, even though it would not work.

"An ingenue," Gladys said, "is an innocent woman. It doesn't surprise me that a boy your age hasn't seen one, and I'm *Gladys*, dear. Comic strips is about the only place you see them, comic strips and private homes."

"I agree with a man I know," said the detective suddenly.

"Beg pardon?" Gladys said.

"Man says innocence is the rarest of commodities in the known world," the detective said. Gladys's face changed, and it was a shame to see.

"Could you repeat yourself, please?" Gladys said. "Sir?"

The detective took his lazy time. "My partner and I," he said, and his sweeping palm said *and our hats*, "we know a man, says innocence is the rarest of commodities in the known world. Says when you find it, grab it, no matter who you have to hire."

"And how do you know this man?" Gladys said sadly. "Sitting next to you, maybe?"

"I know him the same way I know that you drink your coffee

in half cups," the detective said, and his partner lifted the place mat from the table. Gladys looked down for the first time and saw a picture of herself, and then the message in ink: "Gladys comes here all the time." It was true.

"Gladys, pay no attention to these guys," Andy said. "These bad guys are dumb. They think South America is crawling with birds, and I'm going to call the police."

The partner put the place mat down and spread his hands on it like he was healing the sick, which he was not doing. He began to speak. "If someone pours you a full cup," he said, "*Gladys*, the bottom half is freezing cold before you can drink it, on account of your deadly breath of ice. Isn't that right, Your Highness?"

"Kaatu," Gladys said in a mysterious howl, and here we could skip ahead if you know what I mean. It is always tempting to skip past words we do not understand, the parts of a relationship which confuse us, and arrive at a nice clear sentence— "They clearly weren't in love anymore," or "The yellow-billed magpie can be found exclusively in the coastal valleys south of San Francisco Bay, and there are three common words beginning with the letter A that describe it," or "She was wearing some sort of cape," all of which appeared in the report filed by the surviving and more talkative detective. But we cannot skip to that or it wouldn't be a love story. We cannot skip the way we look in photographs, or our own affectations, or the way we like our coffee, or the way the people we love like their coffee, even though they like it some bad, bad way. We must suffer through all of it, without skipping any tiny thing, and anyway it was a shawl she was wearing. She spread it out high so it drooped down her arms and kept saying things we cannot understand. "Kaatu maka, ebbery ebbery fingersauce!"

She stood up from her place, her shawl like bat's wings, and stared down the detective's partner with an elegant disgust we've all unfortunately seen. "I don't love you anymore," she howled, "kaatu kaatu maka!" and she spun out of Andy's diner. When the doors opened the rush sound of the rain came through, like those doors had been soundproof all this time. A blast of cold air gave everyone its fierce attention. It felt colder than it had been outside, but none of the people in the diner had been outside for a while and it had grown dark. It could have been anything, so cold. It could have been the rain maybe. Or—

"Your Highness!" the partner shouted. He put his hat on and left the premises after her in a hurry.

"Oh my god maybe," Andy said. "It couldn't be but maybe."

"The Snow Queen?" Andrea said, so loudly that the carafe wobbled. "The Snow Queen the Snow Queen?"

But now the door had shut, and through the rain and the paintings on the windows they stared. Andrea stared and Andy stared, everyone stared, except the bickering couple so busy wading through the words they wished they could skip that they only had a dim picture of some old woman shouting and leaving, and the cook in his magnificent disinterest, mapping out the world on the griddle where he worked, secure in the very wrong knowledge that he had seen everything before. Nobody had seen this thing, as Gladys faced this man in a hat, and howled something inaudible as he froze in his steps, and finally beheld her.

"Do you think?" Andy said, and put down the coffee.

"That everything in the entire world," Andrea said, "that anyone ever told us, is wrong?" and maybe this is why Mike stared the hardest. It is bad news when the world tells you the bad news that you are wrong, unless you are ten and this happens every five minutes and the only difficulty is that adults spend most of their time pretending nothing much has gone amiss. Mike stared hardest as Gladys raised her shawl again and began the thing no one had seen before.

It was not the rain. It was not the wine. It was not the painted window, which was not blocking the view. Gladys howled and from the folds of her shawl came a spiral something. It was made of flurries, it looked like, white and gray in the diminished light. The spiral spun out wider, wider until it hit the detective's partner and covered him instantly with what had to be snow. It hurt. It hurt him. He was covered and could not move and then the Snow Queen stepped back and was no longer framed in the window.

"What was that, the hell?" Andy said. "What was that outside my diner?"

The detective turned out to be standing flat against the far wall. "That was the Cone of Frost," he said. "I never thought I'd see that in my whole damn life."

Nobody realized that Mike was out the door, although Andrea was staring after him and hoping it was the wine, all she saw. She could not move from her place, this woman who had been drinking, and just so you have some background, everyone in this story is sad. Let's get it straight: everyone here has lost a child, a burden given to so many characters as they walk through a small pinch of paper with the dignified literary weight of grief. It's a gratuitous punch in the stomach, is what it feels like. When Andy learned the news of the car which had not just spun but flipped over on the ice, and so the seat belts, the carseat, the special traction of the tires had not been nearly enough to save him, he sank to the mat like a prizefighter and howled on the floor until his friends pulled him up. *Such good friends.* With Andrea the child died in the crib, downed suddenly like a cheap drink. Mike's little brother died when he fell down the stairs in just the right way and the ambulance arrived too late on a cold, cold night, and his father hardly spoke or opened the mail ever again. The bickering couple would never know their babies, and the frozen partner on the sidewalk could still hear, even through the ice, those last wet and desperate coughs of his tiny daughter as she flailed in the strong hands of her sobbing mother who ran away as soon as it was done, and even the cook did not know that even at this sad moment his girlfriend could not stop screaming from what she heard in that numb whitewalled clinic, and the detective was buttoning his coat and still thinking of himself as the father of a little figure-skating girl who was no good at it. She would stumble around the ice until her ankles made her cry, all the while imagining the perfect 8's, the twirls and flurries of grace, and this detective would stand and imagine it too on the sidelines, as he threw down money for the waffles and buttoned his coat to leave. In the diner these people had frozen in their tracks from being treated so cruelly. Not only their ankles ached, but they were in pain in their feet, and in

"I don't know," Andy said. "If I were you I wouldn't go out there and I wouldn't want to know. Not you."

"I can't believe what I saw," Andrea said. "The therapy I'll need or something. Or, I should sober up, and drive a cab for a living now. You meet people in a cab. A miracle could happen and I would see the Snow Queen again."

The detective peered out of the painted window and banged his head on the glass, hard. It rattled and rattled people.

"Don't do that!" cried the cook. "Watch what you're doing! Pay attention to what's going on!"

"She's gone southside," the detective moaned. "I don't know which direction to go," and this is love, too. If you miss your Snow Queen you might not appear in the love story anymore. "Men grow cold as girls grow old," a song says. "Men grow cold as girls grow old, and we all lose our charms in the end." This is a love story, which must be grabbed in time. Mike knew it, and he ran in the rain on the snow. He had been wearing a sweatshirt this whole time and it was getting heavy and wet. He had the chills as he chased after her, and that's part of love, too. You get the chills when you get close to her, and you run until you slip in a puddle, "Ouch," and the Snow Queen turns around.

"Oh dear," she said. "You're the boy from the diner and you slipped in a puddle. You'll catch cold. You'd better come inside."

"Okay," Mike said, and she pulled him to his feet. "I saw what you did and it was amazing."

"You're wet," she said. "Your sweatshirt is soaked and heavy. I'm worried sick about you."

Where does the Snow Queen live? As it turns out, in a small, cramped apartment on the third floor of a nearby building on the corner of Seventeenth and Church. When love appears it's a supernatural thing like the songs say, but eventually you have to get out of bed, even on the coldest of days, and pay the rent. She held the door open for him.

"Do you have to invite me in?" Mike asked. "Is it like vampires?"

"I should have known," the Snow Queen said, "that a boy your age would have a thing for vampires. As you well know, that's what made my fortune, my boy."

They walked in and saw what she was talking about. The place was little more than some walls and a kitchenette, and everywhere were very large stacks of magazines, and photographs taped to the walls every which way. I told you it was cramped. Mike walked quietly and took it in while the Snow Queen took off her shawl and boiled water for tea. "You should take off your sweatshirt, dear."

"Mike," Mike said, and took off his sweatshirt. "Look, you really were an actress. These pictures are you in old monster movies."

"That was me," the Snow Queen said. "Dracula's daughter. A girl who comes across a terrible secret at her uncle's castle. Look, in this one a ghost falls in love with me and we go to a restaurant. It's a comedy. Here I'm going mad when they're reading the hypnotist's last will and testament, and in the corner a terrible creature is taking me away."

Mike's shirt was soaked too, and he took it off and handed it to her without thinking. "Here you are something else," he said. She found a towel and touched his bare back as she drooped it around his shoulders like a shawl, and he shivered. "You have white makeup and a cape and a cardboard crown."

"The Snow Queen," the Snow Queen said.

"Are you really?" Mike asked.

"How did my lines sound?" she asked back.

"At one point," Mike said, "one time it sounded like you said *fingersauce*."

"Hardly the words of the netherworld of Kata," the Snow Queen said, and unlaced his shoes, sneaker by sneaker.

"Was it fun?" Mike asked. "A movie star? I bet you got to go to parties."

"It's funny you should say parties," the Snow Queen said sadly. "I had this part over there, taped up near the light switch, where I was sort of a ghost grandma. I had a line, 'It's a party!' They had me do it fifteen times, 'It's a party! It's a party! It's a party! It's a party! It's a party! It's a party! It's a party! It's a party! It's a party! It's a party! It's a party! It's a party! It's a party! It's a party! It's a party!' And it never even made it into the picture. Nobody wanted to hear it. You can say something and say something, but still nobody wants to hear it."

"I want to hear it," Mike said, his soaking socks off.

"I was in love," the Snow Queen said. "That was the last thing I was in, and the director fell in love with me, or anyway we had a baby. But the baby passed on."

"My baby sister passed on," Mike said.

"It's a terrible thing," the Snow Queen said. "I've barely gotten out of bed since, and the director too. He couldn't think of anything else but all those monster stories. I ran away from him and wasted away all my money to forget, and if I had one wish now, it would be for that baby back, something to love on these cold days alone."

"If your baby was alive," asked Mike, "would it be my age?"

"Oh goodness no," the Snow Queen said, and then slapped her strong hands on her knees. "If you could have one wish, what would it be for your turn?"

Mike looked out the window down at the street. Most of the signs were dark, and some of the rain was almost hail. "I guess calamari," he said, blushing because he knew it was dumb. "I had it in Santa Cruz and I really liked it, but probably I can't have it now."

The Snow Queen smiled and walked over to her freezer. Inside it was so covered in frost there was only one thing in it. She pulled it out and threw it on the table in front of him. It was a bag of calamari, frozen and pictured on the packaging. Everything she said was coming true. She was a prophetess, something from elsewhere, and this is part of love too. You must believe what is happening, every pronouncement the love is making, or you might as well go back to the diner and wait for someone who has forgotten you completely. "I have a microwave," the Snow Queen pronounced grandly. "It'll be ready in three to five minutes."

In three to five minutes the world can change, and three to five minutes might even be a generous estimate for a relationship between a young boy and an older woman from the netherworld of Kata, if you know what I mean. But all love gets over, and we must get over it. Even Mike, young as he was, knew that the guy he was waiting for at the diner wasn't going to show. The whole world seemed up in that apartment, like the freezer of the Snow Queen might give them a limitless menu if they could just wish for everything they wanted. They grinned at the microwave, Mike especially because he was the one who loved the calamari, but the Snow Queen too, because she was the one who loved him. He was innocent, a rare commodity, and some might say she should leave him alone. But she'd been left alone too long, and who are those people anyway, bickering in the corner and saying such things? Love like this, it was better than sitting in a diner doing nothing, because look what has arrived for Andrea! A man who will treat her badly! Tony!

"Are you open?" Tony said. "I can't tell."

"We're always open," Andy said. "Any diner worth its salt is open twenty-four hours a day."

"I'm in the mood for a drink," Tony said.

Andrea twirled all the way around on her stool, as the diner was the sort of place where that could be done. She was not going to see the Snow Queen today, not again, but in the meantime here was something who could help her through three to five minutes. "I recommend the Suffering Bastard," she said. "It's four parts gin, three parts brandy, one part lime juice, sugar syrup, Angostura bitters, ginger ale, and it's garnished with a slice of cucumber."

"Sounds good to me," Tony said. "Somebody give us two of

those." He would treat her badly, but in the meantime love like this was better. Better something poured over ice, than just the ice outside in a heap by itself.

"We don't serve party drinks like that," Andy said. "This is a diner, and even if we did I wouldn't serve you two that. I've seen a miracle today, and I want to see more of them, so I'm spending the rest of the evening scraping the paint off these windows of mine. I'd make the cook make you a drink, I guess, if we had such things."

"Idaho," said the cook, lost again to us, but nobody heard him because Andy had already started scraping. The scraping was such a horrible sound that the woman in the corner looked up and for the first time realized that she was in this story too, not just the one where she bickered with her ghost of a boyfriend.

"No need," Tony said. "Let's get out of here and go to a bar. You ever been to the Black Elephant, Andrea?"

"See you later, Andy," Andrea said.

"You owe me like twenty-six dollars for all those half carafes," he said, over the scraping.

"She'll pay you later," Tony said, and they walked out together like they were going to a masked ball. Out in front of Andy's was the frozen figure of a man with his hat on, his face icy in the middle of some terrible speech. Toppled, he looked like one of the victims of Pompeii, a city destroyed in a volcano studied by Mike in his classroom a while ago, although now, in the Snow Queen's apartment, Mike was reciting the three common words, beginning with the letter A, often used to describe magpies. Magpies are artful and aggressive birds who are often attracted to shiny things, which is maybe why Tony turned from the dull gray-white of the man on the sidewalk to the brightening shine of Andrea's pretty eyes.

"Who's that?" Tony said, shrugging to the guy.

"Looks like an ex-boyfriend to me," Andrea said.

"Somebody treated him cold," Tony said. Although there was plenty of rain, there was no more sunlight on the street, which meant this lousy day was pretty much over, if you know what I mean. If you know what I mean that's what was happening to them.

"Happens all the time," Andrea said. "It's not the end of the world."

collectively

Saltwater taffy is I guess made from salt water and a whole bunch of sugar, spun or woven or beaten into a substance they sell down by the boardwalk. If you're in San Francisco, as this love story is, you can head south and see it being made in a shack, next to the shack where they sell tickets and next to the shack where they fry up calamari and give it to you for a price. Just follow the signs. You can't miss the signs they put up.

This is love, saltwater taffy. Pretty much everybody has had some. Somebody offers it on a day when you have nothing to do, and most likely you'll take it and put it in your mouth. It unites us, saltwater taffy, but whose favorite is it? Who likes it best? Just about nobody. So why do we eat it? This love story is about this style of love, this sweet thing that exists unasked for, that everybody eats out of the same bag. But also it is about what it says on the shack. I was there myself, and the large sign said: COME IN AND WATCH US MAKE IT.

I did not want to. Some things are private, no matter how many people know about the sugar and the spinning and such, and this love story is about that part of love too.

There's a song called "Please Mr. Postman" or maybe it's just "Mr. Postman." The postman always had it in his head. It was one of the downsides of his job, that and vicious dogs. He explained this to his son as they reached a flat part of the hill, which like a bunch of things was a false ending. If you had a bird's-eye view you could see there was more to it. The postman in effect had a bird's-eye view, from all the days of climbing this hill with mail for everybody.

The son's name was Mike. It was Bring Your Daughter to Work Day, which after much debate had been changed to Bring Your Child to Work Day, to make it more inclusive. It was fairer this way, it united more people, so the postman had Mike with him on his route.

"Most people think it's just delivering mail, just finding the right house and slipping it into the slot," the postman said, "but there's more to it than that." He started to list some things about his job Mike might not know, more or less off the top of his head. Mike sort of listened. "Everybody gets mail, is the thing. No matter where they live. Mail unites us, son, and at a time like this with volcanoes and wicked men we need that."

"My teacher says the volcano thing isn't true," Mike said.

"She would, that teacher of yours," the postman said. "Teachers used to be city employees and they never got married, and now look. They still are. But in my day we all had to stand up and say the same thing to the flag on the wall. Do you do the pledge?"

"I don't think so," Mike said. "I don't think we've had that yet."

"In my day you always did," the postman said. "We would all stand up and say the same thing about indivisible. Blah blah the state of this country. Blah blah blah, blah blah blah blah, Mike. Blah blah blah blah business addresses, or blah blah blah private homes."

Mike wasn't listening, except perhaps a little bit. His father's voice was like the dull sound of the sea. "What?" he said. "What's private homes?"

"You know what private is," the postman said, slipping some mail into the slot. "You can't go in unless you ring the doorbell and someone lets you in."

"Like vampires," Mike said. He was going through a thing about vampires.

"*Not like vampires*," the postman said. "You're not listening, Mike. We've talked about this. We hope this guy will let us come in and—"

"What's the best part of your job?" Mike asked. This was part of the report he had to write, which would be read halfheart-edly by his teacher as she shared a bottle of chianti with her spouse whom she loved.

"I've been *saying*," the postman said irritably, pointing to the next house. "Pay *attention*. The fellow at 1602 is the best part. You're gonna meet him. You're gonna love him. He's a great fellow. Handsome, and pretty tall, and he's made something of himself. I can't wait to see him again."

"A guy? That's the best part?" Mike asked.

"Yeah it's the best part," the postman said, and stepped up to 1602. The house looked like any other house, home to somebody, not to you. It had paint on the outside of it, and windows on the walls. Mike had scarcely any curiosity about it at all. "We're all together on this, Mike. We're all on the same page. You're gonna love him. I love him. I love him like a root beer float. And you're gonna love him like saltwater taffy."

Mike, like a bird, had headed south once. He had walked down the boardwalk, where the taffy is made in small buildings and shops. The sea had nudged his feet and it had been very hot and sweaty outside. He had read the signs, everything they put up for him to read, but still he was unprepared for the man who opened the door. Love can smack you like a seagull, and pour all over your feet like junk mail. You can't be ready for such a thing any more than saltwater taffy gets you ready for the ocean, or Bring Your Child to Work Day prepares you for the lonely times of going to work. But Mike wasn't going to have any lonely times. Not lately, or not in the immediate future. No way, with a door opening like this one.

"Can I help you?" the fellow said, and Mike just loved him. Why wouldn't you? Mike loved this fellow on the spot, like his father said, particularly his necktie and the way that he grasped his hair with one hand, distractedly, as he looked out at his postman. Love flowed through Mike and stuck to the roof of his mouth like a sticky sticky sweet, this fellow from 1602, this man who suddenly showed up on the route and opened the door.

"Hello!" the postman said. "Hello! This is my son. I wanted him to meet you and he did too."

"Um, hello," the fellow said.

"We both totally think you're a great guy," the postman said. "We both love you. We just want to come in for a minute."

"It's not really," the fellow said. "It's not really a good time."

"Just for a minute," the postman insisted, and Mike nodded in agreement. "I have to continue my route because everybody wants their mail, but if we could just come in for a minute, so my son here could get to know you. It's Bring Your Daughter to Work Day. Be a sport, will you be a sport?"

"I guess so," the fellow said, and gave them the benefit of the doubt with an open door. The postman held the fellow's packet of mail out and then flipped it back toward himself and his son.

"I won't give you your mail," the postman said playfully, "until you let us in for a few minutes."

"I already said okay," the fellow said sharply, and Mike flushed a bit. This is love, and the trouble with it: it can make you embarrassed. Love is really liking someone a whole lot and not wanting to screw that up. Everybody's chewed this over. This unites us, this part of love. Mike walked through the door into 1602 and just beamed at this fellow, all smiley with admiration and liking him a lot.

"Make yourselves at home I guess," the fellow said, and just past the door was a sort of living room kitchen combo where Mike could see the fellow cooked and ate and sat on a sofa and put his feet up on a table with magazines. Mike didn't care which ones the fellow subscribed to, because Mike subscribed to the fellow. "I was just going to excuse myself," the fellow said, adorably, "when the doorbell rang."

"Okeydokey," the postman said and led his son into the room to sit. The fellow at 1602 left, and the two visitors suddenly realized there was a woman in the room with them who had been concealed by a floor lamp.

"Hello," the woman said. Her name was Muriel.

"Oh my," the postman said, half-rising from the sofa. "I didn't realize he already had company."

"Yes," Muriel said. "We're having something of a reunion, actually."

"Reunion?" the postman said.

"Here," the woman said, and reached over to the pile of magazines. On top was some mail including an opened envelope.

"Oh, I couldn't!" the postman said. "Not someone else's mail. Put that in your report, Mike. Don't read other people's mail. Your teacher will love that."

"It's okay," Muriel said, handing it over. "Read it."

The fellow at 1602 washed his face more than necessary, as we all do. First Muriel, now the postman and his son. He looked at his wet face in the bathroom mirror. Why was this happening? Why love, today? But nobody ever answers that one, guy. He reached for a towel as the doorbell rang again.

Dear Joe,

I have reason to believe that you are my baby and that I am your real mother. When I was 16½ or 17 I got pregnant and I gave the baby to your parents and said they should never tell anybody. They didn't. You were my little boy, made of sugar and spice and everything nice. I named you Joe for obvious reasons, and as the years went on I was very lonely so I hired two detectives to find you, the source of my regret. I don't want money or anything. I'm a normal person like

everybody else and I just want to get to know you because
you are my baby, baby.
Love,
Muriel, your real mother

"Sooo," the postman said, handing the letter back. "The guy's name is Joe."

"I like the name Joe," Mike said.

"Who doesn't?" the postman said. "And you're Muriel? Well, all I have to say to you, Muriel, is congratulations."

"Excuse me," the fellow said, walking through the room. "I have to answer the doorbell." The fellow kept walking, amazed at his own decision to pretend he hadn't heard what they were talking about. It wasn't true, in any case. The fellow at 1602 looked exactly like his father and overall the letter was suspect. Last week he had received a letter on the same stationery telling him he had won a prize and it was signed "Muriel, your prize deputy." He hadn't answered that one, and now he was thinking both letters were limp ruses to get into the house. But now Muriel was in the house. She was in the house and all she wanted to do was sit on his sofa and get to know him. Where did he work? Where did he find that tie? Did he grow up happy with his fake parents? This is love, the plain truth once you get inside. Like a peacock, we all show off with the plumage. Come in and watch us make it! But then it's just the same story, sugar and spice all spun up. We're all mostly salt water. Love is candy from a stranger, but it's candy you've had before and it probably won't kill you.

"It's just hitting me," the postman said as soon as the fellow was out of the room, "that the name Joe is never on the envelopes I give this guy."

"I have no idea if his name is Joe," Muriel confided with a whisper. "I made up the whole letter, just about. I just love this guy. I love him. I love him and I want to get to know him."

"I know," the postman said. "Isn't he a peach?"

"I love him," Mike said, "and I've only known him for a few minutes."

"That's how it goes," the postman said. "It's like a miracle. You're lucky it was Bring Your Daughter to Work Day. Let's look at his books."

The three lovers shared a look and got a case of the giggles. There was no competition among them but otherwise there was nothing unusual. The books too were nothing unusual: something by Alice Walker, for instance, a very popular author, and several books on things that interested him. They say love is in the details, that it's the little things that make a person special, but then why are the love songs so alike? It's your smile, it's your eyes, I love your eyes and your smile. I like to go to the beach with you, but really the beach is so interesting and pretty that you could take anyone to the beach. The girl singing that song "Please Mr. Postman" just wants a letter from some fellow, and you just make up who the guy is. You're encouraged to do so, to draw up the details that bring you to love him, so why shouldn't you go to his house, where the details live? That's what the guy who delivers the organic box told himself, as he turned off the same song on the radio and stopped his truck at 1602 and rang the doorbell for obvious reasons.

"Just for a minute," the fellow at 1602 said with a sigh. "I already have three people here."

"I didn't want to insist," said the guy who delivers the organic box. He was holding a box of heavy cardboard, filled with organic fruits and vegetables and other products. The gentle hump of a mango, the perky celery, and a plastic container of yogurt were peeking out of the top of the box like they wanted to be with this guy, just lay eyes on him for a few moments, his pretty eyes. "It's just that I think you're totally super and I want to get to know you."

"Get in line," the postman said, and nearly everybody laughed.

"Do you guys love him too?" the delivery guy said, putting the box on the counter.

"Hell yeah," Muriel said. "I love this fellow like he's my own baby."

"I like his necktie," Mike said.

"We're all on the same page, clearly," the postman said, putting a book back where it belonged.

"I've been watching this guy for like six months," said the fellow who delivers the organic box, pointing to the fellow at 1602 with an eager open palm. "Ever since I got on this delivery route. He's a terrific guy."

"I love him," the postman said and winked at Muriel.

"Who doesn't?" the delivery guy said. "He's the rat's pajamas."

"It's cat," Mike said. His teacher's unit on idiomatic expressions had been almost a complete waste of time.

"I knew it was some animal who had the pajamas," said the

fellow who delivers the organic box. "*Cat*. I'll have to remember that. Now, where do you keep your blender?"

"Call him Joe," Muriel said. "It's a name I made up for him, a term of endearment. Try it."

"Where's the blender, Joe?" the delivery guy tried, but he'd already found it, in a cupboard. There are only a handful of places where a blender is kept. If you live with someone romantically, for years even, you could switch to a new person and find their blender within moments.

"Look," the fellow finally said, and everyone looked. He fussed with his hair in that way people love and gave everyone a little smile like he didn't really mean it. "All this is very strange for me."

"Like you're walking on air?" Mike asked.

"No," the fellow said. "Another kind of strange."

"It can't be any kind of strange," said the guy who delivers the organic box. "You asked for it."

"I did not *ask for it*," the fellow said.

"Sure you did," the guy said. "Every week I deliver organic food right here to this house. Look, we have tomatoes, mangoes, beautiful kale, homemade salsa, wild clover honey, celery and fennel and potatoes, and a thing of organic yogurt from the dairy down the highway. Look at all the flavors here. I bring you them because you want to eat them. You signed up for it, Joe."

"And I give you your mail every day," the postman said, "except Sundays and holidays. Why shouldn't I think you're terrific, and stop by to tell you so?"

"I'm putting you in my report," Mike said. "It's for school."

"That's not the same thing," the fellow said.

"The hell it isn't," Muriel said. "I love you like my own son and you don't want me in your house?"

"Yeah, it's my house," the fellow said. "You all seem like nice people, but I'm going to ask you to get out of it. Get out of my house."

"Don't be silly," the fellow who delivers the organic box said. "I'm making you a mango lassi."

"You'd better make a pitcher," the postman said, craning to look out the window. "We got someone else coming up the front steps."

"What the——" the fellow said, but the doorbell rang and he had to go answer it. Once more, this is love: it rings and you open up unless it looks like an ax murderer.

"Maybe it's his wife," Muriel said. "I'd love to meet her."

"Who wouldn't?" the delivery guy said. "I bet I'd love her too. I'm certain of it, in fact. This is going to be delicious. They drink these in India, like at a wedding or if they're feasting. Mangoes, yogurt, a little lime juice if I can find it. I found it!"

"My my," said the first of the three women who walked into the room. It wasn't his wife. None of them were. All of the women were somewhat old and they lived in the neighborhood. "What a lovely room!" she said. "I love how it flows from the kitchen to the living area, and I love you!"

"I knew he would have a fantastic room," said one of the other women, "because he is a fantastic person."

"Come in, come in," the postman said. "The fellow who delivers the organic box is making us all a pitcher of Indian drinks. Stay for a moment and we'll drink a toast—to Joe!"

"What are you adding, clover honey?" one of the women

asked, looking over at the blender. "It looks like this is going to be very unusual."

"Well, I suppose it's a somewhat unusual situation," Muriel said.

"I for one am glad," said one of the older women, and perhaps because of her age the fellow who delivers the organic box turned off the blender and everyone gave her the floor. "I had a story I was going to tell," she said. "I was going to say that I had a rare disease of some sort and I needed comfort. Or that I was anxious for my mail and that I saw the postman go into this house and not come out and so I couldn't wait anymore or I wanted to make sure nothing was wrong. But I'm not anxious for my mail. I'm healthy as a donkey, and no one writes me, just companies hungry for money. Dear Valued Customer, they say, but I know better. Who gets real mail nowadays?"

"It's not donkey," said the fellow at 1602. "It's *horse*."

"Joe gets real mail," Muriel said, and lifted her letter from the table. "I wrote him a real letter."

"Then read it to me," the woman said. "Or make Joe read it. Tell me a story to pass my time. I find you interesting, Joe, so nearly everything you say will be interesting too. I love you. I could say I'm lonely but that's not the only reason. So many days you passed me by, see the tears standing in my eyes. You didn't stop to make me feel better by leaving me a card or a letter. Mister Postman, look and see if there's a letter in your bag for me."

"I hate that song," said the fellow, but let's be honest: that song is an enormous hit. It's most certainly part of a hit parade, and everyone loves a parade. Joe found, to his mild amazement, that he was having trouble not singing along with the love song that was now in the air. "I want you all to leave," Joe said, but he was still adorable to the whole crowd. "This is private property and you're in flagrant disregard."

"Flagrant disregard, get him," Muriel said, or clucked. "Let your mother tell you something, Joe."

"I don't want you to tell me anything," I said. "I'm not—I'm not the terrific guy you keep telling me about. I'm not made of sugar and spice and everything nice. I'm made of rats and snails and puppy-dog tails. I lie sometimes. I have broken people's hearts. I'm looking for love, I'll admit that, but now that it's here in abundance, I'm afraid of commitment and I want you, please, to leave me."

"It's not rats," Mike said, and bit his lip.

"Now look," said the postman. "You've upset my kid."

"Why are you here?" the fellow from 1602 said.

The postman threw the packet of the fellow's mail on top of his other mail on the table in the guy's house. "I'll try to explain," he said, and then he tried to explain the idea that's here. It's an idea we're more or less stuck with. Isn't love a sharing? Isn't it opening your bag of sweets and passing it around, or whipping something up out of groceries you brought to someone else's house? And if it's a sharing, then you have to share it. Love makes the world go round, the hit songs collectively tell us, and the world is full of people you don't know and might as well be nice to because they won't leave. Some of the people you won't like, but every day we wait for the postman and he hardly ever brings something good. Let us love you, the postman was trying to say, this time let everyone love you, but this kind of talk wasn't really his style, so he just said, "We love you, guy. It's your eyes and your smile and your necktie and shoes. You are terrific and we love you, and you're a sport, so be a sport. Take a mango lassi and drink with us." For in the hubbub of things the fellow who delivers the organic box had easily found glasses for eight. They were fancy glasses, not ones the fellow used often due to their delicacy, but why not use them now, even if they break? Why not fill them while they last?

"We love you, man," the postman said, and held out a glass like you'd hold out a bag of something made by the sea. We all want what's in the bag. You'd have to be crazy not to take some. Have you ever had a mango lassi? Thick down the throat, crazy orange, delicious and happy if you like that sort of thing? What else can a fellow do, in the grip of mango and yogurt and fruit, spun up into a substance just like love? It *is* love. It's a part of it.

"Come on, Joe," Mike said, and Joe reached out and closed his hand around something sweet.

symbolically

After the catastrophe I moved out of the city to the California hinterlands to finish my novel, where I had an "unimpeded view," their words. "Hinterlands" is my word. These are all my words, actually.

As you know because you've read my novel, things were pretty sinister for a while. Several famous buildings had been blown up by angry people from another country with varying degrees of success. Sometimes many people had been killed. Sometimes not so many, and also there were rumors of a volcano underneath us. We were maybe living on a volcano, and the big question was what's the next thing, when will the next famous building go, what will happen next. My unimpeded view was a famous building in San Francisco which it seems particularly pointless to identify any further. That's why it wasn't really the hinterlands, where they let me stay, it was just across a bridge from San Francisco and you could see quite a lot of the city, unimpededly, from the empty and grassy field all scrawled out in front of the cabin, including the famous building, but when you have been born in San Francisco and that's where you drink your Campari, that's where you buy your Stephen Spender, that's where you walk with friends and hear about their endless problems, taking secret notes all the while for a novel, then anyplace outside of San Francisco is the hinterlands. It's a real self-centered place, San Francisco, and that's why I had to head out to the hinterlands for a while to get my words together and down on paper.

In the novel you will recognize them as Lucinda and George, but the people who lent me the house were Nora and George, friends of my mother's who have always been great supporters of mine. The place was empty because Nora had decided to travel for a while, and offered me the house because George had been killed in the big fire. The memorial made me sad. So many people were killed that we had to face that George was unimportant, just an incidental and never a target. At the gathering afterwards at the house I sat in the chair where later I would sit and begin my novel of our times, and read to the quieter members of the assembled mourners a poem about George that marked my return to rhyme.

It is from that chair that I saw the unimpeded view of a man with something on a tripod, standing in silhouette at the edge of Nora and George's field. I had just decided to call it a day on the novel and had poured myself some of Nora and George's cabernet, which I was steadily working through, when I saw him, distant and rumpled, fiddling with a tripod and blocking my eyesight. I took the wineglass out with me and crossed to him in the field. I wasn't scared that he was a terrorist, although I knew of course that I would be an obvious target.

A part of my novel discusses how things can get clearer if you get closer to them, a sort of allegorical thing, and that's how it was. Halfway across the field I could see a man a bit older than me, the thing on a tripod a video camera, and that he was rumpled in jeans and a linen shirt which he was wearing unbuttoned over nothing. He was a man with a baseball cap on his head, and also unshaven, but those seemed like things I could fix.

"Hey," he called over. "Am I on your land, man?"

"Yes," I called back. "What are you doing on my land?"

He scratched his chin and shielded his eyes so he could get a better look at me. "Sorry," he said. "I guess this isn't a good time to run around with a tripod on private property."

"Yes," I said. "I guess not." I stood in front of him and took a sip of my wine to show that it hadn't occurred to me to be frightened. "But what are you doing?"

"There's been a threat," he said, pointing out across the bay to the building. "That's the latest threat. That's what they think is next, and there's an opportunity here."

I took another sip and looked him over again. I had been at Nora and George's for just a bit more than an empty week. Crossing the field to see him, sipping wine as I went, made me a gentleman farmer, discovering another gentleman on my property. "I see," I said. "I think. You're making a movie—?"

The guy grinned at me. "Footage," he said. "*Footage*. Don't you watch TV? That's where it said the threat would be. I'm surprised there's not more people out here for pictures, but if I'm the only guy there's all the more for me, right? If they say the building's going to blow, people are going to want to know what it looks like. That's footage. Every station in the world will want it. All the big networks, everything. *Everybody*."

"You're here to tape it?" I asked. "If the building blows?"

The guy shrugged, took off his hat, put it on, pointed at where the building was standing unharmed. "The way I see it is, like, the first time, what did people say to you? Turn on the TV, right? Something's happened, turn on the TV. Somebody's got to take the pictures of the things that are happening. It might sound greedy or something, but if I could stop it of course I would. If I could. But what I can do is, if it happens, I will have the pictures and so people can see and unite, or whatever. Be upset. Know what's going on, because I sold the footage."

"Sold?"

"Well, yeah." He grinned again, and moved one arm so his shirt opened a little more. "I mean, I'm standing out here all day, right? That's worth money. I can't do it for nothing."

"You're going to stand out here all day?" I said.

"If you're mad about the land," the guy said, "I can rent it or whatever. You can have a piece of it. You can have some of the money. You can't be some billionaire, living way out here in an old house like that. I saw when I drove up. Right? Right? You'll take money. Money, money, money, money, money—there's nothing wrong with it."

I took another gentleman sip and looked out at the city I had left, all the characters in my book, so busy and oblivious that they had never done anything for me, not a thing. "How much money?" I said.

"They say thousands," he said. "That's worth it to me, to sit in a field. It's a nice day, even if nothing happens. Right? Look, it's okay, to be on your land, right? Hang out for a bit, if something happens you'll see it, plus some money on the back end, right?"

"I guess so," I said. "I was going to blow off work anyway."

"That's the spirit," he said, and then began to fiddle with his camera again. I sat down on the grass and felt it scraggly around my shorts.

"Do you want some wine?" I said.

He squinted out at the horizon and then made a little frame with his fingers like movie people do in the movies. "It's a little early for me," he said, with the building in his sights. "What, eleven A.M.? No thanks. So what's your name?"

I looked out at the unimpeded city. From the edge of the field I could see places I had been a hundred times, distant and shiny like the setting of something. All ready to go. He and I regarded the city like a lover asleep when you're not, him filming and me taking mental notes for work that was going to blow everybody away. "My name is Mike," I said. "I'm a writer. I primarily write fiction."

The guy was looking through the camera but he nodded, making one last adjustment. "Well, Mike," he said, "have you ever had sex with a man?"

I thought I did a pretty good job of it. We walked back across the field and I didn't do anything like take his hand, and when we reached Nora and George's bedroom I stood in the doorway and bit my lip sort of, like I was nervous and didn't know what I was getting myself into which I've found generally works to my advantage. Adam smiled at me and sat on the edge of the bed and took off my shirt very gently as I stood in front of him, things like that. It makes the sex better. This is the thing when love starts, both people pretending something that will make it happen, the lies all luscious and wet with lonely hope. Afterward he held me which if you have not shaven I do not like and which is easy to get out of if you have set it up previously that you've never had sex with a man so now you're freaking out a little bit and don't want to be held. "Sorry," he said.

"It's okay," I said. Outside it was still plenty sunny and I had to shield my eyes as I scurried out of bed and put my shorts back on, looking at him and leaning against Nora and George's bookshelves. Thick nonfiction poked me in the back, big demanding books on George's area of specialty, astrophysics, which I guess is vital and important but always seems without flair to me, like waiting tables in a restaurant or crawling back to ex-boyfriends on the nights when it hurts you too much to be alone. Adam looked at me like he thought I was cute, which I thought was cute, and I wished again I was a smoker so I could slowly, slowly exhale a nice shimmering cloud at someone as I wrinkled my brow in thought and sketched all my lovers into place.

"So what do you do, Mike?" he asked me. "What are you doing out here in a place like this, a kid like you?"

"I graduated from college almost two years ago," I corrected him. "I'm a writer, I told you. I'm finishing up a new novel."

"A *novel*, huh? How many *novels* have you written?" he asked.

"One," I said.

"One including the one you're working on, I bet," he said.

"How many thousands of dollars have you made selling footage to the big networks?" I asked.

"Sorry, sorry," he said. "I was just teasing you, Mike. I'm a kidder sometimes." He rolled out of bed and stood in front of me, tiptoeing up for a second and shaking his arms out like a dog getting out of the water. "I'm gonna go check the camera," he said, leaning down to put on his sneakers. "I'm gonna take a piss, and I'm gonna check my camera. I left it running but I can rewind and tape over it. Just in case something happened, which I don't think it did because I think we would have heard something."

"You're going to walk out there just in sneakers?" I said. "You look like a dirty movie."

He strode out to the bathroom. "No one will see me," he called, splashing away. "It's warm like California is supposed to be, and we're in the middle of nowhere, kid. This house is in the middle of a field and the neighbors are probably working a stupid job in San Fran."

"I hate when people call it San Fran," I said.

"San Fran is what everyone calls it," he said cheerfully. "I'll be back in a minute."

"When you get back maybe," I said, "we could have lunch or some wine. I could—"

"When I get back," he said, "I'm going to teach you how to suck my cock."

I covered my smile with my hand and he chuckled out of Nora and George's house. The tall grass in the field made shadows on the wall that I knew I could describe in sentences which would have no equal, but I didn't think it was relevant for me to do so. That was the trick, I was seeing, knowing what was symbolic and what wasn't. If the afternoon sun made playful, slippery shadows on the walls *like a group of small and carefree children playing childish and innocent games of childhood*, then you can't include them if you're moving beyond childhood to someone who might figure prominently in at least two chapters of the most important book of my generation. Love is keeping that symbolic focus, each kiss crucial, each step a landmark. I could have read down a list of every important landmark in America and told you what they all stood for symbolically, what it meant if they were to be destroyed. I knew what everything meant and soon everyone else would know too. I just needed to finish it up. I needed to give Adam a name, and nudge all the details into place.

I stood up and got him in my sights as he walked to check his camera and impede my view, and I couldn't decide. David? Steven? Something European like Tomas, but more wistful? I walked out of the bedroom to my desk and paged through my manuscript as I looked at him through another window. More than sixteen pages were finished, but I could still see where I thought he might go just when the phone rang as fucking usual.

"Mommy," I said, before I could help myself, "I said I'd call *you*. Didn't I say that? I'm working and the phone interrupts me. *I'll* call when I'm *not* working, which is hard because I'm working *very* long hours, *very* hard, because I'm a writer, primarily of fiction, and that goes with the territory, but I *will call* so *don't call me*."

"I'm just worried about you, Tomas," she said. "I worry about you. I mean, you just shocked *everybody* on Sunday. *Every-*

body said to me is he all right, they said is he *all right* out there at Nora and George's. You just shocked *everybody*."

"Fiction changes every generation," I said. "It evolves, and some people are going to be shocked."

"But Tomas," she said. "Tomas. I don't understand what that has to do with your shaving your head."

"I told you that heroes always go through *changes*, that that's the very essence of a story, that you must capture the moment when something *changes* because that is what people want to read, and that a shaved head is a *symbol*, that *symbolically* the hero shaving his head is being re*born*, that he is as bald as the day he was born because he is coming to a new *understanding*."

"But you had plenty of hair when you were born," my mother whined.

"You'll understand better when the novel is published!" I shouted. "Then you can read the parts over and over until you *get it*!"

I hung up and found Adam grinning at me. "Sheesh," he said. "I could hear you yelling halfway across the field. Woman troubles, huh?"

I looked at him and he was naked as the day he was born except for the shoes. "Yeah," I said.

"Happens all the time," he said, staring out the window. "All over the world, I bet. Women complaining, taking the money, no wonder some guys want to blow up buildings."

"I don't want to blow up buildings," I said, reaching for him. "I think it's stupid to blow up buildings." This time I let him hold me, although in the novel, no. But you know that of course, because there isn't any Adam or Tomas or anything. There's no wise and sad description of the sun setting and darkening the room in my novel so that by the time we were finished he had to feel around on the floor for everything he wanted to be wearing.

"Checking on the camera again?" I asked.

"Yeah," he said, peering out at the dim field. Then he had a better idea and switched on the TV over by Nora's side of the bed. White children were taking a big stuffed animal out of a box. "Nothing," he said. "They'd interrupt this if they blew something up. No way would kids be opening presents if there was another building gone. On or off?"

"What?"

"The TV on or off? I'm going to pack up the camera and see you tomorrow."

"What?"

"Come back in the morning. They say nighttime's unlikely."

"You might as well stay," I said. "It might happen at the commute. That's early."

Adam threw his shirt back on. "You really like it, don't you, Mike?" he asked. "I'll come back tomorrow and we'll do more. I'll let the camera run again."

"You might as well stay," I said again.

"Nah," he said. "Bad idea, my friend. You better get home too, before whoever owns this comes back and finds a little baldy brat here."

I reached to pour myself some more wine but Adam had drunk it all while I was dozing, I guess, because there was just an empty bottle all sucked dry, a perfect symbol for what was going on. "I happen to own this house," I said.

"I don't think so," he said, zipping up. "I think old people sleep in that bed, because there's pictures of them all over the place. I don't think you own a grandfather clock, Mike, or the three bottles of wine I watched you drink."

"Like *you* didn't have any," I said. The studio audience laughed at something the brats said on TV, another symbolic thing I'd use if I was going to cheapen my work with pop-culture references.

"I think you're someone on the make, like me," he said. "I think you're seeing an opportunity like I am. The thing is, though, I can explain if somebody asks me. Nobody really cares if I'm in their field with a camera."

"I care," I said. "I care if you're in my field. I write my novels here because I have an unimpeded view. I don't want to look at you."

"Yes you do," he said, but he left the room and slammed the door of the house and I just lay there until the end of the episode.

It was a terrible night in the hinterlands. The wind wailed around me like a keening crowd, like an assembly of mourners for the shallow and overrated state of American fiction before my triumphant arrival on the literary scene. I tried to read some of the books I had brought to nourish me during this time in isolation, but I've never been good at reading when the TV is on or when I'm very, very drunk and certain people won't answer the goddamn phone after thirty-two rings. In the morning I decided I'd let myself have a day away from my desk to let the current draft of my novel really sink in, and I was just opening a bottle of wine when I saw something impeding my view of the city where I grew up, in a restrictive and fraudulent household, before departing for a campus that never really welcomed me only to return to San Francisco and find myself completely and totally reborn and shorn of all my previous and toxic influences. I didn't even throw my shoes on. Each blade of grass cut like a blade. I realized halfway there that I was drinking Nora and George's wine out of the bottle, but I thought that was perfect. Desperate times had erased the civility of the gentleman farmer, because it was January 17 and there were two figures at the end of the field, one tinkering with a tripod and the other holding his hands up to the city in the shape of a frame.

There is no mention of Adam in my novel of our times, not even in the discarded drafts in the back of the annotated edition I have all planned. There is no man in jeans and a linen shirt in my novel. He symbolizes nothing. He would never be targeted, even in retaliation. He is at the bottom of the list of things people want to destroy, and so is the woman with the curly ponytail who paused in her operation of the camera to lean over and kiss him on the cheek, and then, in a phony gesture without even a hint of flair, pretend that she just then noticed me in her peripheral vision and give me a puzzled frown like she thought offhand I was dead but the media's so unreliable these days.

"Oh, hey," Adam motherfucking said. "This is Eddie. Eddie, this is that guy I told you I met yesterday, Mark."

"Matt," I said. "*Mike*. I want you off my land. What you're doing is exploitative and wrong and I won't have any part of it."

"You won't get any part of it," Adam said. "It's a free country and if something happens I will get it on camera."

"People want to see this," Eddie said in her stupid bandanna.

"I don't want to see this," I said. "I think you disgusting people are wrong and unfair."

"Adam," Eddie said, "I thought you said—"

"I'll handle this," Adam said. "Make sure the focus is right. They won't pay shit for a fiery blur." Adam stepped toward me and grabbed me by the shoulders and led me down the field a ways, where the city was at a less attractive angle and the building couldn't be seen.

"What's the problem?" he said quietly. "I'm sorry, man, but she said she wanted to come. What am I gonna say?"

"I don't want you here," I said. "Take your girlfriend with the boy's name and fuck her in the fucking woods if it's a free country."

"You gotta chill out," he said.

"Don't tell me to chill out," I said. "I'm a driving force in American literature."

"You're a drunk bald kid in his underwear," Adam said. "Go sleep it off, Mike or whatever."

"It makes me sick that you're selling those pictures."

"It's footage," Adam said, "and it's a free country I said."

"It's not a free country," I said. "I'm scared to live in the city. I'm scared to go home. I'm an important person and that makes me a target. Someone could kill me. Lots of people want to kill me. They're mad at me and they want to kill me."

Adam looked at me then, and if it weren't for his girlfriend he would have been back in the novel, because the view changed. His easygoing gaze changed for me and I thought maybe he saw how important I was, how vital to the American scene. "No one's mad at you, man," he said. "No one wants to kill you. Why don't you—no, let's not drink any more wine right now, okay? Coffee or something. It's okay."

"Nobody knows," I said. "Nobody knows how crucial I am. Nobody calls me."

"It's okay," he said. "It's okay."

"How would you know it's okay?" I said. "You don't know me. You don't even think I own this house."

"You're not in danger," he said. "Look, my camera's not pointing at you, okay? It's not going to happen to you. It'll happen out there." He jerked a thumb across the view.

"You hope," I said.

"Sort of," he nodded. "Sort of, yeah. I guess I hope something happens, because then I'm not standing here for nothing. I want something, you know, important to happen or it's not worth it."

"And I'm not important enough," I said. I wished I had two bottles of wine, and not just for the usual reasons. I wished I had all the right symbolism, two bottles, one of the sweet wine of red relief and one of the bitter wine of white disappointment that I could mix into a sort of rosé in my mouth. I'm very proud of that sentence. "I'm not important enough," I said. "That's it, huh?"

"Importance is the least of your problems," he said. "You don't have any pants on, man."

"Looking good, Adam!" Eddie called. "I got it right in the middle and it's looking good. The sun's shining and everything, right on it. Come see!"

"Yeah," he said and waved. "Are you okay? You want to see it, Mike? Come see."

"No," I said. "In a minute."

"It's okay," Adam said, and walked away from me at the height of my career. He went with his girlfriend and they turned their backs and looked out at San Fran. That's always where the love goes, with somebody else away from me. I just stood in the hurting grass and saw them look. "Come see!" Adam called. "It looks good. Come see!"

"Yeah, come see!" Eddie said. "Come see!" she said. "Come see! Come see! Come see! Come see!" and so I walked over there. I stood in my underwear where anybody could have seen me, but nobody did. Adam and Eddie were looking through the camera, and the camera was pointing the wrong way so I stood there with nobody and looked out at the unimpeded view of the famous building I don't need to designate, neither in my novel nor here. I stood there, January 17, and looked at this thing that people were looking at instead of me. It was a terrible thing, this shift in focus. This is love if it's not with you, a terrible fiery something that makes people look away, and it feels like a punch in the throat. It was terrible, this terrible view, this symbolism too much to bear, unviewed and unpaid for and off camera in the hinterlands. Even in the novel I just stood there, looking at the landmark and feeling the terrible shift, because a few minutes later it was gone.

clearly

This part is a love story forgotten by its characters. If you were to ask them about it, any of them who are still alive, they would remember it again, but not all of it. They would each remember a few details, separate from one another, but the people in this story do not see each other anymore. They have faded even from one another's sleep. No matter where their minds wander, those who are still alive, these people do not cross each other's paths. All four of them have completely abandoned one another.

The woods are still there, though, and protected by law. The trees, tall and close together, and the moss spreading its green dark mossiness, and those mushrooms we should not eat, that's all still there. If you were to ask these forest things if they remembered the story, what would they say? Nothing. The forest does not answer the questions of nature-addled idiots. It is not interested probably. The forest has abandoned these people too. If the forest thinks—and I don't think it does—it thought about these people for a few minutes, while it was happening, and then moved on, as when someone you know tells you a story about someone you don't know, or you notice a fight between lovers on the street who do not know you are there. You might remember a few things—what he drank or how quickly the money was gone or what she lied about—or the next time you see a beer stein, a hairdryer, you might think: He threw this at her. This smashed on the wall, but then what? It is not being thrown at you. You are not the bruised one in this story.

Adam's bare skin, and Eddie's bare skin, are unbruised at this point too, as they kiss fiercely in a clearing. Eddie is a woman and so has more of her clothes off. Adam's shirt is unbuttoned, down the middle, with one shoulder bare, awkward but unnoticed. Eddie's shirt is gone, someplace in the plants which grow on the ground. She is on her back. Her breasts are bare and in the dull gray sunlight you can see her skin as she opens her mouth and moves around. Adam is crouched on top of her, of course. Their coats are nearby because the weather is not warm. The air is like the first bite of a good apple. Eddie's skin is goose-pimply where Adam is not touching her. She keeps moving his hands to different parts of her, moving his mouth to her breast, to her shoulder, but mostly to keep warm. Every part of her grows cold when he is not there. Adam unbuckles his belt and unzips his pants because the plan all along was that they were going to have sex in the woods.

Adam blinks down at her three or four times. His eyes are shot through with red and his penis equally fierce. He looks at Eddie, shifting and arching, and for a moment it looks like something terrible is meandering its way through her, but Eddie is only trying to get comfortable. The floor of the clearing is filled with things, and Eddie feels as if she is sleeping on a bed of macadamia nuts, uneasy and crunchy. Adam lifts one of her legs and then squints and winces for a moment.

"Are you——?" Eddie asks. "We don't have to."

"No, no," Adam says. "No."

"I'm sorry," someone else says. "I'm really sorry." He moves another branch aside and steps the rest of the way into the clearing with his backpack.

What is a clearing, anyway? It is someplace in the forest where nothing is growing, or where something used to grow but nothing has come to take its place. It's supposed to have nothing in it. That's why Adam and Eddie chose there, but now there is another person. At least he is apologizing.

"I'm sorry," he says. "I don't mean to. But my friend is hurt. We fell down. He can't walk. He can't even walk here. I'm really sorry."

Adam lets go of Eddie's leg and it drops to the ground. There is a small marking, or a row of markings, where his hand held her there. Eddie takes her shirt. "What?" she says.

"I'm really sorry," he says. "We need your help. Help. My friend needs your help."

"What—where is he?" Adam asks.

"I'm Tomas," the other person says, even though he does not have an accent. "My friend and I were walking here too. He's only—I don't know—he's by the brook or creek. He can't walk. The two of us fell while we were walking. I need—"

"The forest ranger," Adam says. "The ranger station." He blinks his red eyes.

"I know," the other person—Tomas—says. "But somebody should sit with him. Or I'll go, and I mean you'll go, and I'll stay with him, but I need your help."

Adam and Eddie scarcely have to look at each other. As moral dilemmas go it's not much of one. Adam zips his pants up and hands Eddie her coat which is closer than his. It's within arm's reach.

"I'm really sorry," Tomas says. "I'm—do you want me to step away? I'm sorry."

"Just for a second," Eddie says on the ground. "I need to get dressed."

"I know," Tomas says, and he turns around and takes a few steps into the trees so they can only see his backpack. It is the closest thing to discretion he can do. Adam throws his coat on and laces his shoes and walks away from Eddie like he's ashamed of her. He steps out of the clearing where Tomas is waiting for them. "I'm sorry," Tomas says. "I'm really sorry. There's just no one else here."

Adam gives Tomas a smile made of wire and sort of limps his arms in the air to indicate the way of the world, although he is furious. "We were going to have sex," he says. Why not say it? You're in the woods and you'll never see this man again.

"I know," Tomas says. "Sorry."

"She's embarrassed," Adam says. Now there are three people in the forest when they thought they were two. There are three people in the forest and two of them are men and so they will blame her, the woman, for anything they can dream up.

"Yes," Tomas says. "I'm sorry. I'm Tomas."

"Adam."

Adam and Tomas shake hands, but Adam is angrier still. He did not hear it, the first time Tomas said his name. Tomas is a man who used to be Eddie's lover, six or seven months before

this story takes place. Adam knows this from the stories Eddie
tells, the way you tell stories about people you know. Eddie and
Tomas did not have a bitter parting, and so Adam has thrown
stones at Tomas, as he lay in bed with Eddie and she told stories.
Adam hates Tomas and tried to get Eddie to join him in hate. It
hasn't worked, although Eddie will admit certain shortcomings,
and the two men have not met until now, in the forest, when
Adam has decided that the Tomas in Eddie's stories and the
Tomas in this story are the same man.

"What are you even doing here?" Adam asks. "Foggy. Fog
and rain. Terrible day for a hike."

"I might ask you the same question," Tomas says. It is the
wrong thing to say.

"You can see what I was doing," Adam says and scrubs at his
eyes with one fist.

"What's wrong with your eyes?" Tomas says.

"Allergic," Eddie says, all dressed. She steps out of the clearing and stands with them. Adam can see over her shoulder into
the clearing. Eddie has taken everything with her and there is no
trace, not even in the leaves on the ground, that two people or
three people were ever there. Adam will get home and find dirt
on his shoes, a few small things captured in his jacket, in his
socks, traces of the forest on him, but not the other way around.
"Adam's allergic to something in here," she says. "Something in
the forest."

"Is that so," Tomas says, looking at Adam's eyes.

"Where is this friend?" Adam asks. "Where is your friend?"
He has noticed that Eddie has not bothered to introduce herself.

"Down this way," Tomas says, and the three of them disappear from the clearing completely. They abandon the clearing for the rest of the story to walk together. This is how it is in life and love. In life and love we are with people for a while, and then we join other people, people we have not met, and we walk with them, and we leave behind all the things where we used to be. Sometimes we leave people behind too. Sometimes we walk away from the forest and abandon a person there and never see them again. This happens every day. Every day this happens and scarcely anybody cares.

By the brook or creek is Steven, on the ground near the water with two backpacks beside him. He is almost prone on a small arrangement of fairly flat rocks, with his legs stretched toward the water and his head squinting at the cloudy sun. He looks pale, or perhaps he always looks that way, but he is smiling, with his arms out in a wide stretch, until Adam and Eddie and Tomas walk through the last of the trees, and he curls up and frowns at them.

"Steven, we're here," Tomas says. "I found these people in a clearing."

"We heard you were hurt," Eddie says.

"Hello," Steven says. He looks okay.

"What," Adam says. "What's wrong. What's wrong with you?"

"I don't think I can walk," Steven says, "like at all. It's—it hurts. It's gross to look."

Steven reaches down to his right leg and parts the leg of his pants, which someone has slit right up, cut with a knife or a scissors to see, or maybe it's part of the wound, the same thing that caused it. Eddie gasps, or Adam. From the knee down almost to the shoe, on one neat side of Steven's leg, is a round painful dome of an injury, swollen up purple and black. It has swollen up around a long gash, straight down the leg, although the gash is puckered and not bleeding anymore, as if it happened yesterday and has healed slightly, or is a fake, painted down his leg with thick putty and coloration. But the swelling looks very delicate and realistic, an almost gossamer, tender skin trembling across the wound, so that if you touched it everything would burst into thick blood, and the leg looks very wrong, bent somehow, or maybe that is just the shape of what has happened.

"It hurts," Steven says, and now he looks worse. There is a line of sweat at the top of his forehead, and he turns his head and spits onto the ground. "It hurts a lot."

"Keep it covered," Eddie says. "Keep it covered, I think." She looks around at the brook, which she and Adam had stepped across earlier, or walked alongside, she cannot remember. She wishes very hard that they were still at the clearing, although she had not been comfortable or very enthusiastic. But even bad kissing was preferable to this awful leg, this outrage at the brook. It is unfair that Eddie has to look at this terrible thing, that they all must try to fix Steven's wound just because they are there. She has a thought that she and Adam could say they were going for help but instead just abandon them, leave the forest and go home. It is early, fairly early. Another person would show up, by the brook.

"How did this happen?" Adam asks. Steven closes the pant leg again and covers the wound, and Adam thinks that he must have made a mistake, and that there are two Tomases, one her former lover and another one here in the woods.

"We fell," Tomas and Steven say at the same time. Tomas points up to a small, rocky slope, not many yards away. It looks like something you could fall from, probably.

"We were carrying too much," Steven says, and pats one of the backpacks beside him.

"The packs are heavy," Tomas agrees, though he keeps his pack on his shoulder. "We need to go to the ranger station, but I don't think we should carry him."

"No," Steven says. "It would hurt, and it's not good to move the wound."

"We'll go," Eddie says. "The two of us will go. At the entrance, where we went in. It's not far. Twenty minutes maybe. It's not far. It's not like we're in the middle of nowhere. You can stay here."

"Someone should stay with him," Tomas says.

"That's what I mean," Eddie says. She looks at Adam and then away, down at Steven's leg. "We'll go, and—"

"No, we'll go," Adam says. He changes his thinking again and the anger returns, prickly, moving beneath him and everyone else. His eyes get wide and he has a headache and his body feels wrong. The strain of not having sex, maybe, has helped this anger along, as boys are taught. And maybe a rival, Eddie's old lover returning for her and leaving Adam with a wounded man, all on the pretense of getting help. "Tomas and I will go," Adam says. "You stay here. Tomas and I can go. We'll go quicker." It's the only thing he can say.

"Why don't both of you go?" Tomas says. "Just tell the ranger where we are, or bring him here. It's the brook, right on the path."

"I have a map," Adam says, although neither he nor Eddie have a backpack where it might be. They didn't even bring a blanket, despite their plans, or a bottle of water. "We have a map. Just stay here and we'll go, Eddie. But let's go quickly. There's lots of time before it gets dark, but we should be sure. We'll be gone and back before you can recite the Gettysburg."

"I never learned that," Eddie says.

"Then we'll definitely be back before then," Tomas says.

"What's wrong with your eyes?" Steven says, squinting. He wouldn't ask this, probably, except he is in pain, and distracting himself.

"Allergies," Adam and Eddie say at the same time.

"Something in the forest, apparently," Tomas says.

"It's like that," Eddie says. "Any little thing can set him off."

"Let's go," Adam says, and Eddie can tell suddenly how angry he is. One of his hands is clenched inside his pocket. Why would he leave her here, with this stranger? She'd say something but it doesn't seem worth it. Steven is harmless, with his leg. It is wilderness but popular wilderness, hours before dark. She knows nothing will happen to her, although things have happened to her before, and anyway she will not argue in front of a stranger, and so they go, Tomas and Adam. They disappear into the forest. Later she will think that somebody should have said something. If someone had said something else, the story would have gone in a different way, clearly. Later on Eddie will prefer this other way, any other way. Even now she does. But away they go.

"You're Eddie?" Steven asks. She does not remember if her name has been said.

"Yes," she says.

"Really?" he says.

"*Yes*," she says.

"Thanks for doing this, if that's your real name," he says. "I'm sorry about it."

"It's not your fault," she says. "You fell. Do you have any water?"

"Lots," Steven says, and reaches for one of the packs, but Eddie gets to it first, and finds the water bottle inside, along with an extra sweater and a pair of socks and a folding knife. Perhaps the other pack is heavy. Eddie takes a sip and spills a bit. It is one of those bottles you suck on. She wipes her mouth and hands it to Steven, who takes it but does not drink.

"How long do you think it will take?" Eddie asks.

"I don't know," Steven says. "I'm not good with how many miles. I hope Tomas is okay. He was acting sort of strange. I upset him, I think. It upsets him to look at the leg."

"It's terrible," Eddie says. "I don't understand how it happened on that slope."

"I fell," Steven says sharply, and closes his eyes in a wince. He takes a long sip from the water bottle, possibly to change the subject, and turns his body to accidentally expose the wound again. It must have caught on something, as he fell, a thorny branch or a treacherous piece of rock they cannot see from here.

"Did you say something to Tomas?" Steven asks, and covers his wound again. "He was sort of strange. He was acting strange."

"Tomas," Eddie says, "interrupted us. We were kissing, and—"

"And?" Steven says, and gives Eddie a crude smile.

"And he walked in," Eddie says. All of the people in this story are the same age, more or less. It is an age where they have all had sex already. They have all loved before, and some of them, perhaps, are loving now. They have all had sex, and if you have sex you eventually try it outdoors. Why wouldn't you? And so Eddie does not like this greed to talk about it, even in the woods with no one around. She does not like this guy. Or—and she looks out at the slope again—maybe he is just in pain and trying to distract himself. This is what happens. You meet people who are in pain, in life and love, and you forgive them for behaving the way they do. "We were going to have sex and then he walked in. Is that what you wanted to know?"

"I guess so," Steven says. "I'm sorry. I was only—"

There is a nearby noise, in the trees someplace, as happens in the forest, and Eddie and Steven look quickly into the leaves and see nothing. Although Eddie won't remember this, she moves closer to Steven, close enough so he could touch her very easily, although she has always been in arm's reach. The noise has made her move, as it nearly always does. It is a rustling noise that may only be some branch of a tree, finally giving up on a handful of leaves, or a squirrel, something harmless. But the noise also might be something larger and more dangerous, stumbling as it comes closer, and so Steven and Eddie gather closer to one another and begin to talk closer, too. This happens all the time. You meet someone and talk with a stranger, if for no other reason than they are a stranger, next to you in a diner maybe, or the passenger in your taxi. It has happened to me in the bars of hotels, and in the quieter rooms of parties, when we sit on the coats and place our plastic cups on the bureaus of the host. It can feel a little bit like love, these conversations where we say things that pop into our heads as if they are things we always feel but never say to anyone, but it's not love. Love is, I hope, more than two people sitting down for a while and telling secrets before help arrives. This is just people talking, to distract themselves from strange noises around them as this story gets worse.

"I'm scared, I think," Steven says. "I'll die here."

"No, no," Eddie says, but she thinks of his leg and she does not know. "I don't think you'll die. With something like this you'd bleed to death and you're not even bleeding."

"Isn't that worse?" Steven asks. "Isn't it worse if it's not bleeding?"

"I don't know," Eddie says, and certainly she does not know. If she thinks of the wound, it certainly seems serious. Why else would she be stopped here, with someone she doesn't know, if it wasn't serious and he weren't dying? "If I tell you that you might die, you'll tell everybody later. Tomas. You'll say that this woman waited with you but kept saying creepy things until you got more and more scared."

"Do you *know* Tomas?" Steven asks, but then he frowns and bites down on his own lip. "It really hurts," he says.

"Should we elevate it?" Eddie asks. "Or wash it?"

"I washed it with the water bottle," Steven says, "right after we fell and right before you came. Just distract me."

"Distract?" Eddie says. The wound, she remembers, was not wet when she looked at it.

"Just say something, or tell me something."

"I'll tell you about a dream I had," Eddie says, and this is what I mean. Why would she tell him this? This story does not take place at a time when there are soothsayers. A dream, who cares? And yet we say these things because what would it mean if no one was interested? "I'll tell you a dream I had last night, I think, and I keep thinking about it."

"Does it have specific details?" Steven asks. "I read someplace that specific details can distract you from the pain. Like on a battlefield they give you specific details. Think about your sweetheart."

"Thinking about your sweetheart doesn't sound specific," Eddie says, "but I guess it is. No, this is just a dream, but I'll put specific details in. In the dream I'm dating this guy I knew in high school. I've been on a couple of dates with him I guess, in the dream. In real life I didn't know him at all, not even really in high school. Hank Hayride."

"That can't be his real name," Steven says.

"You're right," Eddie says. "It can't be. I never thought of that. I just woke up and thought that I dreamed I was dating Hank Hayride. But that can't be right."

"Maybe it was right in the dream," Steven says, but Eddie is not paying attention.

"Hayride," she says. "Where did that come from? Hayride,

hayride. Haythorne? Maybe Hank Haythorne? It was Hank something, definitely, but anyway I think someone told me he's dead. But that might be in the dream too."

"This isn't distracting me from the pain at all," Steven says.

Eddie slaps him on the shoulder very lightly, not meaning it, and then keeps her hand there for a second. Steven definitely notices this. She is looking out at the slope where Steven supposedly fell. You couldn't fall from there, and receive a wound like the one she saw. She didn't think so. But what could it be? Why would you lie about that and then do nothing, just sit by a brook and hear made-up stories? Eddie can't imagine.

"So I was dating Hank Hayride," Eddie says, as if changing the subject, "in the dream, and we had gone on a few dates, and then he said we had to talk, or he had something to say to me, or something. I don't really remember. But it was—I think it was *that talk*, you know, when you go out with someone for a while and then you finally have the talk where you tell them something."

"Like you're gay," Steven says.

"No, not like you're gay," Eddie says, "like you're married, or you used to be married and you lost a baby and you're not ready for a commitment, or you need to know what's going on after six weeks of just sort of dating. You know, like the first serious talk."

"I just had one of those," Steven says.

"With who?"

"I don't think you would know the person," Steven says. "I

hope not. It didn't go well. Those talks never do go well, don't you think?"

"I guess not," Eddie says. "I don't know."

"You're always disappointed, I think," Steven says. "Have you had that talk with what's-his-name?"

"Tomas?" Eddie asks.

"No, the other guy," Eddie says. "Adam, the guy you're with."

"No," Eddie says. "No, no. And I guess you're right. I know it will be disappointing with him. We'd probably have it tonight, except now."

"You would go have sex in a forest," Steven says, "and *then* have that talk?"

"Yes, and it would be disappointing," Eddie says. "We would lie, or one of us would, but I'm supposed to be telling you my dream."

"I don't think that guy is good for you," Steven says. "I don't think you should be with somebody like him." Steven reaches down and picks up a stone for no reason and throws it into the water of the brook. "I think you would rather be with someone else. I could tell the second you walked up to me. I could tell."

"Maybe that's what the dream is about," Eddie says, and this is the sort of nonsense I mean. Why would they say these things? It is flirtatious, somewhat, this kind of conversation. But why pretend that it is Eddie's dream that matters, when terrible things are going on? But they do. Steven looks at Eddie and looks at her shirt, which was hurriedly rebuttoned in the clearing, and he thinks to himself, this woman is telling me secrets.

"So we met in this diner, which is a real place in the city. In my dream. And Hank was going to tell me something, which is that he was dead. I guess that *is* more like being gay. But maybe not, because it was causing all these problems. He was telling me that there are certain things ghosts can do and certain things they can't, but all the while—"

"You're very beautiful," Steven says, like he is drunk. Perhaps the pain causes this too, but how many things can you forgive?

"All the while," Eddie says firmly.

"You *are* beautiful," Steven says. "It's okay to say that. I can say that to you. We're never going to see each other again."

This is a weird guy, in the forest, and Eddie knows it, but what can she do but continue with her story? Weird guys live everywhere, and this is part of love, too. If there were more women than men in this story, the women would talk about all those guys to pass the time as it grew darker. They would talk about the men they have met who would say strange, even terrible things, while hoping that they were not terrible. Or, of course, there are men who are really so dense that they say such things whenever the mood strikes them, or whenever they've had too much to drink, stupidly stupidly while walking through the woods, and certainly there are men who do not care if they do things that put women ill at ease when they are alone, or who even, no matter how harmless the day, can conjure panic out of nothing. Steven picks up a stone, this one much larger. He could not throw this one without hurting his leg from the effort, if his leg is indeed wounded. But even this is unremarkable in the forest, which is why this story is forgotten by the people who lived it. How do you forget something? You just walk away from it, those who are still alive. There are so few clearings in our hearts and minds, so few places where something can't grow on top of whatever happened to us before, and this is love too. You are with people and you walk away long after they scare you for the first time, because you know it is happening all over the world. And so we will leave the side of the brook, or creek, and never get to hear that while the ghost of Hank Hayride was talking to Eddie, all the while there was someone scraping at the windows of the diner. It was past January, in the dream, and it was time to scrape off the paintings of Christmas scenes on the windows of the real diner. The paintings would be scraped off, leaving the windows bare and revealing all the people who were talking and drinking inside. As the man—it was a man—scraped at the paintings, his tools made a terrible shrieking sound, and it was this sound that was the scariest part of the dream. When Eddie woke up she mostly remembered this sound, this shriek of a sound, and she knew that it meant that something would scrape away at her and leave her raw, wounded even. Something would scrape and scare her, far worse than her troubles with Adam, who was sleeping beside her within arm's reach. She knew that all of it was over with Adam, despite their plans to go to the forest tomorrow, and sure enough Adam is not with her anymore. Adam has arrived at a field with Tomas walking behind him. The field is grassy and to one side is a pile of segments of a fence which someone has taken apart and stacked up together. All boundaries are down. Far, far from the field is an expanse of

"Just a little bit," Adam replies at once. "I didn't know. It was just for the hike, and we were going to have sex. She loved it."

"I don't think so," Tomas says. "I think you take it all the time, and your girlfriend doesn't know or doesn't want to know."

"Why don't you just say her name?" Adam says.

"I don't know her name," Tomas says. He sighs and takes the water back. He is bored but maybe also a little scared. If they have gone the wrong way it might take quite a while to retrace their steps, and they should proceed, moving quickly, as if Steven is in much danger and pain. "You're the worst possible person I could have found for help."

"What about *you*?" Adam says. "You're lying, too. You said that your backpacks were heavy but you haven't put yours down. There are three backpacks. You have one and there are two by the river. Where's the third person? What happened to them?"

"The backpacks *are* heavy," Tomas says, and by now, after all this time, he is as angry as Adam or anyone else. Aren't there any good people in the forest? This is like love too, that desperate question when we are alone with the wrong people. Where are they? These four people are ill-suited to one another, but is there anyone well-suited, three men choked with dishonesty and a woman still scared by that terrible, terrible shrieking sound, as the paintings are scraped away from the windows and her dream of love is over and she wakes up? Even now she feels like crying, although she has been given no terrific reason to cry. Even now, as Tomas reaches into his pack and withdraws something heavy for Adam to see, Steven is gasping and getting worse, or maybe it just seems that way, after all the time they have spent together. He gasps at his leg when he tries to move it around, and he gasps at another noise in the forest around him, and he gasps at the water as he drinks it down until it is almost empty.

"I think I'm dying again," he says. "It really hurts, and I think we'll have to do something else."

"They're coming," Eddie says immediately, but there's no-body else by the creek but the two of them, and Steven laughs and spits something onto the ground.

"No," he says. "We left them way behind. Do you know that. We left them way behind. It's a song." This is true, what he's saying, although Eddie would have no way of knowing, as the song is obscure and hardly anyone thinks of it. "We left them way behind," the song says, "and when they finally let us out, we tracked down our accusers. And when we finally let them out, they brought up different charges," and this is something that Steven does, too. "It's a song," he says when he's done reciting the lyrics, "but in real life I don't think they're coming. I think we're alone, Eddie, although at least we have water." He looks through the bottle, moving the tiny bit of water from side to plastic side. "I wonder if you're thirsty, like dying of thirst, if you think about all the water you've chugged and squandered. If you think of the water you wasted when you had some."

Eddie tries to think of anything, anything, anything to say. Steven looks very terrible, but then, when she thinks of it, Adam looked terrible too, interrupted in the clearing by a man with the name of her old boyfriend, and his face too, all wrinkled as usual with false concern. She never wants to fall for that again, but what else is there? There is no one who doesn't say something strange. Love is this story, maybe, something happens to us and we are with someone, and we abandon them when we can—we leave them way behind—or we stay, in sickness and in health, as it gets later and darker, quicker than we thought, and colder too, as it has happened one million times before. "There's a song I know," she says. "You don't miss the water till the well's run dry."

"I'm not talking about a *song*," Steven says in disgust, and coughs with pain and puts down the rock. "I mean, if you get old, I wonder. I wonder if you get old do you worry about everything you wasted."

"*You* are wasted," Eddie says.

Steven coughs roughly again, and he nods and looks at the packs on the ground. "All of us," he says, and he puts his hand on her. He puts his hand on her knee.

"Um," Eddie says, and let's leave now. It is clear what is going to happen.

naturally

It was the sort of day when people walk in the park and solve problems. "We'll simply call the taxi company, David, and request a large one, like one of those vans," is the sort of thing you would overhear if you were overhearing in the park. Hank was. He heard that one, and "Let's tell them six and then they'll show up at six-thirty" and "America just needs to get the hell out of there and not look back." Hank lay on an obscure corner of the grass, eyes closed, not moving, getting cold even in the nice day, and he overheard "Maybe we shouldn't move in together at all" and "If taxi companies don't take requests the company will rent you a car probably" and "The guests can gather out on the porch and then come in when dinner's ready" and "Oh my fucking Christ! Don't look, honey, don't look! The man is dead, honey, that's a dead man, oh god somebody call the police."

It was not a mistake. It was perfectly natural, although it ruined the whole day in the park for everyone who was there. Certainly for Hank. It made all the other problems recede for a little bit, although soon they returned, which is as natural as the park itself. Grass, trees, flowers trampled by the paramedics, a few people sticking around to watch with the small wisdom which reaches us in such moments: it is all natural. Someday we will all be dead people but in the meantime we have these problems to solve.

How? Money maybe, money money money, or who knows. "Where's my money? I'm very angry because I believe I am owed some money which you are preventing me from obtaining, I'm going to stab you, or maybe I'm crazy, it's an odd corner of the path in the park and I'm a growling crazy person the government ought to be taking care of, nobody will see it happen." The police asked bystanders who did not see it happen, but there weren't any details. Only a body, what seems like the end of a story to anyone who spoke to the police. "I found him, officer, but I don't know anything else and I must walk around the park and talk with my girlfriend about myself because after all I did not see it happen and I did not know him."

Hank was all packed up, like a song about a man leaving a woman. A zipper closed across his dead face like he had never been there, only a duffel bag. Hank's life was over. He kept his eyes closed, slowly figuring it out and wondering how it would go, surprised that, given that we all wonder it, a bright light or what, surprising that you would have to wait to find out like anything else.

An interval here, nearly indescribable.

It happened. Hank got up while the morgue guy was signing a piece of paper. He saw his own body lying on the thing but to tell you the truth that wasn't what he was most interested in looking at. He had seen himself naked and so had quite a few other people, although some of them do not remember. Hank was more curious that he could walk through the rooms of the place but even this faded almost immediately. Hank moved through this time and did not know what to do with it, those first few blank days at a new job. Where do I go? What do I do? What time do we meet and where do we go for lunch and where are the people who are nicer? He sat on benches and tried to get in a spooky mood. But all the things he could see were all the things you see anyway. People having sex, sure, a couple of times. But Hank had seen movies in which people had sex and those people did not know he was in the room either. We do not want to be in a room and people not to know. Alive or dead this begins to hurt our feelings. We want to be seen. We want to haunt people, if they'll have us, and if they won't have us we feel as sad as we do in life.

And yet it was nothing like life, this thing he was living through. It was as far from life as pizza served on an airplane is from Italy, even if the plane is flying over Italy at the time. People did not see him and so he grew hungry. He did not need to eat, but who does not go into the place anyway sometimes, and order a snack something, just for something to do and because you are not a ghost? The girl at the counter stood and looked at the mouth of a honey bear. It was a clear plastic thing, shaped in the shape of a real bear, somewhat, with honey instead of blood and organs and bones. The girl at the counter was young and named Lila unless the name tag was a joke too, and she was peering into a hole in the fake bear's head to see what the problem was. "It keeps sticking!" she called behind her. Hank overheard her call it as he stood there dimly hoping she would look up and give him a doughnut if he asked. The doughnuts sat there under a clear dome covered in icing and the sprinkles, waiting to be chosen and picked up by the pretty girl's tongs. But Hank felt the thin weight of ignored and left the place without his snack. Woe filled him at least halfway. He had missed his funeral because no one had told him when it was, and always this feeling of what if this is heaven and I'm screwing it up? What if I'm also screwing this up?

This is a love worry, of course. It is the trouble all the time with love. You see the person and you want to cry, "Put down your honey bear and look at me, my darling I dream of! Bring me the doughnut I desire!" But all the time you know the depressing thing: she doesn't even know you exist. Hank kicked a few things around in the street and floated through the door of a private home. A man was opening his mail, who cares. Down the block was the neighbor, an older woman who had sent the letter. There Hank found he could pick up pens, which is where they go when you can't find them. The cat saw him do it. "Mr. Mittens, what's that?" she said. "What do you see, Mr. Mittens, that you behave like that?" Hank gave Mr. Mittens the finger, not for the first time. He walked out holding the pens like a dozen skinny roses for no one he could think of that would see him.

But it turns out someone did. Back at the park Hank was revisiting the scene of the crime in the hopes of haunting maybe. He walked down to the stables where the girls look at the horses and the boys wonder if it's time to go home. Hank steered fairly clear because you never know with horses. He stood on the lawn and cast a shadow over a woman eating cookies on a blanket. The cookies are a favorite of my wife's, dull biscuits with a chocolate picture on top of a boy eating one of the cookies. The boy on the cookie sees the cookie on the cookie, so why wouldn't the woman see Hank? And she did and said, "Hey."

"Hey yourself," Hank said very happy.

"You're in the light is what I mean," said the woman, but she was smiling. "Do you want to sit down so you're not blocking my light?"

Hank got on the blanket and the sun shone on both of them. "Do I get a cookie?" he asked.

"I don't think so," the woman said. "For years my husband ate more than his share of cookies. This is the first time I'm in the park without him. I told myself I'm going to eat all these cookies myself and Joe won't have a single one."

"You'll get sick," Hank said.

"That is the trouble," the woman agreed. "When the marriage is over there's no one to hold your head when you're sick in the toilet. But there were other reasons, you know. It wasn't just all the cookies."

"Of course not," Hank said.

The woman sighed. The joking part with the cookies relented a little, and she stared out at where the horses were living in individual pens. "It was sad, actually," she said, "and it's sad that I'm talking to a stranger in the park about it."

"I guess you don't remember me," Hank said. "I'm Hank Hayride."

"Hank Hayride?" the woman said. "That's your name, or are you the king of a hayride company?"

"I'm no king," Hank said. "We went to high school together. You're Eddie Terhune."

"High school?" the woman said.

"Go Magpies!" Hank said. "You were in Ms. Wylie's class."

"Hank *Hayride*?" she said. Eddie looked up for a moment like Hank was still blocking her light. "Hank *Hayride*? That can't be right."

"It's right all right," Hank said. "I had a crush on you the whole time."

"In Wylie?" Eddie said. "It was her with the chivalry, right? And old poems about love?"

"You didn't even know I existed," Hank said.

"That much is clear," Eddie said. "What was I doing in that class while you were crushing on me?"

Hank looked over at the horses too, and watched a bird land on the fence and then drop to the ground, dead or clumsy. "Fiddling with your hair," he said. "You would take this pen you had which was red with the gold type of a company across one side. The cap was a strange shape like the edge of a pier. I could draw it for you now from the memory of it. You would chew on this thing like a bone and then reed it through your hair, and your hair would curl over it in sort of a waterfall way and you never even noticed."

"Tell me," Eddie said. "Tell me you haven't loved me ever since and followed me here or something scary."

"No no no," Hank said. "I used to look at you and think of that song where it says it's not the way that you smile or the way you do your hair, even though it was probably both those things."

"You're not putting me at ease," Eddie said, "in terms of are you in creepy love with me since high school?"

"The answer is no," Hank said, "because the point is, I don't like that song anymore. It's stupid, the song, and anyway I graduated high school, you know."

"And?" Eddie said.

"And," Hank said, "I've been in other kinds of love. My life has been hard, though, I guess you'd say. But I didn't come to the park to find you. I haven't been here in a while because I got beat up here real bad, like with a knife."

"Oh my god," Eddie said, "but you look fine. You look okay. I guess you didn't die."

Now was not the time to tell her. It never is, right when you meet someone, slap them with a big secret when they're trying to enjoy themselves. It is natural to let the worst parts of ourselves hide in the shade, while the sun shines down on our features like shimmering hair. "I guess not," Hank said. "I guess you brought me back to life."

There is an interval here too, and it is also nearly impossible to write about. A short version would be, Eddie Terhune gave him a cookie. But this is not the description I mean. Something closer is, my wife and I once were in an automobile. We were not married but had moved to New York and were driving some-place where inexpensive furniture might live. We were very quiet in the car, for no reason, and the land outside the car window bobbed by us, flat, unnoticed except for the landmarks which told us where to turn. We were quiet, quiet, quiet, just the engine humming us toward a sofa we might afford, or lamps, and in the quiet my wife spoke up and said something suddenly.

"Cookies," she said.

Why did she say this? We did not care. We laughed the rest of the way, because the point of this story is, it is not the cookies. It is the love. My wife could eat all the cookies and it would not change the love, and if she ate all those cookies I would hold her head while she threw them up, and this too is part of the love. It does not matter if Eddie gave Hank a cookie or not. The cookies do not matter. It is not the cookies that matter, or the doughnuts suffering under the dome, or the horses in the pasture or the honey in the bear or the duffel bag that will close around us when our day in the park is over. There is only the laughing across the land as the car moves you along, on your way someplace with love in the car. It is not the things; it is the way the things are done, and Eddie and Hank fell in love in the way it is done. Naturally they went to restaurants and naturally they went to bed, and they were comfortable in the bed at the end of the evening. Eddie even stood up from the bed without a sheet around her body to get a glass of water. She was thirsty, but what mattered was her body, not shy, in the doorway of the bathroom as they looked each other over again.

"You have a handsome face," she said, "and you haven't let yourself go in the ass department, Hank Hayride."

"No," Hank said. "You're thinking of another guy. Remember Keith, from the swim team? He even had a handsome name."

"Your name is handsome enough," said Eddie. "Are you hungry? Do you want to go out someplace? It's past lunchtime now, or an early dinner. Around the same corner I live on is a magic Chinese restaurant. The Lantern something. Something Lantern. I haven't been there since Joe, when we had a fight. It was a big fat fight, but I feel like I lost that weight, so we could go and have the fried dumplings."

"Sounds good to me," Hank said, "and maybe a sesame something. Chicken."

"Did you really go to high school with me?" Eddie said. "Because I still don't remember you from then and I could check around."

Hank stared at the ceiling and sang the song:

> *We're the Monteverdi Magpies,*
> *And we're here to win the game,*
> *From coast to coast we win the most,*
> *And you'll go down the same.*

> *Ev'ry team is beaten,*
> *And ev'ry player dies,*
> *You stupid geeks will feel the beaks*
> *Of the pow-er-ful Magpies!*

By now Eddie had joined in and flopped down on top of Hank in his sheet. "It's a terrible verse," she said to his cotton stomach. "That second verse with every player dies. I can't believe they allowed it like that yet we all sang it with glee. I was even in the glee club."

Hank remembered her in the sweater they made you wear.

Back then her lips were all with the singing, and now they were kissing him like a miracle. The miracle was, she could see him, Hank, after all this time. "I know," he said.

"I guess death was nothing then," she said quietly. "When I married Joe it was, you know, until we part. But we parted in a Chinese restaurant."

"I'm not sure we should go there," Hank said.

Eddie lifted up the sheet and let it fall parachuted over her like a ghost costume. "Sorry," she said. "Here I am trying with you like a fresh start, and I keep bringing in the ghost of Joe. It's a good restaurant. I won't mope when I'm there."

"It's okay," Hank said, and he knew this was maybe the time to tell her about himself and that day in the park. But he did not want to, which was natural. He could picture the heartbroken scene if he admitted what was known only by Mr. Mittens. Why do this? Why behave this way? There are so many of these ghostly scenes already, the trails of things that did not happen quite. I was in the building days before it collapsed, I walked across that street hours before the accident. I almost married him and now look. I dumped her and look what happened. I'd be rich now, dead, married, happy, run over, covered in lava. I have a dream of what would have happened if what happened instead hadn't. Hank looked at Eddie and dreamt up what would happen if she learned how he was, that instead of blood inside his heart he was only a ghost, slain on the lawn like a dead bird. She would think less of him once she knew there was less of him. Instead he suggested a diner, but Eddie was asleep, her face thick with a nap of dreams. He floated away from her and looked through her stuff. It is natural to do this and natural to stop yourself so the person will not be angry when they awake. Hank did not stop himself.

Dear Joe, the letter said.

The window rattles without you, you bastard. The trees are the cause, rattling in the wind, you jerk, the wind scraping those leaves and twigs against my window. They'll keep doing this, you terrible husband, and slowly wear away our entire apartment building. I know all these facts about you and there is no longer any use for them. What will I do with your license plate number, and where you hid the key outside so we'd never get locked out of this shaky building? What good does it do me, your pants size and the blue cheese preference for dressing? Who opens the door in the morning now, and takes the newspaper out of the plastic bag when it rains? I'll never get back all the hours I was nice to your parents. I nudge my cherry tomatoes to the side of the plate, bastard, but no one is waiting there with a fork to eat them. I miss you and love you, bastard bastard bastard, come and clean the onion skins out of the crisper and trim back the tree so I can sleep at night.

I met a man, Joe, but he is a ghost of a boyfriend compared with you. He will not treat me well, you bastard, and he is already made of lies. He says he went to my high school. He says he's Hank Hayride when I say I could check. But I don't need to check, Joe. I know Hank Hayride died like they say in the paper, like I know how to mix that drink

you like, with the gin and brandy and lime and sugar and
bitters and you fill it with ginger ale and you slice a cucum-
ber if you have one in the crisper. It's a Suffering Bastard,
you bastard. I must have made up my new boyfriend so I
wouldn't be alone in this room. I must be desperate sad, all
without you. Come back to me, you prick. You took all the
pens except this one and you left me all the cookies and none
of it matters without my Joe. God I hope I never send this
letter. I'm going to go to bed now and lose a lot of sleep
over you.
Love,
Eddie

Hank shut the drawer and reset things the best he could so that he'd be undetected. He leaned his forehead against the creaky window and watched people walk by without noticing him. A damp policeman. Two girls returning from someplace, rolling suitcases in a hurry. A guy looking for a newspaper that could work as an umbrella if you were desperate enough. No one.

"Cookies," Eddie said, and opened her eyes. She could still see him and for a minute they were still both happy. "I had a dream," she said, as if there aren't enough supernatural elements in here, "that I had another boyfriend who I think filmed things with a camera. We were making love in the woods," but something happens when you die. You are no longer interested in other people's dreams. "And so the other guy reached in his backpack and I thought it was a weapon, but then I saw it was the same kind of cookies . . ." Her voice evaporated into Hank's disinterest. He stood in the doorway and wrapped the sheet tighter around him like an angry king.

"How long have you known?" he said.

"You bastard you read the letter." Eddie sighed, and dabbed a fingerprint swipe underneath her eyes like she might cry later. "It was in a *drawer*," she said. "It was a secret for a reason."

"How long," Hank said again, "have you known?"

"As long as you haven't told me," Eddie said. "You think I don't read the paper, Hank Hayride?"

"There are five newspapers sitting on your stoop still in plastic bags," he said.

"And," Eddie said, "you were holding my pen in the park. It was part of the whole handful of pens you were holding, a red pen with gold letters and you put it in that story you made up. How could you do that, when I said *first thing* that I was already sad, and with a broken heart? You took me for a ride, Hank. I thought we were going someplace and all the time I knew we were going someplace else, to answer your question."

"Don't look at me, please," Hank said, "like I'm in your light. I know a place with fancy drinks. Let me buy you one, Eddie, and we can sit together."

"A drink won't matter," she said.

"Then have one," he said. "We learned things about each other, Eddie, but couldn't we go out anyway?"

"You weren't what you said you were," Eddie said. "Story of my life, it wasn't what you said." She ran her hand down the wall sadly, like it was the last of the house. "I suppose it never is," she said, "and I'm hungry."

"They have food there, too," Hank said. "Great music and food and fancy drinks."

"No, no, no," she said. "It's raining. Let's break up at the diner, Hank. It's around the same corner. Put your shoes on, baby."

She looked at his shoes and this is when she cried. Hank floated toward her. He knew this must be what she had said to her husband, about the shoes, but what else could he do but put them on? Her gentle blouse was on the chair with her tossed keys, and they went out under an umbrella Eddie had bought yesterday so her hair would survive the season. Outside people hurried. A newspaper came in handy, but not as handy as the guy would have liked, and a little boy was crying on the corner with the wailing you can never console. It is natural, this heartbreak which arrives first when you are young and never leaves your house no matter where you move, but still everyone wants the kid to stop the fussing and shut up.

Inside at least it was dry, although ugly. Hank and Eddie walked past a thirsty-looking woman they did not know, and a lonely boy at the jukebox and sat down as far as possible from the windows, where old Christmas paintings waited to be scraped away. It was not a good day to eat at the diner, dead or alive. Nothing on the menu was tempting, and a neglected chalkboard in the corner suggested that today's soups were nothing. No soups. They unfolded their napkins and I'm sad to say they bickered in the back.

"I'm sorry I didn't tell you earlier," Hank said. "We met in the park and talked immediately, and I guess I didn't want to. I never meant, you know, to hurt you."

"*That*," Eddie said, "is the oldest line in this book."

"Lines get old because people say them over and over," Hank said. "It's the same story—we all lose our charms in the end. I knew when we met with the cookies. I want to love you and take you pretty places. Yes, I have things wrong, but also I can walk through walls if you'll let me show you. Don't abandon this here. Don't find some other boyfriend and leave me alone with only the cats for company." He looked at her and there it was, the panic of screwing up heaven and earth if you say the wrong thing and seal the envelope. Someone can break your heart, leave you dead on the lawn, and still you never learn what to say to stop it all over again.

"I don't think so," Eddie said, and this wasn't it either. "I thought you were nice and I wouldn't be alone but I must have been dreaming. I should have my head examined, wishing you into my life. Someone should peer into my head for letting you into my house."

"You could have told me you knew," Hank said. "If you think you can find a man who doesn't have secrets, then you're *still* dreaming."

"You're a *ghost*!" Eddie cried. "You're *empty* and you have *nothing* inside you. I'm tired of men I have to shape into something."

"I'm tired too," Hank said, and he said no more. He thought she knew what he meant, but the biggest mistake you can make is thinking they know what you mean. If you mean that you are also exhausted and feel dead in the park, and that you ache for a love to pull you to your feet and make you human again, then you must say so. If you have soup to sell you must write it on the chalkboard or no one will buy your homemade soup. Otherwise they think you mean, "I'm tired of arguing and I give up on you." Naturally they will think this, and naturally they will give up on you, and you will give each other up in a grimy diner. Hank was tired and Eddie was tired, and if they were both tired they should have gone to bed, but instead Eddie said nothing, too, just sat and watched her boyfriend vanish from her eyes.

So, the same old story, they decided not to see each other anymore. Hank felt himself fall away as the decision was served up on a sticky plate. He could see through his own body barely, the curl of a napkin through his hand on the table, and the sticky floor through his legs like he was a clear shell, something shaped in the shape of Hank, as Eddie looked up at him and slayed him all over again. He felt the last of him slip away. He will not reappear, Hank Hayride. He was dead to the woman in the diner. He was dead to her.

But there was more, as there always is when the love goes. She was haunted, naturally. Otherwise what is the point, why leave your rickety house, and why this yo-yo world giving us things and yanking them back? Hank Hayride haunted her. Naturally he haunted her, and he should haunt her, for what good are the dead if they do not haunt us, what is the point of these lives? Read instead the names of people who died before I dreamed they would, Amanda Davis, Jacques Hymans, Phil Snyder, Samy Leigh Webster-Woog with his odd and agile dancing like a very bad figure skater on the ice, read the names you think of when you are in the bed losing your own sleep, for the names don't matter. What matters is how they haunt us, when the love has floated away and we're alone in the diner. Over by the windows, the lonesome boy and the thirsty woman were all in a commotion in another story, and Eddie would have another one too. Perhaps she would drive a taxi, or pilot a plane, and once again feel the land shaking happy beneath her. But now Eddie just sat in the back, all the fight drained out of her, and she felt the haunting, and she sipped the bad coffee, and at last in the roar of the rain she gave up the ghost.

wrongly

Yeah, I have a question," said the guy with wicked eyes and a pair of shorts which in San Francisco is widely regarded as wrong. The shorts were the kind filled with pockets so you could take maybe a bunch of tools on a hike. The wicked eyes were the kind they always were: sort of green and trouble. "My question is, I quit. I'm going to quit. I thought this program was my future." He stood up from a horseshoe made of tables where everyone was sitting. The wind blew in from a window and rustled a paper on a bulletin board which was improperly thumbtacked. The paper showed a face with a crown on its head, and when the wind moved it looked like the face was going to throw up. "Are you even listening? But this isn't my future. This is the same bullshit and I should quit right now." He reached down to his place on the horseshoe where three pieces of paper sat in different ugly colors. He brushed them hard so they skittered like leaves do when you kick them. It was unimpressive. Allison was unimpressed, anyway, although she was soft-spoken and said nothing of the sort. "Fuck you all!" the guy said. This wasn't something you could quit really. For one thing, it was optional, although everybody from Graduate Studies in English was there. The other thing was that it was library orientation. The school already had the money, the money, the money of everyone in the room. This was like going grocery shopping and quitting the peas.

"I beg your pardon?" said the library woman who had passed out the three sheets of paper. Her name was something or other.

"I said I'm quitting is what my question is," said the guy. "I'm out of here. I'm renting a crap of an apartment all the way in South San Francisco The Industrial City and now I realize *no way* is this my future!"

The library woman thought this over and decided to move on. "Okay," she said, "let's move on."

"Are you even *listening*?" the guy yelled. His backpack was looped over the back of his chair like the chair, too, was going on a hike. The guy—whose name, for the record, was Steven— yanked off the backpack and tipped the chair over on purpose. "I quit!"

"So quit," said another guy. Allison was pretty sure this guy's name was also Steven. The library woman had made everyone go around the horseshoe saying their names and where they were from and their speciality of study, and Allison thought she'd never been more embarrassed in her life than when she'd said: "Poetry." It was like giving them the money, the money, the money all over again. Linda said it too, or maybe it was Lisa. There were either two Lisas or—Allison couldn't remember— there weren't. There were two Stevens and a Todd and Eddie and nobody would ever forget Bernice. Allison would think suddenly of Bernice far in her future, on her deathbed maybe, and the earrings of Bernice, which would jangle in her future like a neighbor's phone ringing when they're not home and you are, faintly, faintly driving her nuts. The library woman wrote down everything on a pad like the whole room was going down on Allison's permanent record.

"I *am* quitting!" roared the first, crazier Steven. He left the room. The library woman drew a line through something with her pen. Eddie chuckled nervously. Bernice shook her head, and her dangling earrings, very large, also shook their heads. The earrings were in the shape of two heads of William Shakespeare.

Graduate school was a step for Allison, the beginning of a journey but also the end of a journey she'd already taken up north in Washington State. Allison was staring down her future like a hallway, and the light at the end of the hallway turned out to be bouncing off a pair of earrings shaped like the greatest writer in the English language. Allison also had a crap apartment, coincidentally and awkwardly, in South San Francisco The Industrial City, and now she also felt like quitting, but after a certain age you can't quit. Allison, for instance, was that age. After a certain age you couldn't even say where you were from. You went someplace, and lived there. And then you went someplace else. Allison had said, wrongly, that she was from Texas. The library woman had written this down: Allison, a woman from Texas, here to study poetry and poke endlessly at the carpet in her new crap apartment while outside—if, for instance, it was last night—the neighbors argued endlessly over how to get to the airport. "Take a goddamn cab," Allison muttered to herself, shaking a bottle of bitters over a glass she was holding in her hand. But she was too soft-spoken to offer this advice to the bickering neighbors. The bitters, the glass, the ice-cube trays had flown down with her from Washington because she couldn't face a yard sale, and a cab had taken her from the airport, and she'd turned out all right, hadn't she? Hadn't she? Hadn't she? Hadn't she? Hadn't she? And besides, she did want to visit Texas someday. Sprawling and arid, full of millionaires and Mexicans, being from Texas was no less implausible than her actual circumstances, which included a catastrophe of epic-poem proportions in the Pacific Northwest and the ugliest carpeting she had ever seen in South San Francisco The Industrial City. No, you couldn't quit. The whole thing was optional, of course, but everybody, absolutely, showed up to sit down.

For the next forty minutes the library woman explained everything the sheets of paper already said and then, suddenly, she was done. "I'm done," she said. "I'm all done. You can go now to your evening ahead of you."

To Allison, this too, the evening ahead of her, was a long glimpse down a hallway, and she hid in the bathroom. She remembered to steal a roll of toilet paper she kept forgetting to buy but she forgot until she stepped outside into the nighttime that she needed a ride home. Well, not a ride—she had her friend's car with all of her music still all over the floor—but she needed someone who knew how to get her back to the highway that would lead her, wrongly, to her apartment where she lived. I can't imagine I need to tell you who was the only one outside scowling on the steps and tapping a pack of cigarettes against the thick of his shorts.

"Hey," Allison said.

"I don't care about the money," the guy said. "I'm not, what am I thinking of, one of the Jewish people."

Outside there was nobody else. Allison and this particular Steven were at the very top of a long thing of steps. Where do you go when you need someone to tell you where the highway is? It's not like she thought it was a good idea. It was cold outside—San Francisco gets cold, also famously foggy, so you can't get around unless you already know where you're going. Allison held her hand over her purse so he couldn't look through its large rip and see the stolen toilet paper waiting for her ass to get home. "What?" she asked.

Steven turned around and she saw that he had a telephone up to his ear, which was only a small relief. At least he wasn't talking to Allison about the Jews. "Hold on," he said to the other end, and then he turned his bright eyes to Allison. "What?" he said.

"I heard you," Allison said. "I heard you say that you are living in South San Francisco The Industrial City."

"I wasn't bragging," the guy said.

"I live there too," Allison said, "and I was wondering if you could tell me how to get to the highway. I haven't been here long. I don't know where the highway is."

Steven's hand was over the mouthpiece of his phone, and filthy. "Does it strike you that this is a good time?"

"No," Allison said immediately. A good time hadn't struck Allison since a disastrous day with a friend, just out of Seattle. "I'm sorry about it," she said. "I just want to get home."

Steven sighed, and without any further conversation pressed a button on his phone that hung up on the other person who for the record was his girlfriend. "I guess you can follow me," he said. "Are you parked in the stupid lot? I am. I parked in the lot. Let's go."

"I didn't know there was a lot," Allison said.

"We're not supposed to park in it," Steven said, "but anyway, I quit, so who cares?"

Allison looked down: her shoes, too, belonged to a friend of hers. "If I bring my car around," she said, "will you wait for me?"

Steven blinked, and ran his hands down his shorts as if coaxing them longer. Then he looked at Allison, and she saw another glimpse down the hallway. When somebody tells you that a certain boy isn't good enough for you, that person has usually not just moved all alone into a crap apartment in a city known for being south of a city that people have heard of. "What did I just say?" Steven said.

What he'd just said was "who cares?" and nobody wants to hear that. Allison turned up the radio rather than hear it in her head as she drove behind Steven down a spooky road she never would have found herself. It wasn't the same road that took her to the school and it struck her that it wasn't going to take her back to her crap apartment either. It was a trap, maybe; a spooky trap. The road was almost rural, which you can't find in San Francisco much. On one side was a dark golf course sulking behind a chain-link fence and on the other were square apartment buildings with lights clipped to the drains, shining on flat pieces of large lawns tan with drought. Here and there on the fence were dark, exhausted birds who also looked like they followed Steven down the road, but in fact she had a different song going on. The song was a hit from a more recent era, although not a song that Allison liked particularly, and the lyrics kept her absent company as she kept her hands on the wheel and looked through the windshield and saw what was down the road, as sure as the money she'd spent. Maybe Steven wouldn't quit after all, or maybe he'd come to a Graduate Studies party anyway—in either case that would be the next time she would see him. They wouldn't get along, exactly, but they would stand together in equal scorn for Bernice and the other Steven, and leave early for a bar that still had ashtrays. Or maybe it would be a copy shop, the only one in South San Francisco The Industrial City. She'd be making copies of something—the song loped to the chorus, and Allison realized with embarrassment that of course it was *poetry* she'd be copying—and he'd stroll in with a poster of his band. They'd make out, Steven's tongue sour from smoke but worthwhile. Bickering—there was plenty of it in her future, and an old plaid couch he probably owned, the cushions flat and veiny like water lilies. An angry ex-girlfriend to run into, and a time when he would be three hours late and not at all sorry. Would she be pregnant? Allison could not see a baby but boy oh boy oh boy oh boy could she see herself throwing up. She could see the future like an icy prophetess in an old movie, muttering truths that were already printed on three sheets of paper. Allison saw everything, and then, right then in the immediate future, something happened that she hadn't predicted. Steven's car signaled like he was winking at her, and slowed down and stopped by the side of the dark, dark road. So of course Allison had to stop too. "When I was crazy," the radio explained, "I thought you were great."

The song is called "It's All I Can Do."

Steven's car went quiet, and Allison, ten feet behind, turned the key and waited. One car went by, but no others. They were on the golf course side of the road. When she saw Steven's cigarette flick back into the car so he could take a drag, she put the key in her pocket and stepped out of the car. In the future she was standing at his window already, listening to his story of why he stopped, and before she knew it the future was here.

"I ran out of gas," he said before she could ask. "Completely, I ran out of gas. I tried to make it as far as I could."

"You're out of gas?" Allison said. "Didn't you notice?"

"I *did* notice," Steven said, scowling around his cigarette, "but I didn't make it. I ran out of gas. We're going to have to drive together to a gas station and get it how that happens, when they put the gas in a gas can. And then we'll drive back here and I'll fill my car with gas and then we'll drive back to South San Francisco."

"The Industrial City," Allison said, and Steven nodded and threw his cigarette out the window. They were calling it South San Francisco The Industrial City for the same reason I am. It's not because it's the name of the town or because everyone there is industrious. It's because the words South San Francisco The Industrial City are slapped up on a hill, like the famous sign about Hollywood but without even a speck of glamour, so if you are arriving from the airport, your life in Seattle looming over you like ashes from a volcano, you can look out the taxicab window and think, "I am going to live here. This is where my apartment is."

"Let's go," Steven said. "Maybe I should drive because I know where I'm going."

"We're just going to a gas station," Allison said.

"Where else?" Steven said. "Where else would we be going?"

He stepped out of his dead car and stood up. Allison shivered in the rustling wind, and there was a noise from the fence like one of the birds thought this was a bad idea, or maybe it was just one of the trees, groomed and shivering in the nighttime. "You're really out of gas?" she said.

"How many times do I have to *tell* you?" Steven said. "Listen, I've already had a bad day, because you saw me quit, okay? I didn't have to lead you back home. I wanted to go somewhere else. I don't know. I didn't know where I was going to go. But I was doing you a favor."

"I thought you were going home anyway," Allison said.

"Not until I fill my car up," Steven said. "Not until I fix this. I think I should drive. Just give me the keys."

"I don't know," Allison said. "Maybe I should drive."

But Steven was already walking toward the driver side of her friend's car, and she noticed for the first time a limp. "You're lost already," he said, and held out his hand to her. Allison had the key, of course. She had the key in her hand. Not a car went by as she walked to him and gave it up. She put the key in his hand and for a moment their hands touched, and there's a moment like this in a fantastic movie. Ingrid Bergman slips a key into the hand of

Cary Grant, who must go downstairs into the wine cellar in order to defeat what must be the Nazis. Allison and Steven were not in this movie. They were in the outskirts of South San Francisco The Industrial City, which was already the outskirts, and at the end of the movie the love works, despite the Nazis and the poisoned milk and a husband played by which actor Allison can never remember. She slid into the passenger seat, her feet brushing up against her friend's favorite driving music on the floor. When Steven turned the key she saw the same song was still playing, even though the two of them had somehow moved into the future.

"I hate this song," Steven said, peering into the side mirror and turning the car all the way around. Now the apartments were on the right and the golf course was on the left but still the road looked the same.

"It was just on," Allison said. "I didn't choose it."

"Well, choose something from the floor," Steven said. "Christ, this car is a mess."

Allison wondered whether the word *Christ* could be considered the second incident of anti-Semitism she'd seen from this guy, or whether she was still stuck on the first one, the one she'd heard on the phone. She reached down and grabbed a tape and threw it into the machine. The hit from a more recent era stopped and a song began playing that will never be a hit, although it is beautiful. It's a romantic song, but the rhythms skitter all over the place, clicking and whirring like a calculator somebody threw down the steps. "This is worse," Steven said. "What is this? This is some faggot singing with a bunch of drum machines."

"It's my friend's tape," Allison said. "It's my friend's car. And it's a mess because I got this guy to drive it down from Seattle with a bunch of my stuff in the trunk so I could fly. He turned out to be crazy, that guy. I can't remember now why I just didn't drive it myself."

"I bet I know," Steven said with a chuckle.

"And don't say faggot," Allison said. "In San Francisco of all places. What is that, the reason for saying faggot? How can you be in a Graduate Studies program and still say faggot?"

"I quit," the guy said. "It wasn't for me."

"That's another thing," Allison said. "You quit during library orientation. You won't even get your money back."

"I wasn't enrolled in that school," Steven said. "What, do you think I'm crazy?"

"Yes," Allison said. "You, also. Now I do." Outside the road looked the same: the fence was still ugly and the lights on the apartments shone on nothing on the walls. Where was she? Why didn't she just stay in the horseshoe of chairs, or attach herself to the leg of the library woman and refuse to budge until she was taken home and fixed a hot meal?

"Let me tell you what I think about *you*," Steven said, and took a cigarette out of his pocket. "I think you're smart enough to find the highway by yourself but you're too lonely to go home alone, so I think you asked me for a ride. I think you haven't had a boyfriend in months or maybe ever."

"That's not true," Allison said, "none of it, and particularly the boyfriend. What is your problem?"

"I'm angry about things," he said. "I'm going to smoke in here, okay? Does that cigarette lighter work?"

"No," Allison said. "I have matches." She opened her purse and pushed past the library papers to find that she did, in fact, have matches. The fence whirred by. She struck one and lit a cigarette which was hanging out of Steven's mouth.

"Where is this friend of yours?" he said, instead of "Thank you." "Some boy who dumped you but you took his car and all his gay music?"

"Again with the gay," Allison said. "What is it? And no. She's gone."

"Lesbian?" Steven said. "That's okay with me."

"I bet it is," Allison said. "She was a friend of mine. She still is."

"I guess it's none of my business," Steven said, and Allison looked up from her lap. His eyes were sweeping across the windshield, back and forth, even though there was nothing in front of them but where they'd already been. It was the nicest thing he'd said to her. Actually, it was maybe the nicest thing anyone had said to Allison since her landlord said she was easy on the eyes.

"Where's a gas station?" she asked. "I really need to learn my way around this town if I'm going to stay."

"We'll find a gas station in a minute," Steven said. "If they still do that. Maybe since the catastrophe they're not going to give me a can of gasoline. Since the catastrophe I could do who knows with it. You know? Like a gang? Beat up Jews for their money and light the bodies on fire."

"Are you on drugs?" Allison said.

"I wouldn't say I'm *on* them," Steven said, and widened his mouth around the cigarette to give her a little laugh. This was the laugh, Allison could see, that would indicate both a half-assed apology and a cue to change the subject. There had been plenty of Stevens, but the first Steven she'd ever met had a laugh like that, back in junior high. He said he was going to invite Allison to a make-out party but then invited Lila instead, or maybe it was the other way around. Allison only remembers the look on his face when she and Lila waited by the back entrance, near the hideous mural they'd had to paint for Ms. Wylie. It must have been a Wednesday, because the blood on Lila's sleeve made quite a stir when they arrived at Hebrew School. It was very, very easy to beat that Steven up. "Look," he said, and for a moment Allison thought they'd arrived at a gas station, but out the window was nothing. "Not *look*," he said, and reached out to Allison's chin. With not very much effort he moved her head so that she was facing him. "I mean the expression, look. Don't look at me that way. Tell me a story or something. A dream you had. I'm not having a good night."

"Neither am I," Allison said, inching her chin away.

"That's what I'm *saying*," Steven insisted. "We should be keeping each other better company than we are."

"Okay," Allison said, and said it again. "Okay, so where did you get that limp?"

"I hurt myself," Steven lied, "but that's not what I mean. We're flirting, right? I think you're very good-looking. Now you say something."

The song whirred into the second verse. Already they were at the second verse, or maybe it was the chorus, in which the singer insists he won't let go, even if you say so, oh no. Allison has never liked this song, not like Lila, who'd cue it up over and over, her weakening fingers drumming against the steering wheel until she wasn't allowed to drive anymore. Allison wished this is where they were driving, wherever she and Lila were going that night. Maybe it was a party, or maybe they were just going to drive around and cry. "I wish I were someplace else," Allison said. "That's something."

"Come on," Steven said and yanked the tape out of the stereo and—Allison couldn't believe it, but boy oh boy was it happening—threw it out the window while a man on the radio started talking about being an expert.

"I'm an expert," the expert said. "I have a number of degrees on the subject."

"It's obvious we're going to sleep together," Steven said. "You don't need a graduate degree for that. Can't we be honest about such a thing?"

"Did you," Allison asked, "really throw my tape out the window?"

"Not your tape," Steven said with a chuckle of freaky delight. There was either something black in one of his teeth or he didn't have one of his teeth, and Allison realized, with sudden expertise, that she would never know which it was. Quietly, she slipped her feet out of Lila's shoes, which clattered onto the music on the floor of the car. She was ready. She would have to leave all those songs, and the car, but the car wasn't hers, and Jews have it in their blood to leave a place quickly. You never know when it's going to get bad for the Jews, but boy oh boy oh boy do you know when it's happening. Allison saw, spooky as an apparition, the red spotlight waiting for her after the curve in the road, and she knew that was the moment in her future when soft-spoken was a thing of the past.

"I'm going to quit," she said.

"That's what I'm saying," Steven insisted. "Let's just fuck. We can go to either of our apartments. In the morning we'll deal with my car but right now let's quit while we're ahead."

"*Behind*!" Allison said, very very loudly, and Steven twitched his eyes to the rearview mirror. "Quit while we're *behind*!" And the car, Lila's car, rolled to a sloppy stop. The door opened and the night air came in. Barefoot Allison stepped onto gravel, maybe broken glass, and took two quick steps onto someone's lawn.

"Of course there's going to be another catastrophe," said the radio expert. "Do you think this is the first volcano we're going to hear about? And let's not get started on the number of people who, for reasons I have stated, absolutely hate freedom."

"*What*?" Steven said. "We're not there yet! This isn't even my car!"

Somewhere behind them that tape was broken on the ground, but as I said, Allison never really liked it. It was Lila's tape. She—Allison—could survive without that stuff. She could not see far into the future, of course—nobody can. This book only has young people in it because I am not that old. I don't know what love's like with the bulk of so much time, or if the most acute heartbreaks really do slip elsewhere or, as I suspect, stay heartbroken, stay terrible, no matter how many catastrophes go by. "This isn't even my car!" Steven said again. "This isn't even my car, and I have a question! How are you going to go home if you don't go home with me?"

Allison had a question too. "How should I know?" she cried, spreading her hands out wide, but then, when the expert was heard to cry "Oh my god!" and the program skittered to a commercial, she knew of course how. Just because there are more catastrophes on the way is no reason to avoid the ones that are here now, idling in the middle of the road. "I'll take a goddamn cab!" she said. "I should have done that in the first place."

"*Ha!*" Steven said. "You don't know what you're doing!" Then he coughed, around his cigarette, but for a moment it sounded like he'd said "forsooth." "You don't know what you're doing, forsooth," like he was Shakespeare, glittering ugly in the distant past. The lighting helped, of course. The red of the stoplight, and the grainy white from the lights clipped to the apartment drains, and some strange orange light in the sky, all gaped down on her as she took another, another, another step on the wet grass. It was long past sunset, this strange orange light in the sky, and Allison was pretty sure that wasn't west anyway. It was wrong to be barefoot, but these wrongs would be righted. She would find a better curb to stand on, where she could hail a cab or—let's face it—any other savior that might come along. If she waved long enough someone would pull over and take her where she wanted to go. Allison squinted at the strange, catastrophic sky, and took another step, another step, another step, because in the future—she could see it—this would not be happening.

truly

This part's true. A group of men are trying to get an enormous number of potatoes into a café. I know this because I'm sitting at the café where the story is taking place. The potatoes are in boxes, and the boxes are piled in a pyramid and fused together, under a shroud of plastic wrap like they do, a web of ice a Snow Queen might hurl down upon us, if we were potatoes and if the potatoes were in boxes and, um, if there were a Snow Queen. The fused potato pyramid is on wheels, but still the potatoes cannot enter the café. It is impossible. Many men are working on this impossible project. They are pressing their fists against the boxes. They are asking people sitting at tables to move, and a few women are working on this too. Not everybody who is working on this impossible project works at the café, but all of them are certain they can get this pyramid of potatoes to arrive through the small, small door. They are all wrong. It's not an impossible task like climbing a mountain, or falling in love in a nightclub. It's an impossible task like raising the dead. If these potatoes get into the café it will be an actual real live miracle.

But a miracle has happened before, with an object much much smaller than a potato. When I was seventeen and hopelessly in love, I found myself on a vacation, chained to my family in Arizona. In case you're wondering it's a long story. We were visiting Taliesin, a school of architecture founded and designed by Frank Lloyd Wright, about which and about whom at the time I did not give a flying fuck. I was in love and could think of nothing but the love in question, although she—Missi Rubenzik—does not appear in this story. Spread magnificently in front of the school was a path I was sulking through, a swipe of gravel, doubtlessly culled from local quarries, leading up to the building I didn't want to visit. Maybe halfway up, my mother, who appears once in "Particularly," being forced by grown-ups to do a pointless chore, and then again in "Wrongly," in much more dire circumstances, clutched one hand with another, and then looked at me, with an expression of terror, as if I were a phantom. She appeared panicked—she frantically examined the engagement ring on her left hand, so that I wondered, illogically, whether her horror at my uncoupled state had possessed her completely.

"My diamond is gone!" she said. "I've lost the diamond to my wedding ring! I must have dropped it on the path!"

Everyone gathered around her. We looked at the gold setting on my mother's finger, the pointy teeth biting a pocket of air.

"It's gone for good," my father said. "A needle in a haystack."

It was true, as this story is. The path was made of nothing but tiny shiny stones, and even a cursory search was impossible. Now my parents were heartbroken too. The diamonds in my mother's engagement ring had come from the heel of my grandmother's shoe, a place the Nazis didn't think of looking as she led my father and his brother into America, but that isn't the miracle either, although it is miraculous. The miracle isn't the path the diamonds took to get into the shoe, which I would have to invent, beginning with what's-it-called—carbon? a prehistoric creature, tarpitted to death in Africa maybe?—and ending with a German diamond dealer who must have done so much desperate business, or a household tool, let's say a pair of sewing scissors, that my grandmother held in one hand, traveling shoe in the other, as she grimly dug her way out of the catastrophe that surrounded her. But those things aren't the miracle, not in this story.

The miracle is that I found the missing diamond, ten years later in a book:

> A rolling green hill descended behind the house into the valley, and Taliesin spread magnificently in the background. . . . Mrs. Booth clutched one hand with another, and then looked at me, with an expression of terror, as if I were a phantom. She appeared panicked—she frantically examined the wedding ring on her left hand, so that I wondered, illogically, whether her horror at my uncoupled state had possessed her completely.
>
> "My diamond is gone!" she said. "I've lost the diamond to my wedding ring! I must have dropped it on the lawn!"
>
> Everyone but Sophie gathered around her. We looked at the gold setting on Mrs. Booth's finger, the pointy teeth biting a pocket of air.
>
> "It's gone for good," Mr. Booth said. "A needle in a haystack."

We all gazed over the dark lawn spreading toward the evening sky.

"Gone forever!" Mrs. Booth said.

Henry asked for a flashlight.

[. . .]

"Found it!" Henry's voice sailed over the lawn. "Come see!"

Mrs. Booth stood uncertainly as if she believed a trick were being played on her. The look on her face was one of pure wanting to believe—as if she had been told she was about to witness a miracle she should have known was a work of charlatanry.

Over the flashlight Henry's long arm rose again in the air, and he waved the memorial party toward him. "It's worth looking at before we pick it up."

One by one every member of our memorial party knelt and pressed his or her head to the grass to look along Henry's beam. . . . That jewel caught the light and scattered it in a blossom of fire. Green and yellow and white gleams prickled the darkness, as impressive as a rainbow or the aurora borealis. I felt as if I were looking at a spectacular natural phenomenon that had no name yet . . . and I hoped unreasoningly that he would not retrieve the diamond, but that everyone would agree to keep it where we could always gaze on it.

"Unreasoningly" or not, the search party did keep the diamond right where we could always gaze on it. Every time I reread this part of the book—Paula Sharp's novel *Crows over a Wheatfield*—the diamond is still there. Add to this miracle that the scene in Sharp's novel takes place in the *other* Taliesin, in Spring Green, Wisconsin, as far away from Arizona as the lyrics of a love song are from being in love. How did something so small travel an impossible distance? How did a diamond fall from my mother's engagement ring onto a gravel path at Taliesin in Arizona and end up on the lawn at Taliesin in Paula Sharp's novel?

Some say that it's God who performs such miracles, but not in this book. (God appears only once, as the older sister in "Briefly," drinking snitched rum in the good glasses and flirting with the boy someone else wants.) Instead I tracked down Paula Sharp to ask her about the miracle, and it is fair to say, based on an actual real live interview, that she has no idea:

PAULA SHARP: I have no idea. It's a tiny part of the story.

DANIEL HANDLER: Not to me. I'd like to write an essay about it, if that's okay with you.

PS: You want to write about it? You have a magpie's eye if you think that diamond is something to write about.

It would, in fact, require a magpie's eye to notice a diamond on the gravel on the path in Arizona, the setting of one story, and fly it all the way to the lawn on the hill in Wisconsin, the setting of another, and so I read T. R. Birkhead's *The Magpies: The Ecology and Behaviour of Black-billed and Yellow-billed Magpies:*

Attractive, artful and aggressive are all terms which have been used to describe magpies, and they are all accurate. Few bird species outside the tropics can compete with the magpie for looks: its crisp, iridescent black and white plumage together with its elongated tail gives it a distinctly exotic appearance. The magpie's artfulness may be the result of human persecution. [. . .] Not surprisingly the magpie had to adopt a more clandestine lifestyle in order to survive, hence its reputation for furtiveness.

Accordingly, the magpies in this book are so furtive, so eager to avoid human persecution, that you might not have noticed them. But they're there, right from the start:

> the air was also full of smells and *birds* [emphasis mine], but it was the love, I was sure, that was tumbling down to my lungs, the heart's neighbors and confidantes.

They're everywhere, these birds, looking for shiny things and carrying them around in their beaks. How else could one explain the pendant Joe gets in "Obviously," or the envelope of money Helena finds in "Not Particularly," flown in through the rip in her purse? You can follow them throughout the book, flying across lawns, eavesdropping in diners, listening to the radio and tucked into bed, in the forest or in the hinterlands or out the window of a cab, trying to get in the last word:

> Even that *bird* there [emphasis mine], ignoring the Chinese woman in favor of something to eat or make into a nest, could tell you that in chirp language.

But following the birds is like following the taxi instead of the passenger. You might as well emphasize that Chinese woman, whom I first spotted on the subway in New York, where this book begins. My wife and I were coming home one night and arguing like we do. I told my wife I was going to leave her for the Chinese woman at the end of the subway car, and I stalked off and stood next to this oblivious woman until my wife and I were laughing hysterically at either end of the car. We went home happy together, and the woman never appeared in our lives again until I wrote this book.

In an earlier draft, instead of this essay, all of the characters in *Adverbs*—even the Chinese woman—gathered together for a party and decided to play a game. The game is Adverbs, because without a game the party's just refreshments and people talking and there's enough of that in the book already. Someone is It and leaves the room and everyone else decides on an adverb. It returns and forces people to act out things in the manner of the word, which is another name for the game. People argue *violently*, or make coffee *quickly*, and there's always a time when the alcohol takes over and people suggest *hornily* and we all must watch as It makes two people writhe on the floor, supposedly dancing or eating or driving a car, until finally It guesses the adverb everyone's thinking of. It's a charade, although it's not much like Charades. You play until you get bored. Nobody keeps score, because there's no sense in keeping track of what everyone is doing. You might as well trace birds through a book, or follow a total stranger you spot outside the window of your cab, or follow the cocktails spilling themselves from the pages of vintage cocktail encyclopedias to leave stains through this book, or follow the pop songs that stick in people's heads or follow the people themselves, although you're likely to confuse them, as so many people in this book have the same names. You can't follow all the Joes, or all the Davids or Andreas. You can't follow Adam or Allison or Keith, up to Seattle or down to San Francisco or across—three thousand miles, as the bird flies—to New York City, and anyway they don't matter. If you follow the diamond in my mother's ring from Africa to Germany to California to Arizona to Wisconsin, in the heel of a grandmother, in the beak of a magpie, in the gravel of the path, in someone else's novel, in the center of the earth where the volcanoes are from, you would forget the miracle, the reason diamonds end up on people's fingers in the first place. It is not the diamonds or the birds, the people or the potatoes; it is not any of the nouns. The miracle is the adverbs, the way things are done. It is the way love gets done despite every catastrophe, and look—actually *look!*— the potatoes have arrived! They had to slice through the plastic—attractively, artfully, aggressively, to name three adverbs that didn't make it into this book—but the potatoes are being carried inside, an actual miracle! It can't happen to everyone—as in life, some people will be killed off before they get something shiny, and some of them will screw it up and others will just end up with the wrong kind of bird—but some of them will arrive at love. Surely somebody will arrive, in a taxi perhaps, attractively, artfully, aggressively, or any other way it is done.

not particularly

Helena still never got any mail. There was still never any mail just for her, and this wasn't, either. Her name wasn't on it, for one thing, just the address of the apartment she lived in, and the envelope felt thick, like someone was sending her a few million dollars. She could think of no reason, but just the other day she had found a fifty-dollar bill in a movie theater, and there'd been no reason then, either. "Guess what I found!" she'd said to her husband, who was an American named David. She was a British person, originally from Britain, named Helena. Sometimes this seemed like a big deal, a channel between them, sometimes it didn't. She'd waited until they were walking in the park to ask him. "When I went to the movies."

"A mythical creature of some kind," David had said. "I guess a unicorn. That's my guess. Can we now discuss how I will get to the airport with all the stuff I need to take to the airport with me?" Now he was in Canada for his work, which was some kind of job, and now Helena had an envelope with her name not on it. She sat down in her second favorite chair and made a chart.

If the envelope contains one-dollar bills—the movies
again.

If the envelope contains five-dollar bills—another magnum of good champagne, and throw up.

If the envelope contains twenty-dollar bills—the champagne, dinner, and boots in the window.

I forgot ten-dollar bills—champagne and your choice of boots or dinner.

Million-dollar bills—buy England.

The envelope contained a letter, not money. It never does. Helena didn't have any money, what with being broke. She had a job but was fired when the money was gone, and now the money was gone and her husband too, although only to Canada. She thought you needed a passport to go to Canada. In fact she was certain of it. She smoked, a certain smoker, and opened the drawer again to look at the two passports inside. They were different citizens, she and her husband, so it could be laws about citizens, or she was wrong, maybe. Or the love was gone with the money. On the table was a newspaper interviewing a man who had blown up something big. Nobody knows why men do things.

Dear Andrea,
I lost your number but I remembered where your place was.
I'm here saying that I miss our nights of wild love, baby. I
know you miss it too, baby. You are totally hot like lava.
Remember when I totally rubbed you down? I'm going to the

Black Elephant Masked Ball. Meet me there and we'll start
up again like the song says, baby.
Love you,
Tony

The envelope had been thick because it was folded badly around a photograph of a naked man, taken by a naked man. The naked man was standing in front of a mirror with a camera in front of his crotch, although his penis was big enough to hang below. It was also thick. The man's expression was a little squinty, like he was thinking of giving up on the whole thing if someone didn't sleep with him soon, and Helena couldn't think of what song he meant, so she got in the tub and taped the letter and the photograph to the other end where she could look at them. The wall was all puckered from other times she had done this, although she hadn't taped something to the other end of the tub in quite some time. Nights of wild love. Totally hot like lava. It was a common enough name, Andrea. Like David, or she supposed there were other names. She got out of the tub because she had to pee, which was more and more the problem lately. The phone was also ringing.

"It's David," said David. "I'm in Canada."

Helena opened the drawer. "Tell me, spouse," she said, "is Canada a foreign country?"

"Of course it is," David said. "It's like England."

"And is it like England?" Helena asked, looking at her husband in his passport photo and then at the naked man.

"Well," David said kindly, "there's weather. Listen, I'll give you the number of the hotel, but there was some problem with the reservation so it might not be in my name. It'll be under the name of the company."

Helena could not for the life of her remember the name of the company, only that it was stupid. "How is it?" she asked. "The work?"

"Well, it's what they're paying me to do," David said.

"I'm having trouble figuring that out," Helena said. "I don't know what people are paying me to do because I'm not making any money. We're out of juice, David, and I don't know if I can buy any more because there is only a handful left in my purse." They say the poor have dignity but Helena's voice was not dignified into the phone.

"Are you freaking out again?" David said. "Take a bath."

"Tell me something," Helena said. "No, tell me something else. Who used to live in this apartment?"

"You know it was Andrea before us," David said, and gave Helena one of his long, kind sighs, which with long-distance rates cost maybe one American dollar. "Before Andrea I don't know. Early settlers of California, for the San Francisco gold rush. Did I tell you she was driving a cab?"

"Andrea?"

"Last I heard," David said.

"You're jealous," Helena said, and she was crying which was another problem. "I mean *me*. I can't even drive a cab. You love Andrea."

"You could drive a cab if someone paid you."

"*New in town*," Helena said. "*New in town, wrong side of the road*."

"Honey, I have to go," David said. "It's work. I love you. Buy yourself some juice."

"It costs seven hundred thousand dollars," Helena said, and she cried very hard.

"Buy a cheaper kind of juice," David was heard to say. "Andrea, I think this is good for me to be in Canada. We've been fighting and this is like a vacation."

"It's not like a vacation!" Helena yelled, or something. "I'm still here, and you called me Andrea, who you're with!"

"This is what I mean," David said. "Goodbye."

Off the phone Helena felt a lot better, which couldn't be a good sign, but she looked at Tony again. Helena didn't have a lot of men in her life. Her husband, of course, and his friend Ed who married Dawn who was so boring she had an insulting nickname for the two of them and would only meet at restaurants so loud they couldn't talk. Also, there was her neighbor. He walked his dog and Helena would run out in a false coincidence. "Hello again," she would say to the dog. "Hello baby," and cup its face with her hands. The neighbor would smile. "Hello baby," she wanted to say to him, and cup his face with her hands. She could explain that it was a British custom and that she was from Britain, originally. The only other man she had met through an ad. When she was fired— or, more to the point, when Andrea fired her—she found a place on the computer to place an ad. It was free to place an ad so she kept placing them with increasing desperation as the theme.

> *Published novelist available as*
> *editor, ghostwriter, or freelancer.*
> *Rates flexible.*

Published novelist, new in town,
available for a variety of services.
Married. All inquires welcomed.
Reasonable rates. Very reasonable
rates.

I am a writer and please answer this
and send me money. I am flat broke
and I never get any mail. Please mail
me some money and I will do
something for you, I guess.

By the time Helena received a reply she had no idea which ad he was answering, but she met Joe at a sticky diner and had sticky buns. "I think I misunderstood your ad," he said, almost right away.

"Don't be so sure," she said, and why had she said that, and why was she wearing the boots?

"I thought you were looking for a friend or maybe something more," Joe said. "You know what? This is a bad idea. It's just that the love left my life so I answered this ad. I don't know what's wrong. I don't have a lot of money but I'm employed and even you could say I do noble work. There was even a day once, or something, when everybody loved me, but not really since my wife has my love really arrived, if you know what I mean."

"Well," Helena said, wondering if the place served drinks or just wine. "I have the opposite problem, or maybe even worse."

"Listen to you, *maybe even worse*," Joe said. "You have a sexy accent."

"I know," Helena said, and this is another good example of why behave this way? Things just poured out of her mouth lately, like vomit, and sometimes it actually was.

"You're money," came out of Joe's mouth in a new strategy.

"I'm the opposite of money," Helena said.

"No, no, it means you're a good person. I guess it means you're hot, you're money. It's from a movie. Get it?"

"Well, you're a vampire," Helena said. "That's from a movie, too."

"Couldn't we hang out and see where it goes or something?" Joe squinted and scratched his ear like it had an itch and he was scratching it. "I'm not some gross guy. Maybe I'm the male for you. I'm not going to say 'I have a ten-inch cock' or something."

Helena stood up. "You just said it. You just said that exact thing."

Joe smiled and threw down some money for his half of the bill. "Well, I'll never say it again," he said, but Helena never knew if he said it again because the two of them took their searches elsewhere and did not meet for years. Now, though, Helena considered Tony and his story with the wild nights, baby. She has his picture and ten inches is actually a good guess. Her mother would tell her to throw this whole thing away, but Helena decided something herself. This part of the story doesn't have any mothers. They're all gone, the mothers of us all, like the money you spent. Imagine the vanish of the weight if the advice of your mother never existed. They tell us things, unless we have no mothers, and either way things turn out such that nothing you've ever heard is any help. Yes it's love, but how would we love differently, without our mothers? I wrote a book about this and some people thought there was too much sex.

The Black Elephant Masked Ball turned out to be a Masked Ball held at the Black Elephant, a bar over on Grand. Helena found the listing right away. It cost money to go, but there were quite a few of these events lately. San Francisco had experienced its own catastrophe. It hadn't killed nearly as many people as you might think, so the citizens were left nervous and giddy and also thirsty, and it might also explain why Helena bought more cigarettes and fought with people and cried, too. The night of the ball was the same as the night David said he would get home. She could spend the last money handful cooking a meal and waiting for the plane to land, or she could go to the Ball and keep an eye on Tony. She decided to go at the last minute, when she was watching TV. "What happens when the hunter," the narrator asked, but Helena was tired of it becoming the hunted. Why does the hunter have to become the hunted every night? Couldn't the hunter go to the Black Elephant?

Helena couldn't afford a mask but she had a dress as sexy as her accent, and she found a thick black marker and drew a mask over her real face. *Is this a good idea*, she asked herself, in the mirror, *and, also, if you can hear this voice, you're crazy*. She put Tony's letter and naked picture in her purse, which is where Helena kept all her important mail. It was a badly, badly ripped purse and inside was a sheaf of undelivered letters to—drat, she's here after all—her mother. "Ever been to the Black Elephant?" asked the cabdriver, who was not Andrea by the way.

"I'm British," Helena said. "I'm British and I've never been anywhere."

"Well, have a good night," the driver said. Outside, the Black Elephant was a view. The walls were very plain but there was an elegant sign with the name of the place and a terse sketch of an elephant in nice black ink. It was a good sign. Helena paid to get in and Tony Tony Tony was right there.

Inside the light was like that of a lava lamp although there were no lava lamps around. Instead there was a big tank of women employed as mermaids over the bar, and a large screen shining beautiful old movies. Helena watched for a moment as a woman with ice crystals around her eyes decimated a man in a hat with a spiral of snow pouring out of her cape, and then she sat and looked at the list of drinks she could buy. They had everything, and a few things she hadn't heard of. She almost ordered a Motherless Child just for the name but it had egg whites in it, which is very wrong, like wearing shorts in the winter or going on a cruise ship or a decorative animal made of butter or the worry and worry of money while we're trying to be happy and enjoy ourselves. So she ordered a Morning Sickness, which was a mixture of champagne and Italian red wine and this was about as good an idea as drawing a mask on your face.

"Hey, Tony," she said, which was another one.

"Hey," Tony said, over the music. "Do I know you?"

"Nah," Helena said. "I just think you're money, Tony. I think you're hot like lava," and why say these things?

Tony also had a mask on, but he was still Tony, and grinned at her. "I used to say that all the time," he said, "but now it's like you can't tell the volcano jokes or people think you want to blow up buildings."

"I don't want to blow up buildings," Helena said. "I think it's stupid to blow up buildings."

Tony slid on down and sat next to her. "Tony," he said.

"Money, I mean Helena," Helena said.

Tony laughed. "Money," he said. "You drink too much? I like that in a woman. My last girl was a girl I lived with who drank too much. It was a whole year."

"What happened to her?" Helena said.

Tony answered but over the music Helena could not tell "fire" from "fired." "But she was for the birds. Tell me your story."

"I am also for the birds," Helena said. "My mother doesn't exist, and I published a novel last year."

"Like a book?" Tony said, catching the bartender's eye and pointing to himself. "What'd you call it?"

Helena sighed. Why talk about this, with a love story yet to be written? "*Glee Club*," she said.

"*L Club*?" Tony said. "Like the band who does yes yes yes, oh baby yes?"

"Glee *Club*," Helena said. "*Glee*!"

"*Glee*?" Tony said. "You're from England, right? With the accent? 'Cause we don't have glee here, I don't think. What else?"

Helena looked around the Elephant, which was not crowded but certainly not empty. The Masked Ball part wasn't really happening, just a few masks and feathers, but still it was very lovely, and Helena felt good even with a bad drink. "I'm married," she said.

"Married?" Tony said. "So you love a guy already?"

"Well," Helena said, and took a breath because it was a long sentence. "He said he went to Canada but I have his passport so I think he's with his old girlfriend all this time, who I think is the same as your old girlfriend, too."

"They're all the same," Tony said. "They're all the same and it's all the same to me. So you're looking for a little adventure maybe, married lady. What do you like in a guy? Because I keep fit and I know how to give a total rubdown massage."

"Well," Helena said, and had another taste of Morning Sickness.

"You ever been with a woman?" Tony said, and suddenly he was wearing cologne made to smell like a man who gave rubdowns. "With your sexy accent I bet you could get women, too."

"Actually yes," Helena said. "I had this crazy flatmate, or a friend, and sometimes we would drink too much and have a lot of orgasms together."

"Like the song says," Tony said. "Wow. What happened?"

"Well," Helena said, "we turned out not to be lesbians."

"I'd like to watch that," Tony said.

Helena thought of what she and Sam—there's another common name, Sam—usually did, which was sit around and listen to records. "You like to watch two girls, huh?" Helena said. "Maybe you could find another guy who likes that."

Tony put his hand on a space between Helena's neck and her chin, just about where Helena greeted her neighbor's dog. "And what would we do, if I found another guy?" he said.

"You could have sex with him," Helena said, moving her inked-up head.

"I want to have sex with *you*," Tony said. "I don't give a flying fuck about your husband. There must be lots wrong with him if you're alone at the Masked Ball."

"Oh, there is," Helena said, and so she listed them. "He isn't very tall and he says it's all the same to him. Things are all the same to him and he hasn't been fired like me. He likes stupid British horror movies from the 1960s, and Andrea. He is by no stretch of the imagination a good listener, and he flirts with old girlfriends and sometimes he is calm and nice when I wish he'd yell and throw things up into the air and we have no money." In a list this didn't seem enough, so she made up something to make it worse. "And he's a terrorist. He's a deadly terrorist who hates American freedoms. What are your drawbacks, Tony?"

"Let's see," Tony said. "I've been known to make women scream when we're making love. That's probably my biggest problem. It's a ten-inch problem, if you know what I mean."

Helena blushed underneath permanent black ink. This was very embarrassing that he was behaving this way. But David embarrassed her too, and who wouldn't want to be in a relationship where the biggest problem was that he made you scream when you made love? Helena finished her drink. "I really shouldn't be drinking," she said, "especially when it tastes so awful." Most of the chianti was at the bottom, and it made Helena remember this cheap cheap restaurant she and David went to five or six days running in New York. They lived there. "Bring us a bottle of your cheapest chianti!" they would say, which must mean they were not worrying about money. People in love would say such things. Helena would say them if she were in love. She stood up.

"Have another drink," Tony said.

"No," Helena said.

A man in a top hat, a man in a suit, appeared in a spotlight. "We're going to have a dance contest," the man said, and it was loud. "We're having a dance contest. We're going to play a song and the best dancer wins a cash money prize."

"Give me your number," Tony said. "Give me your number you sweet hot as lava baby."

"I forgot my number," Helena said, but she knew where her place was. Tony sent a naked photo in the mail, was certainly another drawback. Yes, Helena had nasty letters too, but she kept them in her purse which slapped against her as she stepped out on the floor. They were playing a song they probably never play in nightclubs. The verses are this:

> *It's not the way you look,*
> *It's not the way that you smile.*
> *Although there's something to them.*
> *It's not the way you have your hair,*
> *It's not that certain style.*

and

> *It's not the makeup*
> *And it's not the way that you dance,*

It's not the evening sky.
It's more the way your eyes
are laughing as they glance
Across the great divide.

and Helena began dancing, because it wasn't any of those things that were leading her home, either. She danced and danced, with the flapping and predetermined motions of a bird flying south. Her purse swung against her because there was no one to hold it, and certain men began dancing in her path, as they will do when a woman is on the floor without a husband for protection. But Helena had no worries about these men or the bag she brought into the club. She knew how to dance even with her baggage. She knew a thing or two about this. She knew who she loved, even if she could not list the particulars of what got her into this kind of love, far from home in another country. But home now was with David and she would fly there soon when the song was over. First let her dance. Let her fly higher than a flying fuck. Let her dance and sing and do all the acrobatic feats required of her sudden glee. She danced like she was going to win the contest, and all the gold medals of figure skating she dreamed of winning when this song was born and that her mother told her would never be hers, would be hers. So she loved him. She just did, immediately and again, often and clearly, naturally and soundly and obviously and many others. She couldn't stop loving him because it was like pretending your own mother was not in Britain, where the song's sexy accent was from. Other people around her were dancing with fancier feathers, shaking the sexy plumage in an aggressive and attractive manner, but it's not the makeup. It's not the makeup and it's not the way that you dance, and this is like love too, where there's only one dancer who will win your contest that night, and they are not particularly the best one. As Helena danced some of the other people at the Masked Ball stopped dancing like they were going to let her win, and why shouldn't she? Why couldn't she go out and flirt with a guy at the Black Elephant and then come home with the contest money? She could not remember the last time she felt so not fat, and the song with its humiliating lyrics of

> *It's not the things you say*
> *It's not the things you do*
> *It must be something more*
> *And if I feel this way for so long*
> *Tell me is it all for nothing*
> *Just don't walk out the door*

kept her in the bright flush of dancing and somebody letting her win. Let her win because she needs the love. Let her dance and win the contest, and let her learn later that you do not need a passport to go from the United States to Canada.

"You won the contest!" the man in the hat said. "You won the contest and you won the prize! It's an envelope full of money! What's your name?"

"Helena," she said.

The man wrote her name on the envelope, H-E-L-E-N-N-A-H, and gave her the money and she held it in her hand.

"There weren't that many people," she said modestly, "in the contest."

"People are nervous after the catastrophe," the man admitted. "People think, If a volcano rose up and destroyed us all in a ring of fire, where would I want to be? Dancing with strangers or home with the man I love? So we have masked balls all the time, but more and more people stay home in the nest. Take the money and go home, baby. It's a hundred gazillion dollars. Go home with the prize money. You won because you are the best dancer at the ball and because you are gorgeous beautiful, and I'm not saying that as a sexy thing baby, because I am totally gay."

"You see that guy in the mask?" Helena pointed him to Tony. "He's gay too and he wants your wild love but doesn't know it. Go to him. Surprise him."

"I'll do that," the man said, and Helena stepped out and into the same taxi with the same driver.

"Nice evening?" the driver said.

"It sure was," Helena agreed. "I won a contest."

"The contest ripped your purse, looks like," the driver said.

Helena looked at her purse and made up something else. "A baby was in it," she said. "An angry baby who wanted to go dancing so it ripped out of my purse." The cab got closer to the neighborhood where Helena lived with her husband. "Now it's in my belly," she said. "I'm pregnant. You're the first person I've told."

"Pregnant with a baby, wow," the driver said. "My lady and I think about having children but I think I have to get over my mother first."

Helena rolled down the window of the cab, which is always

the thing to do on the way home from dancing. Outside it was right as rain and raining the sort of mist that San Francisco offers, and London. Weather, it's all over the world like love. It may be that there was a great divide between Helena and her husband, but Brits swim the channel all the time. Helena opened her purse and tossed the letters to her mother into the dark night. "I'm going to have a baby," she said, but she kept Tony's picture, because the chorus of the song says that if the guy singing it had a photograph of you, as something to remind him, he wouldn't spend his life just wishing. It's a stupid song, but that's not particularly the point of going out. The point is, somewhere someone wants your picture. Helena could keep Tony's photograph in the drawer with the passport pictures, as something to remind her, and instead of spending her life just wishing, she could show the photographs to the baby. "This is your father," she could say, "and this is some bloke I met at the Black Elephant." The baby would know what *bloke* meant because the baby would be Helena's baby, and it would require a passport photograph to go visit its screechy grandmother who was wrong all the time. We all need passport photographs to go anywhere, even though they tend to show us at our worst. But if you don't want to see us at our worst, you can shut the drawer where they are kept.

"Does your husband know?" the driver said, after he had refused her money for good luck. "And does he know your face is covered in ugly ink?"

"He doesn't care," Helena said. "He loves me anyway," and she went upstairs to see if this was so. David sat up from the bed in the dark.

"I was worried," he said. "I got home and you weren't here and you didn't even leave a note."

"*Dear David,*" she said, "*I went out but I'm home now.*" She got herself a glass of water and drank it even though she also had to pee, and this is even another thing like love. We need things and also to get rid of them, and at the same time. We need things, and the opposite of them, and we are so rarely completely comfortable. Helena sat in her second-favorite chair and looked. He was wearing pajamas, but the particulars hardly matter. It wasn't the things he said, and it wasn't the things he did. All over the world are particular people, and you could be happy with probably five or six of them, eight if you're bisexual and everyone is. And so the happiness is not particular, and so you cannot be particular, or all you will have at the end of the night is a purse full of complaints to your mother. *Let yourself win the contest,* the music says, *or there's no point in going to the bar except to drink.* "Listen," Helena said. "Listen and look. We're going to have a baby. I know you weren't in Canada because your passport is here. I think you were with Andrea and it must stop, because this baby is going to win contests. This will lead to a professional modeling career which will enable the baby to put itself through scientist school and cure all the diseases the world's throwing at us. Don't make it sit in its crib instead, writing you letters about lying about Canada."

But David was already hugging her. "Are you really going to have a baby?" he said. "Both of us? You don't need a passport to get to Canada, my love. If you forget, you can get in with a driver's license as long as you make a fuss. I made a fuss, so please you don't, baby. Andrea is sort of mean, and she has that stupid hair, but truly it's that I don't love her and I do you, and what on earth has happened to your face?"

"Is that true?" Helena said, and was breathless and willing to believe that she knew it all along with the love. "I don't even have a driver's license because I'm new in town and everyone drives on the wrong side of the road."

"I'll teach you to drive," said her husband, and Helena imagined that he would have a lot to teach her. So much more gorgeous he was than the song, even in those particular pajamas, that she could imagine he was going to teach her a lot. "I'll teach you to drive and drive you anyplace in the meantime. And the baby, wherever it wants to go."

"It likes the Black Elephant," Helena said and lay down next to him on the bed. He put his arm around her and felt the belly where the baby was currently living. This made Helena need to pee even more, but she kept him there out of love and because of love and because all the stupidest songs are right. Why talk over this music? Helena could think of no reason. Why argue with the way love falls, not particularly, on people who arguably have not earned the warmth it brings in the bed, as fierce and red as the center of the Earth? Helena did not argue. Perhaps she could not, after all the dancing. She leaned against her spouse and stopped her sobbing. She threw her worries into a puddle on the street and let the love deliver itself like an envelope full of money. She clutched it in her hand, the stuff she won, the money she earned, the love she arrived at, everything everything just for her and her baby, baby. She leaned against him and wished for nothing else.

often

The pharmacy on the ship is more like a closet, so the woman working at the pharmacy is a woman standing in a closet, and Allison is a woman standing outside the door of a closet like she's deciding what to wear, thinking what's in my closet? What's this? What's this? And how did this get here, this ugly thing?

"Oh my god!" the pharmacy woman is squealing, because Allison has asked for what she wants. "Oh my god! Congratulations!"

Allison pulls a wallet out of a purse and has a fervent desire, even in these times, that it's a gun. "I want to shoot you," Allison says, but she is soft-spoken.

"What?" says the pharmacy woman.

"You can't tell *anyone*," Allison says, but she knows this is like "turn this ship around and bring me back to San Francisco." Now everyone will know, and she feels fat, too. Almost everyone knows already, the way this woman is with the "Oh my god!"

"Oh my god!" says the pharmacy woman, and Allison looks through her purse again. Where is her gun? Where is her machine gun to shoot people? She hands the pharmacy woman a piece of American currency in the amount of twenty dollars and says, "Instead of change, please give me a gun so I can shoot you." She is soft-spoken but short and full of rage lately, like her whole life.

"No no honey," the pharmacy woman says in her closet. "You sign for it and the bill comes later. You know how to use these things? You pee on it. You pee on it in the morning."

"I hate you so much," Allison says, and the woman frowns like maybe she heard some of that.

"I hope it turns blue," the pharmacy woman says. "When you asked for a pregnancy thing I was like oh my god! I really hope it turns blue for you."

"You too," Allison says, and puts the thing in her purse.

Allison is on a Comics Cruise. The offer came on the phone, which Allison answered on the third ring, like anyone remembers a thing like that. "Hello, I'm the woman from Comics Cruise," said the phone earpiece. "I'm here to offer you blah blah blah. A Comics Cruise is, comic book artists are there. There are panels. Your husband Adrian is incredibly fucking respected in his field, and he is invited on the Comics Cruise. His fans will get a chance to meet with him on a boat in the middle of the ocean. They will get that chance."

"And what do the comic artists get?" Allison asked.

"What do they get?" said the telephone in goddamn surprise. "They get to go on the Comics Cruise!"

"See you there," Allison said, and hung up the phone. This is not exactly how it happened, but Allison went upstairs and told Adrian anyway.

"What?" Adrian said. "A Comics Cruise, do you hate me?"

"She said you were incredibly fucking respected," Allison said. "Sometimes, yes. You could have answered the phone, for instance. It rang three times."

"Like anyone remembers something like that," Adrian said, making a mark on a paper with a pen. "I don't want to go on a Comics Cruise. It's in the middle of the ocean."

"They get you there on a boat," Allison said in anger, and she looked around Adrian's office for a bunch of things she could throw up in the air. They couldn't be important things and they couldn't break. She loved him, after all, but they had been fighting and so she signed him right up for a Comics Cruise. "They pay for the whole boat," she said helplessly. "It's not like they drop you in the middle of the ocean and you're surrounded by sharks. Love me, Adrian, like you used to."

"Sharks?" Adrian said. "I'm definitely not going."

"This is what I'm talking about," Allison said. "You're making me very sad." She was in a chair, thinking about this diner they had been to once, which she had loved but was in an inconvenient place to get to. Why hadn't they gone there again? "Or," she said, "I'm sad lately, and it has nothing to do with that." The diner, she thought. The diner and its menus and seats, everything up in the air. She sat there until her husband looked up at her at least, like he might put down his pen. "Can I help you?" he asked, and here she is. The Comics Cruise is divided into three decks. Everything is on C Deck. Allison is on C Deck, at the Something Bar, with Hillary and Tomas and other people giggling. She needs a vacation, but this is more like hell on Earth than a vacation. Still, it is something like a vacation. In front of everyone are things they won't have to pay for until later. The bar menu is garishly extensive, with drinks like the Neptune Fizz and the Attractive Magpie. They have Hong Kong Cobblers and Tipsy Mermaids and Do Be Carefuls and many people are having Sex on the Beach. They have something called the Gypsy Rose, and they have cranberry juice which they will serve with a twist if you ask. Allison has not asked. There are two schools of thought on what you should drink if you might be pregnant and then again you might not. One is, drink cranberry juice. The other is, why should I drink cranberry juice when I might be pregnant and I'll have to have cranberry juice until the baby comes out of my vagina, I think I'll try the Hong Kong Cobbler. Allison has no school of thought. She's letting her thoughts run around the yard rather than reporting inside, and she is still thinking about sitting in Adrian's office and thinking about the diner, even now. There is a possibility that this is what is making her cry a little bit, but Hillary doesn't notice because she is enjoying her Happy Banana Monkey.

"Earth to Spouse, Earth to Spouse," Hillary says. Hillary is based on a real comic artist whose work my wife hates. Cat humor is prevalent. She snaps her fingers in front of Allison and says it again, "Earth to Spouse." She calls her Spouse because she was behind Allison in the registration line. The registration man said "name" and Allison gave it up. The registration man flipped through a bunch of cards he'd stayed up all night putting into order and boxes. "Hmm," he said. "Your name isn't here and I'm one thousand percent positive these cards are in the exact right order."

Allison looked in her purse for a gun. "You can't be one thousand percent sure," said an irritating woman behind her. "There's only one hundred percent of everything."

"Good point," the registration man said, and they both laughed and the man reached over Allison's head and handed the irritating woman a badge and a packet of stuff. "Hey, Hillary," the man said. "Welcome back to Comics Cruise."

"I'm one thousand percent happy to be here," Hillary said, and Allison couldn't believe it but they laughed again at the very same thing.

"Now, let's get *you* squared away," the man said. Now he was in a better mood, what with laughing so hard at the same thing twice. "Are you a fan or a comic book artist?"

"Neither," Allison said. "I don't really like comic books and I don't draw them."

Hillary had stuck around for this, and the registration man looked puzzled and flipped a few cards, possibly out of habit. "Spouse?" he finally guessed.

"Yes," Allison said. "I married him."

"Are your names the same?" the man said.

"No, no, no, no," Allison said. "When we got married we had all these wedding checks, money people had written to the two of us. We took them to the bank and the bank said it would be more convenient for them if we had the same name. We thought that was ridiculous."

The registration man and Hillary both nodded eagerly. They were both one thousand percent sure that a punch line was coming. Allison remembered when she used to think that, and was amazed that it actually wasn't that long ago. "And then I burned the bank down," Allison said, "with kerosene-soaked rags," but she was soft-spoken and nobody knew about this crime.

"What?" Hillary said.

"I said," Allison said, but then instead of saying what she said she said her husband's name.

"Oh my god!" the registration man said.

"Oh my god too!" Hillary cried, and then put down her shopping bag and gave Allison a hug with both of her arms. Allison decided it was okay sort of like if you're in a car and it topples off a hill you decide it's okay to fall, too. "Your husband is so respected in this industry!"

"Blah blah blah!" said the registration man.

"I'm going to sit next to you at all the panels," Hillary said. "And we'll eat together too and at night they have this wonderful bar and we'll take turns buying each other drinks and stuff!"

Allison looked around at all the lines of people. Many of them were already taking photographs of what was happening. When the phone had said panels on the cruise, for some reason Allison had pictured *panels*, like big blank squares, maybe the walls of a cubicle, or large pieces of cardboard, on display. She thought that would be nice, presumably a break for all the comic book artists who were used to filling in panels with ink. But now, with some people already putting the plastic badges around their necks so they would always have them handy on the Comics Cruise, she saw that of course it was *panels*, with people talking and stating their opinions and perhaps asking questions and preceding their questions with, "I have two questions, and the first question is in two parts." Allison felt herself split into two parts right there on the registration floor, as if her gun had accidentally fired and ripped through her purse into her spine which hurt from the Hillary hug. "I don't have enough money," Allison said. "I can't pay for all those drinks."

"You just sign for them," Hillary said. "You sign for them and the bill comes later. Haven't you ever been on Comics Cruise before?"

"We've never been able to get him," the registration guy said. "We never thought a man of his blah blah would make it to Comics Cruise."

"He didn't make it," Allison said. "I threw him overboard into the sea full of sharks."

Nobody heard her. It wasn't funny anyway, not like that thousand-percent laugh riot, or that "Earth to Spouse" joke Hillary is making now.

"Earth to Spouse! Earth to Spouse! Come in, Spouse!" Hillary says, and Allison clears her throat.

"Sorry," Allison says, and then says it again because she is soft-spoken. "Sorry," she says.

"Hey hey, that's okay," Hillary says. "You have a lot on your mind? Comics Cruise is always food for thought for me."

"I've never been on one," Allison says, to pass the time.

"Oh yes," Hillary says. "It's not a show, though. Do you know or remember? A TV show from when we were kids? It was that show on TV about love on a boat. It was about . . ." Hillary waves her hands in the air and slurps the rest of her Monkey with a straw.

"It was about an hour long," says a voice, and above them is a man who is handsome like a new truck. He has shoulder-length blond hair, if you like that sort of thing, and he is smiling because he needs the practice.

Hillary doesn't laugh, which is sort of a miracle, although not the miracle Allison is hoping for. "That is funny," Hillary says seriously, and puts a piece of ice into her mouth. "Can I use that?"

"Use that?" the man says. "Are you an aspiring comic artist?"

"I *am* a comic artist," Hillary says. "I don't aspire to anything. I'm totally syndicated." She looks at the guy and says the name of her comic strip like you might say the name "Adolf Hitler" if somebody said, "Who's that German guy who was in charge of all the Nazis?"

"Sorry," the guy says, and puts his drink into his other hand so he can shake hands with Hillary. "My name's Keith Hayride. Perhaps you've heard of my strip, *Fair Is Fair?*"

"Heard of it?" Hillary says. "Oh my god!" and Allison looks up at the ceiling to see how quickly it would collapse in a fire. There must be kerosene-soaked rags in her purse, and this guy Keith would definitely definitely definitely give her a light. But where is Adrian? Shouldn't he be at the bar too, instead of maybe hiding in his room? For a while, after the bank fiasco, Allison kept a copy of her marriage certificate in her purse, for identification purposes only. But now Adrian is nowhere to be found in her purse. He has been replaced by a gun, by kerosene-soaked rags, and a pregnancy test. Adrian used to stop by her purse all the time, every day even. That felt like love, to Allison, something she knows is in her purse even if she hardly ever used it.

"This is Allison, Keith," Hillary says, "but her nickname is Spouse because she's married to blah blah."

Keith raises his eyebrows and says nothing. Allison likes that a little bit. "I'm having Sex on the Beach," he says. "It's a party drink."

"Is this your first Comics Cruise?" Hillary asks.

"Yeah, I guess," Keith says. "I'm sort of looking forward to the panels I guess. Although a lot of the people say stupid things at those things."

"They're just trying to ask us questions," Hillary says, like she's petting one of her cats and calling it a nickname. "I think it's nice. Comic fans don't get that chance very many times."

"I guess so," Keith says, looking around. Someone takes a picture of them all at the bar together, and Allison blinks in it. "Some of them seem like kids."

"There was a children's author cruise too," Hillary says, counting something on her fingers. "The theme was 'High Art and Low Art.'"

"That won't get you laid," Keith says and chuckles.

Hillary takes the straw out of her Monkey and drinks some more of the wet ice. This doesn't pass the time, so Allison decides to speak up.

"All my life," she says, "people told me what would get me laid, but I never did it."

"And?" Keith says.

"And I never got laid," Allison says, but is this a mating dance

or not? If someone is answering this question it's not Allison.
For a while in school she was all about the ornithology, mostly
because of a professor. "For all organisms the single most important aspect of their lives is to reproduce, for if they leave no de-
scendants they are evolutionary failures." But then she switched
to English and got her Ph.D., and then she met Adrian because
they both were always copying things at a copy store, and now
look at her. Past the bar is a dance floor the size of four mat-
tresses pushed together in the center of the room, and somebody
is playing dance tunes, so people will dance. She loves Adrian
very much, but how did the mating dance leave her here? She
thought there were more steps to it than that.

"Oh my god!" The pharmacy woman is here and now she is
wearing sunglasses and three other people, one of whom is inching her hand toward a camera tucked into the waistband of her
pants. "Have you told them?"

"Told us what?" Hillary says, and laughs for a minute like
she's getting ready to laugh later and wants to make sure it's
ready.

The pharmacy woman claps a hand over her mouth and her
friends laugh, sure enough. They're all comic fans, although
clapping their hands over their mouths will not save them from
kerosene-encouraged flames.

"Told us what?" Hillary says. "Told us what told us what told
us what?"

"She's pregnant," the pharmacy woman says, and how could
this happen? Allison never should have let her out of the closet.
More and more in the news, in the country where this whole

thing takes place which is America, there are random gunmen and they shoot up whole rooms of people. But why are they never here, where we want them? Why don't they shoot up a whole room just when Allison wants them to?

"Oh my god," says one of the friends of the pharmacy woman. "With your husband and what he does. He writes about it and now it's true! You must have been waiting for many years!" Everyone thinks this over and makes some joyous noises.

"I hadn't thought of that," Hillary says. "Oh Spouse I mean Allison this is so exciting for you."

"You know what I hadn't thought of?" Keith says, but the pharmacy woman and her friends have found some stools so they can get their chance to meet comic book artists in an informal setting. They decide to sit in a half-circle, like half a bunch of sharks, like there is only half a chance Allison could go some-place else. "I hadn't thought that everyone who works on the cruise would be a fan of comic books, " Keith says. "I'm pretty sure they didn't make that very clear on the phone with the Comics Cruise woman."

"Yes, wasn't she awful?" Allison says, but instead one of the comics fans is explaining they needed waitressing experience.

"Or an equivalent," she says, and then she pulls the camera all the way out of her waistband because this is her chance. "They didn't just take everybody."

"This way we don't have to pay," the pharmacy woman says. "Plus it's not very difficult. Have you seen that pharmacy? It's just a tiny room. It's about the size of a bathroom, really."

"It's such a big responsibility," Hillary says.

"It's just handing people things," Allison says. "One of those Monkeys could do it."

"I mean another life," Hillary says, and then reaches across the table and puts her hand on Allison's furious stomach, apparently so she can think about it some more. "Another life. I don't know if I could do it."

"I could do it," Allison says, but she has no idea if anyone can hear her. "I need another life, actually."

"So it's really true," the pharmacy woman says. "It really turned blue?"

The song ends, so even a soft-spoken woman can be heard. "I was definitely blue this morning," she says. "But then, I'm blue most mornings."

"Blue most mornings," Keith says. "I really like you, Allison. I think I like you. Can I use that? I'm going to use it."

"You won't believe what they make us do, on the Comics Cruise," the pharmacy woman says. "Okay, first of all we have to show up five days early, okay? And on the glass windows? By registration? There were these stupid Christmas paintings from the Christmas Cruise and guess who had to take them down? They gave us a scraper thing to do it. Scrape scrape scrape, just to meet you."

"And your husband," says the woman with the waistband.

"But Christmas was a long time ago," Allison says. Everyone frowns, so they must have heard her.

"Christmas was just the time before," says the pharmacy woman. "It was just Christmas."

Allison thinks through the ice in her glass, the stained napkin of the Something Bar. How is she here? It was just Christmas? "Smile," says the woman with the camera. "Smile or cheese."

Tomas lifts his head from the bar at the flashbulb, perhaps thinking it was the end of the world. "I want another drink," Tomas says, "but the bartender is an enormous fan. This is like some sort of anxiety dream."

"Oh my god!" the pharmacy woman says. "I know a great game, Oh my god! It's Dream or Real. We each say something that's either something that happened to us or a dream and we guess it. You say, 'Dream or Real' when it's over. I learned it from someone else."

"I don't want to play," Allison says.

"I'm guessing that's Real," Keith says. "Do I score a point?"

"It's just a party game, or drinking," the pharmacy woman says. "There's no points. I can't believe I'm getting to play with comic artists oh my god."

"I'll go first," Tomas says, and Allison stops liking him best. She has not liked a thing about him, including his work, which she read a few pages of in Adrian's room. Everybody was a vampire or was afraid of vampires, and they all lived in a rainy town where the sun went down every night. But he brought a bird in its own cage, with a sheet over it so no one could see the bird and the bird couldn't see anyone and the whole thing was a secret bird. This was a customs problem, and it meant that Allison was able to skip parts of the argument in the registration room, particularly when the bird started shrieking. The customs problem ended the discovery that a Spouse was taking a free cruise to

Alaska while the famous comic book artist lurked at home with a pen and the fans did not get the chance they were working at the pharmacy to get.

Since then Tomas has not been so reliable. He talked at the panels, and everything he said was tinged with the unreliability of someone who would bring a bird on a cruise ship. "I was hiking with two friends of mine," he says now, "deep in the woods outside of San Francisco, when one of us tripped and fell and hurt his leg very badly near a stream," and Allison skips this part too, migrates as far away from the woods as she can with the same mystery that grips her throughout. Why are there so many moments like this, in her love story? Why is it that there are so many ways it can go? Why can't it just be the same thing, over and over, like a John Donne poem run off at the copy store with the receipt stapled to the bag, an identical John Donne poem for everybody in the classroom to ask the exact same questions about, so that sometimes you go home and drink a bottle of chianti and shout things up to your husband like, "Dissertations aren't the same thing at all, because I have to work really hard on them!" Allison definitely loved him then, that nice guy Adrian. She loved him when he left his stack of work on the table by the cash register and she looked at all those panels. His first comics were about the end of the world, a time when volcanoes became angry and burned everybody up in Detroit and Los Angeles and other cities where Adrian had lived. *Hell on Earth*, nine issues numbered. She loved them, one through nine. She used to sit in her bathtub and read them several times, listening to the rustle of the pages of panels in the empty tub. It was too hot to take a bath and she loved him. Adrian scrawled two sentences on two pieces of paper and held them up for her, lines of dialogue. They were almost the same, but Adrian spent the whole day convincing her to care about them. She would waste every day with him and his shoulders, drooping under his shirt, as he would lean down and pull her out of the tub by her beltloops. Why couldn't every moment be a copy of that? Instead, unfortunately, always, there are several ways to do everything, and this is evidently the way Allison's story has gone, with a Comics Cruise heading north for a state she has no interest in visiting. How could it go this way, with Adrian? Look at herself, she is dancing with Keith in the emptying late bar. They are dancing to a song with lyrics.

> *Every day I think of you, baby,*
> *And every day I cry.*
> *It's hell on Earth without you, baby,*
> *Do you want to know why?*

And the chorus goes,

> *Why are you dancing with Keith, Allison?*
> *Why are you at a Comics Cruise?*
> *Is this good for the baby, baby?*
> *Why did you order the hummus platter,*
> *and didn't it taste gross?*

By the time they were married Adrian's comics had shifted slightly, like the crust of the Earth. Now the comics were about a young man and his wife and they had adventures, but all the adventures were about having trouble having a baby. They would rob banks, and aliens would fire lasers at them, and the woman would pull all sorts of lifesaving props out of her purse, but never never never could they have a baby, and that was always the bittersweet end of the story. Allison didn't love these as much as the end of the world, but this was the path of the ship she was on. "What is it?" she asked him, after a fight she lost track of. Allison had thrown something up in the air. "Is it that you want a baby?"

"Baby?" Adrian said, and threw down his pen. "Maybe someday," he said, and what was she talking about and why was she asking, and now the song is over and Allison is asking the bartender something.

"What?" the bartender asks.

"Hong Kong Cobbler," Allison says, instead.

"Are you sure that's good for you?" Keith asks, who is apparently standing beside her.

"It's for you," she says to him. "I've been drinking cranberry juice all night. Dream or Real? Dream or Real?"

Keith chuckles and looks over Allison's shoulder and makes a little jiggling motion with a clasped hand, like he is running a pen through the air. "I don't think so," he says. "Morning will be here early. First thing in fact. I'm going to chuckle again at my own joke until the bartender brings the bill."

But it comes, soon enough, and he signs it with a pen it turns out he had with him all this time. "Hummus platter," he says. "I forgot we had hummus and we ate it. I wouldn't say it was racist, Allison."

"I'm an enormous fan," says the bartender. "And of your husband's too, ma'am. Congratulations by the way. With his work I thought maybe you guys wouldn't. I mean, how would that come about, you know?"

"It's a common story," Allison says, hoping she is still as soft-spoken as she thinks of herself. "My husband ejaculated inside my vagina."

"I think it's time for you to go to bed," Keith says. "I'll take you." Surprisingly, he is right. The dance music is now playing a song from many years ago, when Keith was surely some handsome boy in high school. The song is "Come and Get My Heart" by The L Club, from their first album *Introducing The L Club* on L Club Records. "Yes yes yes," Keith hums, "oh baby yes," and Allison thinks for maybe the first time about this baby. Her stomach feels the same, even after Hillary put her hand on it, so it is easier to think about the baby living in her purse, the lint like placenta and an umblical cord that can keep your glasses hanging around your neck if you've become that sort of person. But the baby must be careful. It should not play with the gun or the kerosene-soaked rags or the little vial of ashes Adrian gave her. This was back when people were always mailing Adrian little vials of ashes because of the volcano stories. Now it's fertility workbooks, and she and Adrian sell them back to the bookstore on grumpy cardboard mornings, the books in a box in the back of the car they bought together, 60–40 because Adrian made more money at the time. And now. Allison gets to her cabin and when she sees that Adrian is still not there she feels sick to her stupid, raging stomach.

"I'm going to throw up," she tells Keith, and lurches past the porthole to the bathroom, which is scarcely bigger than a closet. The toilet was designed by Norwegians who have a theory about how easy it is to use, but Allison thinks to hell with it, and leans across the empty bathtub and her own vomit buckets out of her.

"Oh," Keith says.

Allison turns on the Norwegian faucet so some of it will run down the drain, and takes off her shirt which is stained. Where is Adrian? The first time she threw up with him he held her hair like no one ever had, the gentle hands of someone who draws the apocalypse happening. It was Christmas, and her bad clams were like something buried in the center of the Earth. And now? Allison throws her purse to the floor.

"Are you okay?" Keith says.

"I just threw up," Allison says, "or didn't you hear me? I'm fine. I'm married to one of the most respected comic artists in this Volcanic Age. The trouble is, it never occurs to me that people are anything but nice when I meet them."

"That doesn't strike me," Keith says but is getting her a glass of water.

"But then, they only have to say one thing and it all goes down the drain." Allison feels the cool porcelain of Norway and leans down further into the tiny tub, as if the thing she's going to say next is what is really bothering her. But it's not what is bothering her. She just threw up, is what is bothering her, and alone in the middle of the ocean. "One day," she says, "Adrian was listening to me speak sharply about something, and he didn't even put down his pen. You know, I have several poems by John Donne committed to memory, so it upsets me."

"Ssh," Keith says, and she sips the water down. "You're talk-ing very loudly, Allison."

"I do too!" Allison says. "Where, like a pillow on a bed, a pregnant bank swelled up to rest the Violet's reclining head, sat we two, one another's best. He's my best, Adrian."

"Are you really pregnant?" Keith asks. "Are you really preg-nant and do you really love that husband?"

"I'm writing my dissertation," she says, "and the center of it is this theory that it's none of your fucking business. Often I do. Yes. Often I love him and he is always my husband."

But Keith is taking her glass away. Allison looks back up and realizes with a sort of giddy horror that he has also taken off his shirt. His careless chest looked nothing like Adrian's, with hair trailing down like smoke from someone's mouth. How early are the handsome taught such things, to lumber into a room where a woman is already having a bad time, to let the party drinks con-vince you it's a party? What reasons can dissuade such wrong wrong things?

"I just *threw up*," Allison tries. With two people in the closet it feels like the pharmacy again. And, is she pregnant? But Keith is running his hand on Allison's shoulder in a way very strongly suggesting that she actually pay crucial attention to this very mo-ment.

"Shall we dance?" he says.

"No," she says.

"Yes we did," Keith insists. "We were dancing. I saw you."

Allison nods a very little bit. "I heard the song," she said.

"Yes yes yes," Keith says, "oh baby yes," and the hand moves to her belly.

"Another song," Allison says. "The one by that band, from when I was in high school, that saved my life the way songs do. 'Whatever I do, I'm just passing the time, to get to you to pass the time with you.' That's what I mean, Keith Whatever. Go away and I love him. Often I do. And the other times—"

"The other times are a vacation," Keith says. "You're on one now."

"The other times are hell on Earth," Allison says. "When he's not here there's arson and gunfire, and sharks and the bartender is an enormous fan." She looks up and the closet spins, like it, too, is an enormous fan. "I can't go by myself. I need his help."

"That's quite a story," Keith says, but he takes his hands off her. "Can I use that?"

"You can use everything," she says, and dumps her purse all over Scandinavia. "I don't need anything here, like my wallet stuffed with cash they won't take, and these linty mints, and if you want to put your glasses around your neck there's a cord just for that. Here's some tissues if you're sad, and a pregnancy test."

"Oh my god!" Hillary is standing in the doorway of the bathroom which on one hand is surprising but there's the other hand, too. "Oh my god you guys. Turn on the TV! Turn on the TV!"

"Don't you knock?" Keith says and puts on his growly shirt.

"There's been a catastrophe," Hillary says, but Allison can't see her stupid expression from her sad location. Allison washes the last of everything out of her mouth and pushes the contents of her purse together in a heap. "I hate you," she says very quietly to Hillary. "Your comic strip is incredibly stupid and badly drawn, and you announce all of the jokes twice. Like the title of the comic will be, 'The Masked Ball,' but it will give away the punch line before you can even read it. And you, Keith, the heads of all your characters are stupid big, and don't dance so close with your denim erection." But Allison is soft-spoken and nobody hears this kind of prayer, where you pray to the specifics of a person. Please, Adrian, with your shoulders and your lovely drawings of the end of the world, pick me up by my beltloops and rescue me off this boat, in the name of the can where you keep your pencils, and your haircut, Amen.

Not today. Allison pulls herself into the bedroom where Hillary and Keith are staring in horror at a blank screen. "We don't have TV," Allison says anyway. "We're in the middle of the ocean."

"Of course we have TV," Keith says. "Haven't you ever been on Comics Cruise before?"

Slowly, slowly, the screen shows them a city on fire. "It's San Francisco," Hillary says. "That's where your husband lives, Allison. It's just like his work."

"I live there too," Allison says, but she is on a ship right now.

"The pharmacy girl told me the news told her that it was a volcano," Hillary says. "This is really spooky, Spouse. First a volcano like his old comics and then you're pregnant like his new comics. And it's happening on Comics Cruise!"

"Flip the channel or turn it off," Allison says. She lies on the bed, which was her plan anyway, like a pillow. "I want to skip this."

"You can't skip it," Keith says. "Something like this is on all the channels although I don't for a minute think it's a fucking volcano."

"It is a fucking volcano," says the guy on TV. "It's hell on Earth. Look at this footage we got of it and you will say holy motherfucking shit!"

"Holy motherfucking shit," Keith says. "Whoever got that footage must have made a bundle."

"Oh my god," Hillary says. "We will stay on Comics Cruise forever and ever and ever until this is over, and I'm so terrible to be around, aren't I?"

Allison is on the bed and trying to listen. Adrian should be here, on the ship in the middle of the ocean, or she should be there, throwing up in her own bathroom. It's bigger, San Francisco, and more of her things are in it. Allison looks off to the purse pile in the room she'll pay for later, if what the registration guy said is true. They don't want her by herself. They don't want Allison to show up without her husband, everyone knows this, and Allison doesn't either. This can't be happening, and look at that stuff: the wallet, the mints, the tissues. There's no gun to shoot her way out, or even a baby to keep her company. She has nothing to get her off this boat, and please, please, look at those ashes of his on the floor. It has been often. It has not been often enough.

"Allison, you've got to see this." Hillary is jumping up and down like a monkey, and Allison looks wistfully back at the purse for something to kill her with. Please, not the ashes. "Oh my god! Oh my god! Oh my god! Oh my god! Oh my god!"

"There are no survivors," says the television, "or maybe there are. Obviously we're not going to be one thousand percent correct about every little thing at a time like this."

Allison puts a hand on her stomach. She feels fat, but maybe it's just her. Maybe she's by herself. "Help me," Allison says, but she is soft-spoken, and everyone she loves is so far away.

barely

You have to be careful when you say what you like two weeks before your birthday. You say birds you'll get birds. You say the new album by the Prowlers and you better not buy it yourself because it will be waiting for you in the bag from Zodiac Records, at a ten-percent discount on a Monday, Wednesday, or Friday afternoon, when the boy from the Winsomes works there, with his curly red hair and that tiny little beard all bass players grow, giving ten percent off to anybody who smiles at him cute. Two weeks before don't say anything you don't want because boy will you get it. Boy you better be careful.

It was the week everybody got really into the Clientele album that Andrea and Sam had to leave the apartment one morning so the landlord could finally repair the glass shower door the other Andrea walked into the night of the Zumpano show, so the two of them decided to sit out front on the sidewalk with a pitcher of margaritas and sell stuff they didn't want anymore on a blanket. Sam sold the skirt her mother sent every birthday, three of them, and the limited-pressing seven-inch single by the Unsuspecting Motorists, "I Am Here." The single is rare but Sam didn't really like them anymore since they dropped their guitarist for a boy with curly red hair and a tiny little beard. It was eleven A.M., too early for the naked lady across the street, so of course Andrea and Sam ended up talking about Egg. "I like him," Andrea said. "I'd give him a ride to the airport if he asked me, but I'd be very surprised that he asked."

"What's-his-name was a boy like that," Sam said, forgetting for a moment and sipping from the pitcher. From her bedroom window she could hear the faint sounds of the first Katydids album. No one remembers that album but Sam. It wasn't on loud enough to hear really but Sam didn't think she could call to the landlord to turn it up. Andrea and Sam had lived in another apartment, over by the zoo with the other Andrea—as if two Andreas weren't enough trouble, it was also when the radio just wouldn't stop with that Waltzing Pneumonia song "Andrea Says"—and they became friends with the landlord because he called them both "Chicky chicky," mostly Sam. But then Andrea and Sam got a letter from him which started "Dear chicky chicky sexy," and it contained some snapshots, and so they moved. In the new place they had not as much room. It was harder to move around, or to move in, even: there were still boxes. They were marked FRAGILE from the last move but now they held different things. They weren't fragile anymore, hadn't been fragile for years, and you could shut up about it because they knew how that sounded.

"I wish you wouldn't call him that," Andrea said, as if they hadn't been quiet all this time.

"What's-his-name?" Sam said.

"Yes," Andrea said, "because he has a name. Steven is his name, by the way."

"Can I keep calling him Egg?" Sam asked. "You'll grant me that, right?"

Andrea sighed so loudly that the two boys looked up from the crate of comic books they were looking through. Andrea and Sam had found the crate as is, in the apartment when they moved in, and every sidewalk sale they lugged them out to attract boys. "Yes, Sam," she said, and gave Sam a look that approximated enormous patience. "Egg."

Sam reached across the card table and flicked her thumb at her black badge sitting there, decorated with a wavy, hand-painted yellow line. She'd found it outside the Black Elephant one wealthy evening, and now it skittered toward her roommate but stopped halfway like it had lost interest. "Those comics aren't for sale," she told the boys, and held up the pitcher. "Margarita?"

"Tony," replied one of the boys, moving on. It had been like this for years. Andrea and Sam had known each other forever, or at least since the first Morphine album which was almost as long. Somebody someplace had introduced them by having a birthday party they both crashed. It was at an art gallery with paintings on the wall. At the time Sam lived in South San Francisco The Industrial City but still she knew enough that when a guy named Tomas stood up and said that there were a few things everyone needed to know before he read from his unfinished novel and the first thing was that it was a work-in-progress, they left together like they had plans. Zodiac was closed but Andrea and Sam convinced the boy to reopen and they bought an album each, at ten percent off, while he put stacks of dollar bills into waiting rubberbands. Almost immediately they had a tiff—Andrea wanted to buy the Fallen Airlines album *Give Up the Ghost*, and Sam thought they were terrible except the debut—but it ended quickly and they both thought themselves slightly victorious. There was going to be a lot of that. Late-night San Francisco doesn't offer much food but Sam taught Andrea this tiny sushi place across from Seven Gables that she later tried to teach Sam about. Andrea and Sam pushed a platter back and forth between them, offering larger and larger sums of money for the other to eat the worst kind, when they slap a piece of cold omelette on top of some rice and hope it will pass for sushi in the land of the blind. They invented a game of making a list of songs with hilarious unintentional parentheses. Their favorites were Tammy Wynette's "I Wasn't Meant to Live My Life Alone (with Vince Gill)" and Johnny Cash's "Where Were You When They Crucified Our Lord (with the Carter Family)."

Boys, like Frank Sinatra they'd had a few. Andrea had a drunk guy named Ben who was an activist after a few beers. He'd call department stores and pretend he was going to stop by for a mink stole that same afternoon, and then suddenly shout "Fur is murder!" and hang up while Andrea and Sam laughed and played the Salad Forks album. The whiskey he took to bringing over didn't last, either. "I always thought alcoholics would be *fun*," Andrea said wistfully the night she dumped him and went with Sam to the Tish Brothers show to celebrate. Ben had turned out to be the opposite of fun, and smashed a speaker in his rage on his way out. For a while Andrea and Sam listened only to the Phil Spector box set, which was in mono, but finally they relented and spent the money.

Sam had the houseguest. He'd arrived about the time the Spinanes broke up. He was somebody's ex-something and ended up staying weeks, and all day long. They'd all play Andrea's old board games she'd rescued from the divorce and say less and less to one another. For a while, under the spell of a compilation from Don't You Love Me Records, the houseguest slept in either bedroom while deciding who to sleep with. Andrea and Sam agreed it didn't matter who he chose. He chose Sam, and so for a while it was like that. Then one night he got tired when Whistledown took forever to start their show because the banjo couldn't be amplified to their satisfaction. The houseguest was tired. Sam said she'd go on to the Smoke Room where Brad Wooly was rumored to be playing Burt Bacharach covers. She never understood why he was gone when she got home. She never quite got why he wasn't waiting on the couch with a nature program on television.

The houseguest got married out in the wine country, the week before *Ruins in the Country* arrived at Zodiac Records, and Andrea and Sam were stunningly invited. It was the fanciest envelope that had ever arrived in their apartment, and it was inside another one. Sam wore one of the skirts her mother sent her, but they ditched the wedding early and went back upstairs to the hotel rooms. They took off their shoes halfway down the corridor and carried them along with the bottles of wine the caterers had given them, and walked to their room turning all the DO NOT DISTURB signs over so they read MAID, PLEASE MAKE UP ROOM. Inside they left bare footprints on the TV screen as they stretched out on the floor and listened to the Asking Prices and the Stone Roses and *Perfect Teeth* and *Ev'rything's Coming Up Dusty*. The hotel room had a tiny, unsatisfying stereo, and Andrea and Sam talked about their vanishing list of friends.

"Well, the other Andrea moved to New York with that guy obsessed with Bob Dylan," Andrea counted, "and Kate's never gotten over high school, and Carla Louise drives a cab now I think and so is never free at night or during the daytime. Ed and Dawn are now Dead and Yawn, but what's-her-name from England we still see at Barrelhopper shows."

"She's no friend," Sam said.

"I wish you'd work that out," Andrea said. "Clark still works at Zodiac, and Porky's still over at what's-it."

"None of those people are friends," Sam said. "We don't even know Porky's name."

"It's Porky," Andrea said, and took both bottles. "A mouthful of champagne and an extra sip of chianti is my recipe for a rosé cocktail you make right in your mouth. What's your point?"

It struck Sam, boy not for the first time, that she and Andrea were more like a lesbian couple that had broken up than whatever it was they actually were. Over the years they had developed a layer of sincerity over the irony over the sincerity. It was an irony sandwich, then, which tasted mostly like sincerity, like a cheap, bad sandwich. They grew their hair until it was time to get it cut, and they lived together in yet another apartment with a bathroom floor nothing could get clean. Up went the Elvis Costello poster, the one everybody had. While listening to the Hummingbirds they had seen a hummingbird which they interpreted as a sign, and so together they purchased a hummingbird feeder and together they never put it up, planning to lure hummingbirds with abundant charm rather than sugar water. Together they named the hummingbird Hummers but Hummers never appeared again, at least not when they were looking, and together they had managed to get Sam fired from her job for using the office scanner and printer. They had scanned and printed, over and over, a title in parentheses from a Beatles album, in the prim and beautiful original 1960s font: (This Bird Has Flown). They'd printed them out on stickers and ran around their neighborhood, adding them to signs which kept appearing stapled and taped to telephone poles. The signs advertised a lost parakeet. Probably they would not have been caught had they not left Sam's keys and the bottle of gin and the two bottles of tonic and the lime and the bag of ice and the knife they had used to slice the lime on the receptionist's desk where they'd been fortifying themselves waiting for the scanner to work. They'd done this together and told no one.

"I thought of someone else," Andrea said.

"Mike, I thought of him too, and give me the wine," Sam said. The Dusty Springfield album had reached the particularly sad song, when Dusty says she's been wrong before. The song called for more wine always.

"Okay, Mike too," Andrea said, "but I was thinking of the naked woman across the way."

This woman was not a friend either, but she had friends. What she did not have was curtains, and Andrea and Sam would watch her from across their cheap street. Sometimes the views were disturbingly intimate: the woman's boyfriend would cook, while the woman would pick lint off her jeans or read the side of a box of tea, not speaking, or friends would arrive and leave after only an hour, helping her hang framed prints on the wall. But more often the woman was alone and would walk around naked for some reason, neither beautiful enough nor ugly enough to make sense. Andrea and Sam would watch all day and not understand it.

"We've never met her," Sam said, although actually the woman had come to a sidewalk sale and bought a skein of yarn neither Andrea nor Sam could remember owning. "I think we don't have friends really anymore. It's like we're the left-behind canaries from that book our moms used to read us."

"It wasn't canaries," Andrea said. "Something else was left behind." Andrea's mom was actually not much for reading to kids. She was more the type of mom who would teach you how to shimmy. "Do you wish you were downstairs in the rented hall, with a husband or whatever they call those boys nowadays? Did you see his uncle stuffing money into a birdcage they set up so people could stuff money into? Wedding after wedding after wedding and then yours—your wedding? Would that make you what they're now calling happy?"

"No, no, no, no, no, no," Sam said. She tried to grab for a pillow but it was all the way up on the bed so she stuffed nothing over her mouth and nose.

"Then cheer up," Andrea said, "if you have nothing better to do." In the months since the release of the Magpies' first single, "How Good Are You," San Francisco was rumored to be anticipating a catastrophe, natural or man-made no one knew, debated in the papers in an increasingly spooky tone. Andrea pictured the two of them living through whatever it would be, or maybe in some desperate race against time, stuck in traffic or on an island with no way to get across, with either Andrea or Sam driving and either Andrea or Sam sick and dying in the passenger seat. Andrea shared these stories before the first sip of anything at all, but it was tougher, in Sam's opinion, for Andrea and Sam to keep projecting the sense that they were sharp-tongued survivors of a million dangers when in fact nothing much had happened. They'd discovered they'd been at the same show many years ago, when Prince had joined the Bangles onstage for the song "Manic Monday" and a sloppy, ill-rehearsed cover of "Gotta Whole Lotta Shakin' Going On," but more and more this seemed like it wasn't enough. More and more it seemed like less and less. "At least we don't have Hank Hayride's problems," Sam said out loud. This was a joke about someone from Andrea's high school that Sam hadn't even met, but someday, San Francisco being small, that would happen and hilarity would likely ensue.

But not today. Today was the morning after the Sinways show, and Andrea and Sam were drinking Belgian beers in the Pour House and playing the entire Cottontails album *How Can You Believe* on the jukebox. In front of them was a loose pile of cash they'd come by through selling the books they didn't want anymore to Page Through Books. They'd sold *Ivanhoe* and *The Color Purple*. They'd sold *The Magpies: The Ecology and Behaviour of Black-billed and Yellow-billed Magpies*, which was actually a library book, and *Crows over a Wheatfield* and *Sir Gawain and the Green Knight*. They'd sold *The Harvard Dictionary of Music* and *The Red Badge of Courage* and *Beloved* and another copy of *Beloved*. Sam had wanted to sell *Glee Club* and Andrea hadn't let her, but they'd sold poetry by John Donne and Wallace Stevens and Elizabeth Bishop and Stephen Spender and at least four books of advice, and *The English Patient* and *Heaven Is a Place on Earth*, which was quite popular at the time. It seemed maybe only *Lipstick Traces* and *The Forthright Girl* and *Hangover Square* were sitting lonely together on the shelves. "I just drank *Treasure Island*," Andrea said. "Long John Silver down the hatch."

"I guess we should have kept that one," Sam said meanly. "For Egg, I mean. That's a boy book, what with the treasure hunt and all the blowjobs."

"There aren't any blowjobs in *Treasure Island*," Andrea said. "That's *The Sea Wolf*, and will you do one thing for me?"

Sam narrowed her eyes, which is a good trick. "You said that five things ago," she said, and then—"What?"

The song "Girl Hurricane" started, and a few others at the bar looked up in recognition. This was the hit. "It was dark all day and getting darker all the time," the hit says. "I was sitting in a rocking chair, drinking gin and lime." Andrea finished her beer. "Be nice to him," she said.

Sam made a noise like she'd had a baby and the baby had fallen into a volcano, years and years ago but still sad.

"Why don't you like him?" Andrea said. "Why aren't you nice to him? He doesn't have any of the things."

Late one night over a Nick Drake album they'd made a pact not to touch the things wrong with boys: Money, Mommy, Slutty, Druggy, and Gay. It was an informal pact, but it had turned out not to be enough. You might think, as the song goes, that it'd fallen apart when Egg arrived, but it actually started when a very popular band who refused to have their name here released a new single, with lyrics Sam didn't like. "You want me?" the song asked, or maybe it was the singer. "Well, come and knock the fucking door down. I'll be waiting, with a gun and a pack of sandwiches." Sam couldn't believe it was *sandwiches* and not *cigarettes*. Who on Earth would think to bring a pack of *sandwiches* someplace where you had to knock the fucking door down to get in? To cheer herself up she got a movie she liked and watched it—*The Snow Queen*—on TV. That was the day Egg arrived.

"I met this guy Steven," Andrea said. "He was at the Laundromat if you can believe it. We're going to see the Friendly Skies."

"But they suck," Sam said.

"So do all my clothes," Andrea said, walking in front of the TV, "but I'm going to wear something. Listen for the doorbell."

"Our neighbor isn't wearing anything," Sam pointed out, flapping her wrist at the bare boobs across the way, but Andrea was already splashing in the shower and leaving a mess. Sam watched a scene or two and then suddenly it was the scene in which Egg walked into their apartment for the first time without knocking.

"It was open," he said and then looked at the movie. The first thing that bugged Sam was that he would say "I'm really into" whatever the topic was. "I'm really into movies," he said.

"Andrea will be just a minute," Sam said. "Margarita?"

"Steven," Egg said, walking around the apartment.

"*Sam*," Sam said.

"Okay, Sam," Egg said. "Sam like a guy?"

"That's right," Sam said. "Sam like a guy. I'm Sam, a guy."

"*Hummingbird feeder!*" he said. The unopened box was on top of a stack of fragiles. "Maybe I'll call my band that. Hummingbird Feeder."

"You have a band?" Sam said.

"Not for real," Egg said. "Just, you know, to think about. Hey, Andrea's great, huh?"

"I've known her for years," Sam said, "but you never know."

"We all have our faults," Egg said.

"Look," Sam said, but Egg looked at *The Snow Queen* so Sam turned it off. "I mean *look*," she said. "The expression. I know you. You hang around the Laundromat and eavesdrop until you can just parachute into the conversation the one time someone does their laundry without their roommate."

"That's not me," he said mildly. "I was at the Orbit Room. Andrea bought me a drink."

"The Orbit Room," Sam said, "is *right next to the Laundromat.*"

"Chinese women do my laundry for me," Egg said. "I'm an electrical contractor. We have a minute so I'll tell you. You know how a building goes up, at first quickly and then stops while they putter inside? That's me. I'm why."

"Well, thanks for wasting my time," Sam said.

Egg laughed the Egg Laugh: *Ha!* just once. "Here's where it gets interesting," but Sam never heard that part. Andrea walked in wearing the dress from the place Sam couldn't go anymore because she yelled at them over something that, at the time, was completely worth it. Completely. Egg shut up and looked at her like a bird hitting the window.

"Where's the poo-poo?" she said to Sam, gesturing to her hair in her hand.

"He arrived just now," Sam said.

"That's not what I meant," Andrea said. "Steven isn't the poo-poo. I mean that sticky hair stuff."

"You don't need hair stuff," Egg said and took her face in his hands. They kissed grotesquely. It was a small apartment, so it was hard for Sam to look elsewhere. Somewhere in the stack of records on the new speaker was a song called "The Dream of Evan and Chan," a whirring, buzzing song about going to hear a band play. It's a love song, sort of, with the singer insisting that he won't let go, he won't let go, even if you say so, oh no. But it's also a song about a dream, and at the end of it the telephone, ringing ringing ringing ringing on, wakes the whole band up from the dream, and the dream is over. Sam knew the song was in there someplace, and she also knew—like it came to her in a dream—that if Egg listened to it he'd think it was just some faggot singing with a bunch of drum machines. And also, Sam just knew, he'd say this. Sam could hear him say this even over the clutch of her hand on the remote for the television, tighter and tighter until the little plastic buttons begged for dear dear life. Sam had no mercy for the little plastic buttons, not with Andrea and Egg kissing like that. They could beg all night, but she wouldn't let them go, even if they say so, oh no.

At last they stopped.

"I'm taking your purse," Andrea said. "Mine still has that rip."

Egg was looking at the stack of records on the new speaker. "What's this?" he asked. "It looks like the eighties." It was an album by the Clash entitled *Sandinista!*

"The money," Sam said. "Take the purse but leave me my money."

"I did, except you don't have any," Andrea said, and she still didn't have any on the day of the Retro Pop Gala at Stirrup Park, so Egg lent her the money for a ticket and Andrea paid for the sushi they ate afterwards. They were ganging up on her. The place was almost empty and everyone was trying to be nice.

"I'm really into this restaurant," Egg said.

"I taught it to Sam," Andrea said, feeding him something.

Sam ate her Volcano Roll in fury. If Andrea and Egg weren't in love, it was safe to say they were planning on doing that later. Maybe she wasn't feeding him something this instant, but it was Sam's story, she was realizing, and no longer about the two of them. "Tell me something," she said to Egg.

"You don't have to," Andrea said quickly.

Egg picked up a piece of ginger and put it on his finger like it was wearing a little hat. "I'll tell you something," he said agreeably. "Do you mean a joke? Do you want to hear the story, or joke, about the people who found money in the street? Oh, wait. I blew it already."

"It's okay," Andrea said. "We know that one."

Andrea and Sam had never heard that one. Sam in particular was so broke that she would definitely remember something about finding money in the street. She gripped her little cup, which was likely imported. Millions of people live in Japan, a good portion of whom must be unhappy and devoid of money, and yet the bottles of sake are always so small. "Change the subject," Sam said.

"I think I'll change the subject," Andrea said. "What should we do for Sam's birthday?"

"Out of the neighborhood," Sam said, "that's for sure."

"If we go out of the neighborhood, Mike probably won't come," Andrea said.

"I don't care." Sam turned her empty cup over but kept her hand on top of it like it might leave. "Those bird signs keep getting stapled up no matter what we do. Petey the parakeet. 'Answers to Petey.' It depresses me. They're never going to find that bird."

"It's flown," Andrea agreed.

"No, no," Egg said. "Birds like that, when they get lost, there's a flock waiting for them in the park. They flutter around together. It was in a magazine, pictures of it."

Magazines. Listen to him. "Bullshit," Sam said. "I'm in the park all the time and never seen that. It's a story. People walk around and solve problems, is what the park's for, and there's horses for girls to look at."

"Nope," Egg said. "There's all the pretty birds in the flock in the park. All the parrots people lost, and bright-green parakeets like Petey, canaries, toucans, all those black bird what's-its, who steal the shiny things." He wiped his mouth with a napkin, and then, slowly, wiped his mouth again. "What is it, Sam? What do you want for your birthday?"

Sam let go of her useless cup. "A bird," Sam said, suddenly and dishonestly. Her birthday was two weeks away. Egg gave Andrea and Sam both smiles, and clicked his chopsticks together like novelty teeth.

"Okay," Egg said for nothing and ate the piece of cold egg.

So then for a while it was him in the story.

The Clash's album *Sandinista!* was an absolute favorite of Andrea and Sam's, for damn good reason. It is very long. It's on two compact discs in my house, or on three vinyl records at Andrea and Sam's. Egg was right about it—it does look like the eighties, although it was just 1980 when it arrived. It's a scruffy album, and the Clash was very much into Jamaican reggae at the time, so there's lots of that, and dub, which is like reggae but instrumental and less able-bodied. Andrea and Sam had sprawled on the couch night after night, laughing and arguing over whose turn it was to get up and flip the record over, and the first time the houseguest kissed Sam, right on the right shoulder, she would never forget that "Somebody Got Murdered," her favorite song on the whole album, was what was playing, but still Sam had to admit that the album seemed a little long. Sometimes. If she tried to listen to it all, without anything else happening in a room all lit up with insomnia, the album seemed to stretch its dubby fingernails far out late into the night like it too wanted to do something better that evening.

But it was morning when it happened, and it was the Katydids album playing again, with Sam curled on the couch like a semicolon and Andrea moving Sam's feet so she could sit in her towel and talk about the new shower door, and then Egg walked in, which meant he must have a key because Sam never forgot to lock it anymore. He had something with him that at first looked like the ghost of a midget. Sadly, though, it was a cage he was holding with a small sheet over it. "Happy birthday to you," he sang in a fake British accent, "Happy birthday to you." Then he stopped before the part everybody likes best, the part that goes "Happy birthday dear," and then says your name. But Egg just put the cage on Sam's lap. She peeked in and saw what there was to see.

Oh god, or somebody, what is with the terrible things? If you made a world why not a better one? Why must we do the best we can if you didn't, Mr. or Ms. Perfect? Could you not find a kiss for us when we're up, O finder of lost pets, instead of the kicking when we're down? With all the stories, all those lost birds heading south when it gets real cold, is this really how your work must manifest itself on Sam's lap?

"The bird guy says his name is Lovey," Egg said, "but you can change that. It's a lovebird, sorry for being corny."

"I thought those had to come in pairs," Andrea said.

Sam put the sheet back down. "Shut up shut up shut up," she said.

"Not this one," Egg said. "It's a rare bird—*ha!*—like you, Sam."

"Fuck you," Sam said.

There is a part of the first Katydids album that is somewhat inexplicably in Japanese, right toward the end. "Steven, would you excuse us for a minute?" Andrea said.

Egg stood up. Sam might have been able to stand it if he'd just walked into the kitchen but he stopped and took the box marked "Hummingbird Feeder" with him, for something to do, and that clinched it. He was too dangerous to be in Sam's story any longer.

"He'll slay you," Sam said very softly. "I know him, Andrea. You'll go on some hike with his college buddy and they'll just do it. You'll vanish. You'll disappear and I'll be here alone on the couch listening to the Katydids album."

"The album," Andrea said ominously, "is almost over."

Sam sighed and looked at the towel Andrea was wearing. It was impossible for her to imagine the ways terry cloth could be as beautiful as it was. "I know," Sam said, "that I'm turning into a creep. I *know* it. But also, I'm right about Egg. You will vanish, Andrea, into the woods."

Andrea leaned down and held both of Sam's arms at the wrists with almost no pressure at all. "Listen to *me*," she said. "You are *barely* being nice here. I *barely* like you the way this is going." The *barely*s, Andrea and Sam both knew, were a lie, a tiff they couldn't tape together. They looked at one another like a pair of parentheses. From the kitchen, over the Katydids, was the sound of Egg opening a box.

Sam got off the couch and took her new bird with her as she walked out of Egg and Andrea's irrefutable happiness. She dragged herself down to the sidewalk, where outside like a miracle, gazing down at his shoes on the ground, was Mike, a friend of hers.

"Hey Sam," Mike said. "Are you selling comics today? Is that a bird? Wanna see some ants?" Mike was ten years old and lived in the neighborhood with a sad and cautious dad.

"It's a lovebird," Sam said, planning on giving it to him. But first they would talk. "Do one thing for me, though. Mike, let's not talk about the love part of the bird. Let's just hang out."

"But I know lots about love," Mike said.

"You don't know anything about love," Sam said. "You're young and you've had no experience. Your experience is like, how many kinds of gum have you had."

"Seven," Mike chimed in immediately. "I know about love. I got taught it by my girlfriend."

Sam could not hear the Katydids anymore. Either it was over or Egg and Andrea had switched records as soon as she left, or she was simply too far away. There could be a simple answer. Overhead the weather was strange like something might happen, but there was a whole flock of nothing in the sky. "You have a girlfriend?" Sam asked.

Mike blushed, but "Yes," he said. "You're the first person I've told. She's older than me. She's way older."

"That's nice," Sam said. "Tell her happy birthday, your old girlfriend."

Fuck him. Fuck that bastard kid. She could give the bird to anybody. She knew the whole damn city. She could get a job driving a cab, and when people leaned up to give her the money the bird could peck out their eyes, or she would drive it south for the winter when it got cold, out of the kindness of her heart. She knew the names of each and every one of the Marvelettes. She had lots of people in the neighborhood. She crossed the street and knocked on the door of the opposite place.

Love is a story, usually a love story. The main characters are what matter. The guy who works at Zodiac doesn't matter here, and Porky doesn't matter, or Helena or the houseguest she married or Mike or Egg—none of these people are in Sam's story. The main characters are Sam and her friend. Sam heard the bare footsteps, and then the woman opened the door. Thank god she was wearing a robe. The ugly terry cloth sagged, though, and if Sam cared to turn her attention to it she could see one boob. On the wall was a print you could not see from the opposite apartment, but Sam had seen it before. It showed a woman in the woods who looked not unlike the woman who lived in the place. She had a big dumb smile.

"You found my bird!" said Sam's last friend. "Petey! Petey!" and somebody help her, this is the only story Sam is in.

judgmentally

In the United States, where this love story is set, we all get to make decisions about love, even if we're not citizens or if we don't know what we're doing. If you get into a taxi and you fall in love there, no laws passed by the government of the United States will prevent you from making a fool of yourself. If you have someone in mind for the prom, you do not have to submit this person to a vote. If you want to be a lover, that is your call, no matter your mother's advice or what the song on the radio is going on about. The love's yours, in the United States, for the time being.

If you'd rather be a criminal, however, we have a different system for that. In the United States, twelve people get to decide if someone's a criminal or not. There's not anything that anybody can do about this. It's not the same twelve people—it's different every time, like a dozen eggs. Also like eggs, it's a process that's been described as messy. Joe had eggs that morning, a big breakfast.

A big breakfast weighs you down in the United States, not what you want to eat if you're going to work at stopping a disease. Nonetheless Joe had eggs. He worked at a place called Stop AIDS Now, a political and/or social organization the aim of

which is to stop AIDS, a terrible disease that has killed millions
of people and which is spread through two acts much associated
with love: having sex and having babies, now. At the time of this
writing, let's face it, nobody knows what to do about this.
There's drugs but they don't work, and there's bigotry which for
some reason works real well at the job of making everything
worse, and people keep on performing acts of love and then dying, all over the world all over the place. Joe's job thought that
enough was enough, among other strategies. It was a worthwhile
job and so paid not that well, but Joe told himself he didn't need
much money, which is a common and surprisingly not-that-
difficult thing to do. Eggs are cheap. Joe tried to stop AIDS now
Monday through Friday except when he was sick or really
wanted to go to a movie instead of to work, or was called—summoned, they call it—for jury duty. What happens with jury duty
is, for a week maybe you get to be one of the twelve people who
decides if someone's a criminal, maybe nothing happens. Neither is really that taxing. Thus eggs.

Character description: Appropriately tall. Could dress better.
A body you could like if you liked that sort of thing. Using a
United States metaphor, if everyone in New York City is staunch
and traditionally heterosexual and up and down the West Coast,
from Seattle to San Francisco, there is nothing but lesbians and
gay men, put Joe in maybe Kentucky. There are men so handsome that to pretend Joe did not notice and desire them would be
wrong and absurd respectively. Everybody notices. Not to mention curiosity, which is normal as omelettes and consumed at
least as often. But Joe dated women and was married to one once.

Very nice person. Worked hard. Had big lips. Represented to Joe qualities which were enviable and true, mountains of etiquette and integrity, lakes of charm and goodwill and resourcefulness, well-chosen outfits of tenderness and shiny cloth, all these desirable and inutterable things which no one can list in love. Buttons, the way she buttoned things. Aluminum foil looked better on things she had cooked. The way she said, when she said it, "Put your shoes on, baby." Conversations, the interesting people she brought home or knew in childhood or who ate at her diner or she overheard in the park. Several friends who told jokes that were funny when Joe heard them. Paying for things with cash or a credit card, this woman's hair, the wild laugh at certain lines in a movie. "What am I, an acrobat?" would make her laugh, "It's a party!" would make her laugh. Kissing all the time which the lips are good for. Sense of envy from copassengers in elevators, from plants even, from houseplants on the very good days. In the United States this often leads to weddings unless you're gay, although this too will change, for how could it not, and perhaps it has by the time this is published. For six years love reigned over Joe and then something else, a new phase of the button moon. The chicken of love laid another one. Her elbows suddenly were ugly. There wasn't enough money, or maybe the night the restaurant closed around them, Chinese men in tuxes putting the chairs up on the tables like big spiders in a museum, closed for the day, closed for the evening, the lights turned low and the shimmering music off and two coats and only two coats standing off to one side on a glum rack of pinging wire hangers, while they fought, husband and wife, until they were both in tears.

These are the things we must know. This is information relevant to the case and the only judgment there is is: Joe—yes—Joe is nice. He's a nice guy! He's our hero! Let him have the eggs! Toast, hash browns, he ate all of it and never once thought about his wife. It was okay. Nothing tasted great, not even Top Ten in eggs, but it was time to go. The summons, they called it a summons, said 8:30 A.M. and it was criminal not to show up.

Jury duty is, you sit in a room to see if you're going to end up doing something, a room humming with nothing while people someplace else and invisible to you decide things. It's just like work, but you're not at work: you're a juror, maybe. This is your brief new job. Doesn't pay well.

Eventually you are called into a room, as we all are. Joe was, via number. His number was a hundred something and they called 104 through 110, which was him. He paid attention as he walked out of the room. What would happen now that his number was up? Nothing probably. But nevertheless the hallway was like a drum roll. He had been doing nothing for a long time, though they'd given him several breaks. He had a perfectly natural and appropriate sense of narrative suspense and desire: maybe he would be *sequestered*, a sexy word.

Courtroom, the usual thing, flags. The United States like all disobedient things has a father, and the father of the United States hung over the place where the judge sat, like a big full-color dollar bill wincing all over the proceedings. Joe took a seat, everybody took seats, take a seat and wait for the judge, when the judge comes stand up. That was not Joe's favorite part, to tell the truth. Joe wasn't crazy about the idea of a judge, spending his middle to late age deciding whose fault it was. Back in the restaurant, there was only one moment of any peace. "I don't think it's anybody's fault," she said to him, and he realized he'd never forget those red chopsticks with the curled yellow dragons. "I don't think it's anybody's fault," and as they faded from one another this was the only thing that made it easier to get back to sleep when he woke up and found that it was still two years later. It wasn't anybody's fault and Joe didn't like standing up for a judge who might decide otherwise, but you had to. You had to slide on down the bench and everyone slid on down the bench. Joe was next to a guy with somebody else on the other side.

"Hey," the guy said.

"Hey," Joe said back. Some people had been talking in the bigger room but Joe had just sat and let the eggs take care of things for a while. Maybe now though, Joe felt summoned to do some talking.

"Do you mind it," the guy said, "if I talk over the pros and cons of working the night shift?"

Joe tried to decide. The guy had big fluffy earphones down around his neck like he might listen to some music later. The vest had stains. On one hand, it would be boring. On the other hand, also boring. "Sure," Joe said.

"I'm not working right now," the guy said. "Are you working?"

"I work at Stop AIDS Now," Joe said.

"AIDS?" the guy said. Also, he was ugly. "The thing fags get?"

Joe decided that fighting bigotry wasn't his job that day, what with jury duty. "Yep."

"That's rough," the guy said. "You gay?"

"Nah," Joe said. There had been three or maybe four very attractive people in the larger room, not relevant to the case.

"So I'm not working," the guy said. "Not a lot of jobs since the catastrophe, but I've been offered a couple of things and they're night shift. You know?"

"Where?" Joe said.

"Supermarket," the guy said. "It's night shift. There's things to load but they're not that heavy because you have a thing to wheel them around in. You know, here's the lettuce. I did that before. But the place is crawling with rats."

"Well," Joe said.

"Yeah," the guy said.

"Rats aren't nice," Joe said.

"They suck is what. They suck is what the rats are doing there, so what do you think?"

"I don't think you should take that job," Joe said.

"There's more you need to know about my situation," the guy said.

"I'm not going to give you any money," Joe said.

"That's not it either," the guy said, "but my other choice is medical transcription."

"Okay," Joe said, but only because it seemed like he should do something while the guy wiped his lips with the palm of his hand.

"I sit in a room and listen to tapes," the guy said. "That's all I do. That's the whole job. The Jewish people work there. Everything that the doctors say, like white male with no preexisting conditions. Appears to be cysts. Stuff like that. Very rare case. Nomenclature and incision, surgery right away. I do this and I look at all of the Jewish people and even though it's nothing personal I know they are going to steal me blind. I'm surrounded by the Jewish people who want to steal all the money is what's happening. They are Jewish and they are willing to break the law."

Joe felt willing to break the law, although there are so many laws it is essential for the purposes of this case to differentiate. Joe was ready to break the law prohibiting prayer in government buildings. Joe didn't want to decide something for himself, like could I please move somewhere else. He knew the odds. Not when there's a flag. Nonetheless the longing, the prayerful sort of longing that does not stop when you know the house is empty and the last of her stuff is gone. The longing for the decision to be made for you, while you lie with the minions on the floor, please, please, please. Please powerful something. Some sword of justice. Some truthful brass gong. I will light any incense. I will renew my driver's license fifteen times. I will never ask for any other toy, this is the only toy I want, please please will someone lift me out of this room. Could I please be lifted. Could today be the one. Could some large fist stop it for a second and open up the great palm of everything I started dreaming of as soon as I knew this would not last, could I be plucked, could something just pluck me out and up and over and through and away and any other parts of speech you would demand of me. Judgmentally judgmentally judgmentally I would believe in you and swordfight others who did not, any necessary sacrifice if you were in the mood for that. I would give anything. Open my wal-

let and lungs. Take anything, you requisite criminals, you sum-
moning thieves of this terrible place where every story seems to
be set. I will drive you to the airport, O Lord our God, first thing
in the morning if that's when the plane is. Take all my breakfasts
away from me but *let the jury duty end*. Don't make me listen to
the guy any longer. The guy keeps talking. Will not the King or
Whatever of Hosts read my name out loud from the Book of
Love?

"Attention if I read your name out loud," the woman said too
loudly. "Then you are excused from official jury duty for the
year. If I read your name you are excused. Joe is excused. Several
other people are excused. I will read their names out loud incor-
rectly and real slow."

Joe! For the year! He stood up while other people were talking. They could not move their legs fast enough he was stumbling over them out of the bench so quickly. "I thought all
week," some people said. "How come her, and not me? Why
couldn't you tell us in the big room, and not me? Why are babies
dying in faraway lands?" Not Joe. Joe didn't ask a thing. He had
after all promised not to in his prayers. Below the portrait of the
father of the United States: In God We Trust. If we trust Him
then we don't point out that he doesn't exist. It is rude. We
promised. We take his impressive hand and we go out of the re-
volving doors to the sunlight of the bus stop of the downtown
district of the city. The light shining on Joe is the prettiest thing
in any book you have ever read. Thank you, thank you, thank
you, you are dismissed.

They say love's like a bus, and if you wait long enough another one will come along, but not in this place where the buses are slow and most of the cute ones are gay. "I could take the bus," Joe said out loud, "but a taxi is better. Taxis are better than buses." This felt good and a taxi pulled up due to the fact he was raising his hand, which in the United States means please pull up, taxi.

He got in. Filthy but so what? Taxis are better than buses. "Where to?" the taxi driver said who was a young lady hoping maybe this day might be the miracle.

"Um," Joe said. "I don't know. I just got out of jury duty. Everybody thinks I'm in it for the rest of the week. I could go anywhere."

The lady said, "Look, buddy," and then she turned around and the milk of human kindness flowed into her veins. "Well," she said, and smiled at his grin. "Where are we going to go?"

"The best place in the city is the Black Elephant," Joe said.

"On Grand?" the lady said. "That's your favorite place?"

"It's the best place," Joe corrected. "The places in the city are ranked as follows. The Black Elephant. The Shanghai Express. Stirrup Park. My friend Mark's apartment. The Eden Fruitery. Lambchop's Diner, why did I not have breakfast there this morning? I'm crazy. It's the sixth-best place in the city and the best place to have eggs."

"Lou's Kitchen is better if you want eggs," the lady said.

"I don't want eggs and no it isn't. Then comes the museum and then movie theaters, all in a row: Rialto. Cinema Experience. And so on."

"You seem very sure of yourself," the lady said, and they smiled. It was a judgment call to smile but they did it. They smiled like they already knew each other and the way the story goes, like they already liked each other but hadn't been in each other's company for years and now—*now*—now was their miraculous chance, but first they would pretend not to recognize each other, because why the hell not.

"I am," Joe said, "certainly sure of myself. I am certain."

"So you want to go to the Black Elephant?"

"I never want to go anywhere else in my whole life."

A squawk on the taxi radio distracted the lady from maybe realizing anything more about Joe for the moment. She picked up the speaker device and spoke into it, saying "Yes" and "No" and "No" and "The Black Elephant" and "The Black Elephant" and "Down near Wyatt" and "No" and "No" "Eleven" and "Nowhere near there" and "No" in a voice curdled with talking to someone she didn't like. Joe loved the listen of it, the beat of her annoyance, and realized he was syncing it up with the song he was thinking about anyway. The song is called "Lady Cab Driver" and the real lyrics are like this:

> *Lady cab driver can U take me for a ride*
> *Don't know where I'm going cause I don't know*
> *   where I've been*
> *So just put your foot on the gas—let's drive*
> *Lady don't ask questions, I promise I'll tell U no lies*
> *Trouble winds-a-blowin' I'm growin cold*
> *Get me outta here I feel like I'm gonna die*
> *Lady cab driver, roll up our window fast*
> *Lately trouble winds are blowin hard*

And I don't know if I can last
Lady I'm so lonely I know that's not the way to be
I don't want isolation but the air it makes me cold
Drive it baby drive it, drive this demon out of me
Take me to your mansion honey let's go everywhere
Help me girl I'm drowin' mass confusion in my head
Will U accept my tears to pay the fare
Lady cab driver, roll up your window fast
Lately trouble winds are blowin' hard
And I don't know if I can last

and that's it. Those are the whole lyrics. "Did you hear that guy?" the lady asked. "That's Drecko. He tried to fire me last night and now he wants me to do him a favor."

"He's a terrible person," Joe said. "I challenge him to a swordfight and anybody else who tries to fire you."

"I like you," the lady said and laughed with her hair needing combing.

"I like you and I like taxis," Joe said. "Taxis are the best way to travel. I'm only going to take taxis from now on."

"That'll be expensive," the lady said.

"I should be earning twelve times my current salary," Joe said. "I'm doing the most important work on Earth. People are dying every day and people are still stupid about it. Those people—it's a long story—are the worst people on Earth. Drecko is one of them."

"He sure is," the lady agreed. "You know, I'm not sure the Black Elephant is even open now."

"Sure it is," Joe said. "An impressive hand is carrying me through all seemingly locked doors."

"You're acting kinda kooky," the lady said. "Are you drunk? A religious nut?"

"I guess I'm feeling religious," Joe said. "I guess I'm starting a religion that believes taxis are better than buses and tipping you fifty dollars is a religious sacrament. Why can't I start a religion? Lots of people did it a long time ago, and where are they now?"

"Dead," the lady said.

"When you were talking to Drecko," Joe said, "I was thinking of that song 'Lady Cab Driver,' do you know that song?"

"Everybody sings it to me," the lady said.

"It's the best song on Earth," Joe said. "I'll buy it for you on CD. It's my new hymn. It's the best song there is and it makes me happy just to think about it. How many happy people do you think there are in the world? Twelve?"

"I don't know," the lady said. She shrugged and the two of them watched someone very old and very short walk slowly in front of them. Character description: Chinese. Old woman. Not lonely. Has groceries she paid for herself, Joe would judge. Anyone normal would judge. This is it, the job we are given, to form some specific and inexplicable judgment, to prefer the delicious food that is offered to the selfish money we might otherwise keep. Even that bird there, ignoring the Chinese woman in favor of something to eat or make into a nest, could tell you that in chirp language. Love is a preference, and Joe found one as he was summoned to do. He found the love story he preferred, although he didn't render this judgment officially until three years

later when he and this cabdriver right here lay laughing and naked over how giddy he was during the miracle, during the blatant
afternoon they met. "My friends sure aren't happy," the lady
said, thinking about what was said instead of what was walking
which was her right as a citizen. "My friend Joe used to be happy
I guess, but then he got heartbroken."

"I got heartbroken myself," Joe said. "At the time we said it
wasn't anybody's fault but it was mine. I'm guilty of that most
certainly. But at least she got happy again. I'm happy to say she
got happy again although it makes me sad to admit it, if you
know what I mean."

"I know what you mean and what can you do?" the lady said.
"My old boyfriend got sued by his own mother."

"I rule that the mother is at fault," Joe said. "She's a terrible
criminal, that mother, and so is your old boyfriend unless you
don't think so and have evidence to the contrary. What are we
thinking? A volcano could destroy this town tomorrow, or guys
with guns. Or both. Of course there's going to be another catastrophe."

"Of course," the lady agreed, "but both? I don't think that's
likely."

"Likely?" Joe said. "What are the odds that I'm in this
cab?"

The lady smiled the same smile, but Joe wasn't tired of it. No
one ever got tired of this kind of smile, this smile of recognition
but pretending not to recognize one another, to keep it strung
along, to make the story more interesting as everything happens.
Like a song on the radio, if you know what I mean and who

doesn't. The right song, hitting your ears from the shuffle of everything else they play out there. The world could end waiting for it, just some song on the radio, but then one day you click the button and it's on, and all the traffic in the world can't matter. Nothing can drown out this song, and look! Out the window the two of them could see it: finally finally finally, a truck was pulling up in front of a café and unloading a mountain of potatoes, shiny with plastic wrap, so some wondrous chef could cook everyone breakfast. "From where I sit," she said, "the odds are one hundred percent."

Joe leaned back in his seat. "You're the best person I met today and I am going to the Black Elephant and I'm going to be happy every day beginning at eight-thirty sharp. It's my job."

The street stopped whizzing by and the lady cabdriver turned around and pointed at a number showing on the meter in red electric lights. Electricity was invented in the United States if you believe such things but you don't have to. Nobody has to. The lady pointed at Joe's number and held out her beautiful, beautiful open palm. Never seen anything so beautiful, never never, Joe and the taxi in the middle of a big fat blessing.

"You've arrived," she said.